***The Christus Experiment* by Rod Bennett**

He's been divinized, demonized, demythologized, and decoded. He's been spoken for and spoken against, the best loved, least understood, most controversial figure in human history. All of which makes Jesus of Nazareth the single most tempting target for haunted Georgia billionaire Anson MacDonald and his pricy team of time-traveling scientists and historians. What if you could capture Christ?—bring him to our own time, make him sit for modern questions and get his answers on tape? Would he do miracles? Start a revolution? Would he disappoint his followers—or disappoint the skeptics?

These questions become a good deal more than academic for three unsuspecting outsiders brought to MacDonald's secret compound for close encounters with his mysterious guest. Sylvie Fortune, the beautiful but wheelchair-bound police psychic, has longstanding issues with the failed Messiah of her childhood and insists on hanging these around the neck of MacDonald's visitor. Security analyst Carter Nichols, brought in to investigate the leaks that threaten Jesus' safe return to his own time, grapples with the threat of attack by fanatics and the social unrest that could erupt when the truth about the Christus Experiment is revealed. And most frightening of all, Rabbi Jakob Silverberg, assigned as the Nazarene's Jewish chaplain during his 21st century stay, begins to uncover a sinister plot to change history, slowly realizing that someone (or *something*) could very well be using MacDonald's time machine to enslave the future forever…

ROD BENNETT

THE CHRISTUS EXPERIMENT

WONDER *Magazine Press*

To

Jim Henry III

A hero of mine

CONTENTS

Acknowledgements

This book is a spiritual and psychological adventure story full of wild and irresponsible religious conjecture, equally indefensible whether taken as theology or speculative fiction.

There's really no excuse for it at all, unless perhaps it's the same excuse Chesterton once offered for his own paradoxical religious writing: "There seems to be some sort of idea that you are not treating a subject properly if you eulogize it with fantastic terms or defend it by grotesque examples...I think [on the other hand] that the more serious is the discussion the more grotesque should be the terms...So far from it being irreverent to use silly metaphors on serious questions, it is one's duty to use silly metaphors on serious questions. It is the test of one's seriousness...It is the test of a good religion whether you can joke about it." *The Christus Experiment* then, is offered as a serious joke, so to speak, in the Chestertonian vein, with hopes that no one will be tempted to mistake either its "silly metaphors" for actual theology or its serious questions for mere tomfoolery.

Those who know the works of C.S. Lewis, Arthur C. Clarke, Dr. Ronald L. Mallet, Paul J. Nahin, or Robert Riskin will find their distinctive influences throughout. Much more direct credit is due to people like Jim Henry III,

Mark Shea, Jim Peavy, Rabbi Scott Sekulow, Fr. Geoff Horton, Lint Hatcher, Mike Aquilina, Robert G. Bennett, Gary & Kathie Lundquist, Gary Jansen, and Cari Hawks Foulk, all of whom provided active help in one way or another. The author also tips his hat to Ronald S. Ligon, Brad Linaweaver, Renee Bondi, and Catherine Metheringham, a very nice group of folks who inspired this book in various ways whether they realized it at the time or not. Astute readers who have "read a science fiction book or two" before this, might also notice a couple of hat tips interwoven into the text itself. Finally and most profoundly, the author owes a debt of gratitude to his longsuffering family, wife Dorothy, son Jack, and daughter Martha.

The author also thanks you, the reader—really, the most important link in the entire chain. May you find sound answers to your own Christus Experiment, on whichever timeline you happen to occupy.

G E N E S I S

"Time is a sacred thing…it is an emanation from that place where eternity springs…It is a clue cast down from Heaven to guide us." – Juan Eusebius Nieremberg

1:1

He had to admit it.

Even for someone like himself, who had always done exactly as he pleased and had scrupled at precious little during his short, mad whirlwind of a life, *this* thing—this raid, this escapade, whatever you might want to call it—had undoubtedly been the most thrilling, the most terrifying, the most gratifyingly transgressive caper of them all. It ended hours ago, yet he couldn't sleep, he couldn't eat, he still couldn't do anything but lie there on his bed thrashing around, replaying every delightful instant of it over and over in his head. It went without saying, of course, that he couldn't tell anyone. Yet the urge to do so was entirely overpowering, so much so that he'd even considered making the long drive into the city in the middle of the night, just to sit among people, at a bar or a restaurant or something, saying nothing but simply having seen what he'd just seen and done what he just did. There'd be an almost sensual pleasure, he guessed, even in that—just sitting there quietly among them, looking at their silly, complacent faces, knowing how their heads would explode if he *were* to tell.

He'd squelched the suicidal thought, obviously. It became instead an elaborate fantasy he'd been toying with in lieu of counting sheep, almost like the sex fantasy one might construct during a more ordinary sleepless night. He created, to begin with, the perfectly ideal victim: a contented, cow-eyed young woman from some bucolic Middle Western state, good-looking enough to project an air of self-confidence, yet pumped so full, in reality, of unfounded retrograde opinions (adamantly held, of course) as to have felt herself secretly vulnerable all her life. She would need to be intelligent enough to grasp a little of the science he'd sketch out to make the story understandable, yet just pliant enough to accept it without allowing inordinate skepticism to break up the narrative flow. She would become enthralled right away, he had decided; fascinated both by the adventure itself (little knowing, at first, the point toward which it was aiming) and by the adventurer, so full, as he was, of enthusiasm, expertise, and personal charm.

He'd tell of the terrible yawning pit that had opened at his feet—a well between worlds, made possible by the exploitation of forces so exotic that Einstein himself had hesitated to believe them possible. Next, she'd hear of the corresponding hole that had opened in another sky; that weird, consciousness-bending hole out of which had fallen, like spiders on a web, a dozen man-shaped figures in black ready to work their will on someone else's world. How the scene might have been understood by the illiterate horde of Semitic aborigines who'd witnessed the event on that end he wouldn't venture to say. He could only paint the picture from his own perspective: the incomprehensible plunge through the centuries; the sudden rush from blackness into twilight as he and the other "spiders" dropped on their ropes into the Temple square like the falling of a theatre curtain; the deafening crash of silence as a smothering sea of Hebrew chant was choked off mid-phrase. He'd recollect the moment of touchdown; how they had instantly spread out to form a circular perimeter, just as they'd been drilled to do in their extensive paramilitary training; how the apparent leader of their group, a huge commanding black man in his sixties who must have seemed an exotic Nubian or Ethiopian to the crowd, blew his whistle and barked his orders. And then he'd describe, best he could for this imaginary young woman of his, the most vivid memory of all—the pungent oriental spice that had instantly filled his nostrils, something he'd never smelt before, a fragrance which might even have become literally extinct in the centuries since but which would, in his mind at least, stand forever as a touchstone for that particular slice of antiquity. Finally, he'd finish his intro with a flourish by recalling that first long look at the Holy City herself. This had been the Feast of Tabernacles, the annual ceremony of Illumination. In accordance with established ritual, a band of brilliantly vested priests had just emerged to light the four great golden candelabra, symbolic appeal to Jehovah for deliverance and redemption. Now, the hundreds of lights on these massive lampstands had sprung to life one by one, and their flickering glow flooded old Jerusalem, making her cobbled streets look like literal streets of gold. Not just anyone, he supposed, would grasp the significance of these descriptions at first; not just anyone would, as he hoped, begin to suspect—with the appropriate tingle of astonishment and horror—exactly where all of this might be headed. This girl would. Just as he'd given her the needed smattering of science, so he'd supplied her already with enough Sunday sermons in her past, enough half-remembered Bible classes and half-digested fundamentalist theology to stand her in very good stead here as well…and, of course, to make the crack of the whip really sting when it finally came.

Yet how to broach the big moment, the first appearance of the Prophet, the Chosen One, the whole damn point? How, in short, to say *Ecce Homo* to his theoretical girl in that theoretical bar? How, indeed. To come right out with it like a rabbit from a hat might provoke not just disbelief but some kind of cognitive shut-down, a psychological unwillingness to "go there" in the modern parlance, which would ruin his fantasy completely. The same thing happened, after all, in much more mundane aspects of life. He himself remembered, for instance, the day when he, as a teenager, had toured the house where Franklin Roosevelt died, the very bedroom. They'd told him the place was kept exactly as the great man left it—and, in fact, there in the bathroom rack hung the very toothbrush the President had used a few hours before his passing. FDR's toothbrush. He'd stared at it…and disbelieved. It couldn't be, could it? Surely this was a replica, an artist's conception. Otherwise, the humdrum little thing would prove that this mythic figure, this character out of a book, had occupied the same world that he occupied, the same plane of existence. And *that*—though there was no rational ground for the feeling at all—seemed entirely impossible. How much more then, with *this* Man, this figure out of a much grander book, so much more the subject of legends? How could she not balk? Yet such was his task on this sleepless night.

He'd approach it from an oblique angle, then. He would avoid using the Man's proper name to begin with, just call him Teacher or Rabbi or something. And then he'd paint the Rabbi (with some measure of truth) as a political figure at first, interrupted while addressing his tremendous and rather volatile personality cult. Perhaps he wouldn't mention, however, what a delicious thrill it had given him personally to cut the gentleman off in mid-sentence; that was a detail which, while destined to be conveniently forgotten by the Man's supposedly infallible chroniclers, he himself would cherish forever, but which might, he supposed, come off as rude or ill-mannered to his intended audience. Better to emphasize instead the hard-won facility with language he had acquired for the trip; the Man was sermonizing, after all, in Second Temple Aramaic, a tongue dead for all practical purposes since the fall of Masada and not at all easy to learn at this late date. Yet he had understood the preachments easily—and butted in just as easily with understandable words of his own. Here, however, in recounting that initial face-to-face exchange, all foreplay, he supposed, must necessarily come to an end. Just as the crowd had realized by this point that it was he himself and not the big African who was the true leader of the interlopers (having likely assumed already, given his coloring and European features, that he was a Roman and thus one of the accustomed "boss men" of their world) so too with the girl would it become pointless to attempt any further finesse. There was nothing else to do now but simply blurt the thing out word for word, just as it had actually happened, letting any complacent faces go well and truly slapped, and allowing the Emperor to stand fully revealed in all the glory of His fancy New Clothes:

"Are you Jesus of Nazareth, the carpenter's son?"

"I am."

"You'll have to come with us for a while, sir."

Now, if she was the kind of girl he took her for (and somehow he felt sure that she was), his companion's consternation would be audible at this point, just as it had been from the Jews. She might even lash out at him, as some of them had. How incredible, for instance, had been the moment when—as two of his men in black came forward and took Jesus by the arms—an unknown disciple in the front row had been stirred to action. The simple, swarthy fellow saw what looked to him like a kidnapping…what was, in fact, a kidnapping. Rising to his feet, he'd pulled a sword from under his cloak. He hadn't reckoned, however, on the tremendous powers of these dark angels from the sky. One of them produced a fat, square hand weapon no one would ever have seen before and pointed it at the would-be defender. A tiny red spot of light appeared on the man's chest; a thin ribbon of wire sprang out, struck him, and sent him crumpling to the pavement in convulsions. A second disciple produced another sword. He, too, rushed forward to strike. This one might have succeeded where the other failed had not the Nazarene himself called out in a loud voice.

"Cephas!" he'd cried, once again in Aramaic. "Put away your sword! Whoever lives by the sword will die by the sword. Allow it to be so for now."

Chagrined, Cephas (later to be called Peter in Greek) had withdrawn obediently. Another man called out: "Master, what does this mean? Where are you going?"

"I have other sheep, Philip," the Man replied, "that are not part of this fold. I must bring them also. Then there will be one flock and one shepherd."

Suddenly, even his own mind reeled at the recollection. He balked at the outrageous whopper himself and felt foolish for having told it, though his memory of the actual event was only a few hours old. His lady friend wouldn't stay to hear how he'd produced a weapon of his own (though of a much more benign sort)—the big, black pneumatic injection gun with which he had zapped the Nazarene off to dreamland for ease of handling. Nor would she stick around to hear how the sleeping Messiah, without any help at all from Georg Friedrich Handel, had ascended into heaven on a Coast Guard-style rescue stretcher. He'd have to spin his finale for the bare walls as well, telling how he and his team had followed the Messiah into the 21st century, hoisted back up the same ropes they'd come in on, leaving the hole to close beneath them with the sound of a strangled tornado. Delightful as his secret might be, it was simply a tale too good to tell. Nobody with any self-respect would sit for such a patent, barefaced lie, however true it might happen to be.

Abandoning the hopeless fantasy scenario, he rolled, for the umpteenth time, heavily over on his bed.

And as he did, the pleasing fantasy was all at once replaced by worry—worry and shame. What if his patron, his mentor, were to hear him carrying on like this? He literally shuddered at the thought. He could never admit *these* kinds of feelings to anyone, least of all to him. It had all been done, he agreed, for the purest and most altruistic motives, in the name of science and in the pursuit of truth. Of course it had. And the results of the experiment—to be obtained in the epoch-changing weeks ahead—would be processed carefully by sober minds, and released to the world when deemed appropriate for the betterment of all mankind. All this was true. All this he had and would continue to enthusiastically support.

Yet here in the isolation of this endless night, the blessed thought of yanking that particular oriental rug from under the feet of the world kept him charged like a live wire. *No, Virginia, there is no Santa Claus.* Here are the facts—read 'em and weep. God, what a moment that will be! The thought made his heart pound with adrenaline, like the heart of a jackrabbit in a trap. And now he realized anew, of course, that normal sleep was out of the question—tonight, and perhaps tomorrow night as well. Resigning himself to this fact, he turned at last, sat up in bed, and switched on the bedside lamp. Slipping into his house shoes, he stood up, stepped out of the bedroom, and started down the hall to the lab. Obviously, there was nothing for it but a good old-fashioned shot in the arm—literally.

He laughed to himself. Thank God for illegal drugs. And needless to say, he *didn't* mean the One sitting quietly, even then, in His cell in the building next door.

A D V E N T

"Subtle is the Lord, but malicious he is not." – Albert Einstein

2:1

From lonely Mount Nebo in the south the great mountain range winds north through the lifeless desert, its course paralleled to the west by the meandering Jordan River. The Jordan carries water sweet and clean from the well-fished lake which is its source and deposits said water unceremoniously into a dead salt sea. In between stands the Holy City, its great white Temple climbing toward God, most sacred spot on earth to the faithful. Carter Nichols could see the spires of it from the back seat of his limo, sparkling in the early morning sun. Across the runways to the south the rolling oasis of the Wingpointe Golf Course was visible, too, where clean cut Mormon businessmen were already moving onto the back nine. Nichols smiled, but the smile passed quickly. It all made perfect sense here in Salt Lake City, didn't it?—where wandering 19th century pilgrims had found a homeland as desolate as the biblical Sinai and named its landmarks accordingly, where their great-great-grandchildren built this modern international airport for the silvery angels of the jet age to rest their weary wings. Ancient history isn't always ancient then, is it? It's restless, agitated, resentful of its prison in the past, looking always for new ways to reassert itself, to reach forward into the future and trouble the present with strident, unchronological claims. So why shouldn't the reverse be true as well?

One of those angels—a whistling Gulfstream V—was sitting on the tarmac just ahead, awaiting his arrival. Nichols gathered his things as the car rolled to a stop alongside. When the driver opened the door for him, he steeled himself, hesitated, and then shoved his bad leg—the one with enough screws to open a hardware store—out into the cold spring daylight. Grunting and hissing, glad that the aircraft noise smothered these embarrassing sounds, he took a death grip on the doorframe with his good left hand and then hoisted the rest of himself out in one quick, painful spasm of effort. Once erect, however, Carter Nichols stood straight, without crutches, proud to again look something like the vigorous young professional he had been when last seen around these parts. The sleeve of his jacket covered the only remaining visual reminder of his late incapacitation: a right forearm encased in a cast from elbow to wrist. Drawing in a long invigorating draught of the chilly air, he stepped confidently toward the boarding ladder.

Rocklynne, as Nichols might have anticipated, was waiting there with one of his men (name of McCandliss, if memory served)—waiting to frisk him, even though the two had known each other as business acquaintances for nearly eight years. Nichols grinned and lifted his arms obligingly; it was all SOP, of course, and completely routine. Due to the high ambient noise level any potential observer would have watched the scene play out as a silent movie. Nichols was tall, boyish, a blue-jeans-and-tweed type in his mid-thirties who looked as if he might have worked for Bill Gates at some point. The other man was straight, square-shouldered, also tall, but heavier, with the hard, unspoken dignity one often notes in black people old enough to have survived segregation. His BDU pants and black polo shirt showed Rocklynne for just what he was, a very seasoned private policeman trying to look casual. The men shouted a word or two of small talk into each other's ears, finished the formalities quickly, then climbed the steps, retracted the ladder, and sealed the door behind them.

The enclosed interior of the plane engulfed Nichols in warmth and silence again; it took him several moments to become aware of the soft wheezing of the ventilation system, the soft murmur of conversation inside. An attractive flight attendant offered to take his jacket. As he gingerly extracted the plastered arm and surrendered the coat, he glanced around the cabin for traveling companions. There were only two, excepting the pilot and security men; an elderly gentleman in the front row wearing a yarmulke and a small, black-headed woman seated in the back, her face buried in a paperback book. Nichols recognized the gentleman immediately.

"Rabbi Silverberg!"

Smiling, youthful eyes looked up out of a gray and friendly face. "Hello. Have we met?" The voice carried just the barest trace of a middle-European accent.

"No, I don't think we have," said the younger man. "I'm Carter Nichols. I designed the security system for the MacDonald site."

"Mr. Nichols knows all of us, Rabbi," offered Rocklynne in explanation. "Better than we know ourselves."

"Everybody gets a background check, I'm afraid," Nichols continued, "and I have to do all of them. Which is why I know to ask about your wife—Lydia, I think—and your, what was it, *eighteen* grandchildren?"

"Nineteen!" beamed the Rabbi. "And all very well, thank you. Would you like to see some pictures?" His hand moved threateningly towards a back pocket.

"Some other time, Rabbi, some other time. What's become of Rabbi Mintz?"

"I'm afraid Rabbi Mintz took ill," Rocklynne responded quickly. "Had to pack out early."

"Gee, I'm sorry to hear that. Nothing serious, I hope?"

"We hope not. Still waiting on an update. He left early last week."

"A bit too early, as it turns out," said Silverberg.

"That's right!" said Nichols. "Tomorrow night starts Passover, doesn't it? And our visitor doesn't go home until, what, Saturday?"

"Which is why they had to call in the 'B-Team'," said Silverberg, in a self-deprecating tone. "It isn't strictly necessary, of course. In fact, it's a little unusual. Passover is a family celebration for the most part."

"Mr. MacDonald is sensitive about that sort of thing," interjected Rocklynne, as he took the seat next to the Rabbi. "Doesn't want it to be said that the man lacked for anything while he was with us."

Silverberg agreed. "Certainly not 'the consolations of his religion,' as he puts it."

"Well, I'm sure you'll do a wonderful job, Rabbi. Ought to be a fascinating experience to say the least."

"Indeed."

The flight attendant reappeared from the cockpit, interrupting politely. "We're all set for departure, gentlemen, so if I could just ask you to be seated and fasten your safety belts."

"Oh, absolutely," said Nichols, breaking off the chit-chat immediately and turning his attention to finding a seat. Characteristically, his gaze drifted quickly back to the woman in the rear. She'd dropped her novel now and was fiddling with a set of miniature headphones and a tiny white mp3 player. Nichols noticed first that he didn't recognize her at all. This in itself—in such sharp contrast to what had just taken place with the Rabbi—was a striking surprise. The girl's appearance was striking as well, exactly the last sort of person he expected to see on this particular airplane. First of all, she was young—in her mid-to-late twenties, he guessed. The black hair falling onto her shoulders, a wild and unkempt mane, was an obvious dye-job and meant to be recognized as such. Also jet black, a huge baggy sweater was trying to swallow up the rest of her. Her complexion would have been considered unusually fair if she'd been wearing a party dress, but set against all this ebony it looked like literal porcelain. The effect was further accentuated by the blood red nails at the ends of her slender fingers and the multiple silver studs which pierced the delicate china cups of her ears. Suddenly, the girl became aware of his presence. She looked up into his face for an instant or two…before subtly rebuffing his convivial expression and vanishing back into the book. She was beautiful, Nichols decided, or would be, anyway, if only she looked just a little *healthier.* Her big, intelligent eyes were a luminous blue, but slightly watery, touched with red around the rims, and underscored by distinct dark circles. Nichols wondered how much of it was just part of "the look." In any event, he did finally what any of his friends would have foretold under the circumstances; he stepped impulsively to the back of the plane and sat down beside her.

"Carter Nichols," he announced, offering his hand. "With Tech Services."

The girl looked away from her book reluctantly, a fat second-hand copy of "Mansfield Park" by Jane Austen.

"Sylvie Fortune. Of the Mayflower Fortunes."

Nichols smiled. "There weren't any Fortunes on the Mayflower."

"There weren't? Well, I can't say I'm surprised. My parents lied to me about everything else, too." She finally took the proffered hand.

"Pleased to meet you, Miss Fortune."

"Call me Sylvie."

2:2

The plane rumbled into motion, rolled out onto the runaway, and was airborne inside of three minutes. Sylvie and Nichols were pressed into their seats firmly as the craft strained for altitude.

"Oh, God," said Nichols suddenly. "'Miss Fortune'—I walked right into that one, didn't I? And you're sick of hearing about it, of course. How does somebody like me get out of the trap tactfully?"

"Most people don't use 'Miss' anymore."

"That's true. Once again, I'm behind the times."

Abruptly, the plane banked to the west tilting the cabin to a near-45 degree angle. The bright shafts of morning sunlight coming through the windows played across the opposite side of the compartment like golden spotlights.

"I've got to tell you, Miss—uh, Sylvie. I'm very surprised to meet somebody on this plane I know nothing about. Who invited you along, if you don't mind my asking?"

One of the beams hit Sylvie full in the face; she put up her hand against the glare. "Hudson, I think the name was. A woman."

"MacDonald's private secretary? Wow. I'm impressed. What do you do?"

"Police work."

"Really? What sort of police work?"

"Investigations."

"You don't say."

Nichols was officially intrigued now. And the answer seemed evasive. The plane leveled again. Sylvie reopened her book and stuck her nose firmly back into it.

2:3

"They tell me you're former Army, Rabbi."

"That's right," replied Silverberg. "Retired Colonel. Twenty-five years in the chaplain corps. Yourself?"

"Marines," said Rocklynne, with the usual pride.

"I thought so. You looked like a jarhead to me."

Both men smiled at the ritual continuance of that long-running feud. Clearly, they'd make very congenial companions for the duration of the flight.

"How did you get involved in all of this?" the Rabbi asked.

"Corps threw me out. Mandatory retirement after thirty-three years."

"Quite a change of pace."

"Not really. I spent my whole career guarding high security sites. Nukes, mostly. Submarine bases. In a lot of ways, this ain't nothin' but a change of uniform."

"Family?"

"Married to the Corps. She dumped me, though." Again, both men smiled. "I guess I was ripe pickings for Mr. MacDonald's recruiters. How 'bout yourself? How does a Rabbi get mixed up with a bunch of Christian apostates like us?"

"Oh, I needed a hobby, I suppose, once I retired from the Army back in '87. So I got interested in biblical archeology and First Century religious sects. Wrote a couple of books. Published a paper back in 2001 on an odd little group of quasi-Christian Jews called the Ebionites. That's what got me noticed by the MacDonald group."

"Got a surprise visit from Dr. Mason one night, I bet," said Rocklynne.

"Dr. Roberts, actually. They only had a few questions, really, but they did sign me up."

"In blood, of course," added the former Marine, wryly.

The Rabbi looked into Rocklynne's face earnestly. "It *is* an astonishing thing, isn't it? I'm here in the middle of it now and it still seems like a dream."

"Well, don't worry yourself, Colonel. You stick with me and I'll see you through."

2:4

When the jet reached its cruising altitude, tail to the rising sun, Nichols extracted his briefcase from under the seat and took out a book of his own: a thick, leather bound copy of the King James Bible. Sylvie glanced over immediately and the sight of all that Scripture caused her to interrupt her own reading. Seeing her watching, Nichols began to read aloud. *"When Jesus knew that his hour was come that he should depart out of this world unto the Father, having loved his own which were in the world, he loved them unto the end."* After a brief pause, he closed the book and turned to Sylvie. "That's an exceptionally stirring piece of English, don't you think?"

From over the top of her dark circles, Sylvie's eyes flashed. "Mr. Nichols," she said, "I'm not bothering you. I didn't object when you sat down. But please don't start preaching Jesus at me, okay? I don't want to 'get saved.' Been there, done that. So please—let's just go back to our books, all right? If you don't mind."

Nichols answered shortly. "No, I don't mind. To be completely honest, I don't really give a damn whether you get saved or not. I'm not a Christian."

"You're not a—well, what are you, then?"

"A libertarian?"

Sylvie's features softened. Her tone became apologetic. "I am so sorry. It's only that, well, you threw me off with your little Bible there. I'm touchy, I guess. I get a lot of heat from the Bible beaters in my line of work."

"Don't mention it," said Nichols. "It's just that I haven't read the New Testament in a while. Figured I ought to bone up. You know, under the circumstances."

Nichols smiled what could only be described as an "insider's smile" but the girl's face remained blank and uncomprehending.

"Circumstances?"

"You don't—uh, you haven't been out to the Site before, then?"

"No, I haven't."

"I'll be damned. I mean—well, that's got to be a first."

"What is?"

"There's usually a pretty thorough, um, orientation, I guess you'd call it."

"So your square peg," concluded Sylvie, eyes flashing again, "doesn't fit my round hole. Is that what you're saying, Mr. Nichols?"

Nichols was caught short, but only for a moment.

"Oh, I wouldn't necessarily say that. Not at all. Only—well, let's just say you've got an interesting day ahead of you. Miss Sylvie Fortune."

2:5

Nichols was good-looking as geeks go. Definitely. And Sylvie'd been glad to learn that he wasn't some kind of fundie throwback. He had a nice smile and she'd have liked that back in the days when she still gave a damn about such things. And he smiled in spite of it all, like Sylvie still caught herself doing from time to time. That was interesting. He smiled in spite of the underlying buzz of sadness she could feel radiating off him, like infrared heat, whenever she looked his way. His come-ons, too, had been pleasingly subtle—that was nice. Of course, he'd be backpedaling like crazy within the next hour but that was okay, too. Truthfully, she'd been glad for the company during the brief seventy-five minutes of this flight, though they'd spoken very little. Just having a live body so close seemed to scare the haunts away, made a little bubble of warmth in which to briefly nest. Though her eyes were still scanning the words, Sylvie's thoughts, she now realized, had strayed far from Jane Austen. She closed the book and turned to look out the window.

Just as she did, the engine noises were altered and with a gentle downward lurch the small craft shifted unmistakably into descent mode. Yet the view outside the window was still wilderness—a miserable, treeless wilderness of uniform brown, punctuated only by the occasional yellow blotch of a sandy dry lake bed. Sylvie had seen a film once about the atom bomb test sites of the 1950s; this place looked exactly like that, and she figured you could probably get cancer just from breathing the air out there. Craning her neck a bit, however, and looking ahead along their flight path, something else entirely came into view. A strange, shallow inland sea was shimmering in the distance, looking just like the traveler's mirage one hears about in the desert. And now, directly below the plane, she noticed a recently laid band of lonely two-lane blacktop, aimed at the oasis like an arrow. A few more minutes and signs of a human presence came into view. Situated along one shore of the brilliant blue lake was a tight cluster of modern buildings, with a water tower rising above them. The buildings seemed very new, high-tech even. Strangest of all, the entire complex was ringed by a perfect circle of white, as if some stupendous giant had clapped half a cocoanut shell over the place and then pulled it away, leaving an encircling stamp more than a mile in diameter. What was this ring? A fence? A wall? It was still too far away for Sylvie to make out. She turned to Nichols, who was still poring over St. John's Gospel.

"Where are we?"

He leaned into Sylvie's personal space for a moment, smelling of Old Spice as he peered out her window.

"That's Pyramid Lake down there. About an hour north of Reno. Anson MacDonald owns this whole area. Close to 1700 square miles."

"He publishes a newspaper, right?"

"Three hundred and ninety of 'em, in fact, worldwide."

Nichols's casted forearm was propped on Sylvie's armrest now. The sight of it moved her to comment.

"How'd you hurt your arm?"

"Oh. Little difference of opinion."

Sylvie raised an eyebrow. "Really?"

"Between my car and a bridge abutment."

"Damn."

"You should have seen me a couple months ago. Just barely missed out on life in a wheelchair, they say."

Just then the flight attendant appeared in the aisle and, leaning into the seating area, spoke quietly to Sylvie.

"I wanted to let you know, we'll be passing through a weak magnetic field just before landing. Part of the research. It's nothing to worry about, but it does affect some people oddly. If you start feeling dizzy, try closing your eyes and tilting your head down."

Sylvie had little time to question this peculiar announcement; the plane was on final approach. Looking ahead, a private airstrip could be seen inside the white ring, but the ring itself was still a mystery. It was clear now that it did indeed rest on the top of a solid white wall encompassing the whole site. Its actual function, however, appeared to be scientific. She watched it draw nearer and nearer. Finally, the edge of the ring raced past her window at 130 knots. The instant this happened, Sylvie felt more than dizzy—she felt her eyes roll back in her head and her stomach leap with a violent rush of nausea. Oh, God. What had the lady said?—*tilt your eyes down and your*—what the hell was it? Relief came quickly, though, without her following any instructions. Another second and Sylvie's whole body went completely limp, as though someone had simply switched off the current. Her head fell back heavily against the headrest and her mind went blissfully to sleep.

2:6

Even before Sylvie opened her eyes again, after a period of weightlessness and disorientation that felt like an eternity, she knew by the smell in the air exactly where she was: it was in her own bedroom, in her own home. Isn't it amazing how the sense of smell brings this kind of recognition so quickly? The plane trip over the desert had been a dream, then. She willed her heavy lids to open, then allowed her sleepy, unfocused gaze to drift slowly across the familiar ceiling above. Warm California sunshine was coming through the Venetian blinds, creating a series of golden bands and alternating stripes aimed at the wall below the foot of the bed. These lines, in turn, directed her attention downward to the familiar dressing table standing against that wall, standing reassuringly where it always had…except…

Except, no! Sylvie's eyes widened and she sat bolt upright in the bed. This wasn't her home, after all! Not anymore. This was the idyllic, silly, suburban, and completely wonderful bedroom of a naïve teenage girl. This was Sylvie's own bedroom, in fact—as it had looked in another time, another place, another world, when Sylvie herself had been another person altogether.

She swung around and stood on her own two feet without a second thought. Rushing over to the dresser she began to examine the girlish treasures that were arranged there, each in precisely its proper place, each exactly where Sylvie remembered placing it. A brass trophy with her name on it, awarded to the Girl's Swim Team Captain of 1998. A favorite plush bunny from Knott's Berry Farm. A framed photo of herself, at 14 years of age, standing with a group of friends under a banner reading, "Methodist Bible Camp - Summer 1995." A valentine from David Blankenship. Sylvie felt her throat tighten and her eyes well up with salty tears. She hadn't seen, hadn't even thought about any of these things in years, in centuries, in eons of geologic time. How could they be here? How could *she* be here? Had she dreamed, along with the desert flight, a whole alternate life for herself, a whole decade of unreal events, an early 21st century that hadn't really even happened yet? God, what she wouldn't give to believe that were true! And yet—there was an item on the dresser she didn't recognize. Something alien, out of place. She put out her hand, half expecting it to vanish like smoke, but it didn't. It was a corny little vacation knick-knack out of the 1960's, an old-timey snow-globe with a plastic Christmas manger scene inside. Across the base of it were the words, "Bible Land Wax Museum - Hot Springs, Arkansas." Sylvie shook it up instinctively and watched it do its thing. She had no memory of this at all. She'd never been to Arkansas. It wasn't hers, never had been. It was completely out of place, dislocated like herself.

With this thought, Sylvie turned for the first time to the dresser's mirror, to get some sense of exactly what "herself" might still mean. Standing in it, looking directly into her own eyes, was a startling perfect image of herself as a 17 year old. Her hair was its natural color, loose and mussed a bit from sleep. Her eyes were clear and bright, her face as innocent as a blank sheet of paper, absolutely beautiful, radiating raw health and youth. It was like looking at the familiar face of an old friend who had died. Methodist Bible Camp might have been yesterday.

Sylvie grew numb at the sight. As she did, the snow-globe slipped from her fingers, dropped to the floor, and shattered.

2:7

The vision ended with the chirp of an airplane's tires on a desert runway. Nichols was still there, speaking to Sylvie with concern, his hand resting on her forearm.

"You okay?"

She opened her eyes and looked around uncomprehendingly. "God," she finally said, wiping her eyes, trying to get reoriented. "What in the hell was that?"

Nichols called out to the flight attendant. "Could we get a glass of water back here?"

Silverberg and Rocklynne turned around in their seats to see what was happening. Nichols took Sylvie's hand and held it tightly. "You're not going to throw up are you?" he asked. "I barfed all over my shoes the first time."

The jet taxied to a halt on MacDonald's private airstrip. Out the window, a welcoming committee of three separate vehicles could be seen driving up to meet it; a white van, a black Mercedes sedan, and a security Jeep with a logo on the door reading "Central Electronics Service—Unit 16." As they arrived, Rocklynne rose, opened the door, and lowered the steps. Meantime, the flight attendant had reached the rear of the cabin bearing Sylvie's water glass. She accepted it and took one or two small sips. Rabbi Silverberg rose to disembark as Nichols stood and offered Sylvie his hand. Attempting a weak smile, she politely but firmly declined.

"You go ahead."

2:8

For a man just out of physical therapy, Nichols got down the ladder with surprising agility. It was important that Fuller should not start thinking of him as diminished in any way, or in need of replacing. And sure enough, there was the Boy Wonder now, emerging from his expensive car, looking like a million dollars as always, immaculately and expensively business casual. Fuller was no older than Nichols, he just acted older. And it seemed natural on him. You simply looked into those blue hawk-like eyes and found yourself saying, "Yes, sir" without meaning to—and with complete sincerity. They said he was a genius of some sort, a child prodigy—and with doctorates from at least three prestigious universities, in disciplines as diverse as neuroscience, biophysics, and information theory, it was easy to believe. The man had certainly demonstrated, at any rate, a stunning knack for sniffing out and involving himself in the very most cutting edge scientific endeavors, from stem cell research and the Human Genome Project to gravitomagnetism and this current foray with Mr. Anson MacDonald. Nichols started across the gap to meet him, pushing himself to look stronger than he actually felt. Fuller met him halfway and offered his right hand. Displaying the cast, Nichols carefully substituted his own left.

"Still on the mend, I see," said Fuller, with a studied warmth. "Well, thank you for coming, Mr. Nichols. We've got quite a little mystery for you out here."

"Don't mention it. I'm intrigued myself, to tell you the truth."

Silverberg stepped up from behind.

"And Rabbi Silverberg," beamed Fuller, offering another handshake. "I can't tell you how much we appreciate this, sir. Let me apologize again for the short notice."

"Think nothing of it, Lance. I'm honored to be here."

Nearby, a very different man was emerging from the white van. Tall, fit, just on the wrong side of sixty, Caleb Donophan might have been a rancher or a writer of western novels. Dressed in blue jeans and cowboy boots, he wore his grey hair in a ponytail between his shoulder blades. His eyes, also gray, were clear and intelligent, and his voice had something of the young Henry Fonda in it, a quality not all thirty-somethings would have picked up on but which Nichols did and liked. Nichols knew Donophan far better than he did Fuller, and was less frightened of him, though his resume was no whit less impressive. Close friend of Carl Sagan and John Wheeler, author of over sixty papers in the fields of elementary particle theory, X-ray physics, quantum gravity, and plasma spectroscopy, Donophan was, nevertheless, a modest and unassuming gent with a pleasing countercultural air Nichols had always enjoyed. He turned and called out to him brightly, again offering his good left hand.

"Dr. Donophan!"

"It's Caleb," the scientist insisted.

"That's right. I forgot. First name basis."

Donophan took the hand awkwardly, causing both men to smile at the predicament. "I just don't like sounding so grown up," he said.

Nichols laughed. "I missed you last time I was out."

"When was it?" asked Donophan. "February?"

"January 9th!" Nichols exclaimed.

"That's right. You were in an accident."

"Three days before the extraction."

"Well, you got here just in time. You know we're sending him back on Saturday."

Standing with his back to the plane, Nichols suddenly noticed that something behind him had caught everyone else's attention. He wheeled around just in time to see Sylvie, seated in a wheelchair, being unloaded from the jet using an elaborate lift device. A tartan throw was draped over what he could now see was a pair of emaciated lower limbs; tucked lifelessly to one side of the footrest below was a pair of old-school basketball shoes with hot pink laces. Rocklynne was standing to one side, lowering the electric platform using a hand-held remote. It was Fuller who finally broke the silence.

"So this is Miss Fortune come to call at last."

"Miss *Sylvie* Fortune," Nichols corrected.

With her chair now on the ground, Sylvie headed toward the group under her own power, Rocklynne trailing behind. She sidled up alongside Nichols, catching his eye for just an instant. He looked away quickly, afraid of staring. Then, afraid of having patronized her with a show of pity, looked back—looked her square in the eyes, in fact. And as he did, he spoke out to Fuller and the rest.

"Gentlemen, this is my new friend, Sylvie Fortune. Apparently she's expected. Sylvie, this is Dr. Lance Fuller, administrator hereabouts, and Dr. Caleb C. Donophan, the chief technician of the project."

"Welcome aboard, Sylvie," offered Fuller. "Did you have a pleasant trip?"

"Actually, she, um, tangled with the containment field, I'm afraid."

"You do look a little blue around the gills," said Fuller, not without the trace of a smile.

"I'm alright," Sylvie answered shortly.

"It's quite a phenomenon, that barrier. Blocks all radio or cell phones, too. I like the privacy myself, but it does tend to cut us off from civilization. Have you any bags to unload?"

"Just a little carry-on," said Sylvie, holding it tightly in her lap. "I hope they told you—this is just a one-nighter for me. We agreed to that over the telephone."

"That's right," concurred Fuller. "And that's still the plan. You should be able to finish up before supper."

"I don't think you're going to be here very long either, Carter," said Donophan to Nichols. "Just between you and me, I'm not convinced there's anything wrong with the security system."

"Oh, I'm inclined to agree," added Fuller. "But Mr. MacDonald wants it done, so…"

"Done it shall be," finished Nichols. "I'll get started right away."

"Master Sergeant Rocklynne will take you directly to the security center. And you, Rabbi," Fuller continued, "I'll be escorting you to the Research Complex to finish your orientation." He opened the door of the Mercedes;

Silverberg entered the plush vehicle and fastened his seatbelt. Nichols and Rocklynne stepped toward the Jeep.

"You're going to be riding with me today, Sylvie," said Donophan. "This is a brand new van with a wheelchair lift in the back, just arrived this morning. Still got the sticker in the window."

"Wow," said Sylvie dryly. "Can I keep it when we're finished? I haven't wrecked a new car in several weeks. Which reminds me, you don't do blood tests on your overnight guests, do you?" Donophan paused and then smiled a sincere, quizzical smile, wondering just how much of this joke was genuinely autobiographical. Nichols wondered, too, having overheard at a distance. He spoke softly to Rocklynne as they entered the Jeep.

"Boy, she's one of a kind, isn't she?"

"Man, you hadn't seen anything yet."

2:9

The inside of Fuller's car, heavy with the smell of fine leather, was as immaculate as his own personal grooming. From the passenger seat, Silverberg watched him buckle his safety belt and then insert a Mozart CD into the console. All of his movements were smooth and elegant, as if he kept some small portion of his intellect at work constantly, calculating in advance the most efficient path of his hands through the air. He turned the ignition switch and the well-oiled German machine purred quietly off the airfield. Soon, it was rolling down the streets of what might almost be a tasteful Lake Tahoe resort development. The buildings were all beautiful, done in the appropriate Nevada ranch style.

"That's the Commissary there, Rabbi. Breakfast is at seven, lunch at 12:30. Dinner starts at six and is available until nine. If you're keeping any special diet just let the chef know in advance. Pick up any phone and dial 88."

Turning a corner, a different street came into view, much like the first. The overall impression was that no expense had been spared. Even a few bristlecone pines seemed to have been transplanted simply for the shade.

"This is South Street," continued Fuller. "Over on the right is 'E' Building, that's where you'll find the conference rooms and offices. To our left is 'F' Building, which is all the maintenance shops and support facilities."

"Where is the, uh—machine located?" Silverberg asked.

"Directly at the center of the Compound. I'll have Dr. Donophan set up a tour if you'd like."

"I think I would like that. You know, I must admit, Dr. Fuller, even though I've followed your updates very closely I'm still reeling at the thought you've actually done this."

"People felt the same way when the first transatlantic cable was laid. The idea of standing in a parlor in New York City and talking to someone in London seemed like a miracle. Now we're speaking to someone from across a sea of time instead. Either way, you get used to it pretty quick."

2:10

Donophan played Woody Herman rather than Mozart, but otherwise Sylvie's tour of the compound was much like the Rabbi's. He took her past the hotel/dormitory where, she was surprised to hear, he'd lived for most of the last five years. He showed her the carefully groomed beds of mountain wildflowers beginning to bloom—the delicate white chickweed flowers and wild blue iris. Finally, he took her to the rear entrance of 'F' Building, where he carefully completed all the elaborate rituals of hitching and unstrapping, unbinding and unbuckling which were involved in the offloading of her wheelchair. As he did so, Caleb Donophan made, once again, his customary plea to be referred to only by his first name, a custom to which the dark-eyed young lady one third his age finally promised to adhere. Caleb then piloted Sylvie smoothly through the outer doors of the plush facility before halting at a security checkpoint. One of Rocklynne's officers greeted them there, another polite black man named Burgess, wearing a more obvious security uniform; he took charge of the chair, positioning Sylvie in front of a blue photo backdrop. "Just a quick picture for your ID badge," he said.

"Great. This ought to be fetching," said Sylvie, as the man tinkered his big square camera into position. "Hey," she pled, "can I have a week or two to freshen up before we do this?" A flash went off and Sylvie saw her new digital picture instantly on a nearby computer monitor. "See what I mean," she finished. "My old milk carton picture was much nicer."

Donophan chuckled. "You're funny, you know that?"

"Oh, you just caught me on a good day, is all. Some days I'm like George Bailey on Christmas Eve. Only the goddam angel never shows up."

A printer buzzed for a minute or two, then spat out Sylvie's new ID card. The guard handed it to Donophan who attached it to a lanyard and dropped it around her neck.

"No kidding," she insisted. "I'll have you reaching for the Midol by tomorrow morning. Just wait."

2:11

Carter Nichols strode purposefully down the busy central hallway of the Protective Services office, a euphemistically named suite of rooms that served as central police station for the entire compound. Shadowing him was his on-site point man, Will Jenkins. Jenkins was a bit younger than Nichols, shorter and stockier, somewhat more blue-collar than his boss, accustomed to stringing cables and turning screwdrivers. The two were carrying on a running dialogue as they walked, Nichols in too big a hurry to turn and make eye contact, Jenkins flipping through the pages of a heavy clipboard.

"You've been over all the event logs," Nichols queried. "No door alarms, no motion triggers."

"None," replied Jenkins firmly. "And we've gone back six weeks already."

"Keep going. All the way back to Day One, if you have to. OT's not an issue. Use Henry and, um, Stone. And Chan. Get out your fine-toothed comb."

Tech Services employees were everywhere, most of them looking as busy as Nichols and Jenkins. Almost all of them attempted some kind of eager greeting, having seen neither hide nor hair of their convalescent boss in the more than three months since his accident. He'd left the site about six o'clock one morning after a brutal all-nighter—it was during the final crazy push prior to extraction. The next thing anyone knew, Nichols was in the hospital and Jenkins was in charge 'til further notice. "Carter!" called out one of the techs. "When did you get in?"

"Not now, Paul. Staff meeting at seven—I'll get with you then."

"No flags or tamper alerts, either," continued Jenkins. "Ran that myself."

Nichols frowned. "How about trouble alarms? Power failures?"

"Ditto."

"I need a cup of coffee."

Nichols hung a quick right into a staff break room, but stopped quickly in the doorway. An elderly gentleman in black was sitting at the snack table, wearing a clerical collar, nursing a cup of tea and chatting with a companion. It was the Right Reverend Randolph Young, retired Episcopalian bishop of a big Northeastern city. The other man Nichols recognized as Stiles, the linguist.

"Oh, hello," called out the cleric. "It's Mr. Nichols, isn't it?"

"That's right. Nice to see you again, bishop. Don't let us interrupt."

"Not at all, not at all."

Nichols turned quickly on his heels and escaped. A couple of steps down the hall, he confided his relief to Jenkins in a low tone of voice.

"That was close. I don't know if you've had the pleasure yet, Will, but that man will bore the paint off the walls if he catches you. He's like the Ancient Mariner."

"Really? He never bothers me."

"I made the mistake of asking him a question once. About the theology. After that it was off to the races."

Jenkins grinned, still keeping pace. "His book went to number three on the New York Times best seller list."

"I saw that. *Christianity Without Christ*. What the hell does that mean? Christianity without Christ is like rock and roll without sex and drugs. I mean, geez, if you don't believe the stuff anymore why not just go ahead and say so? Get on with your life, for God sakes."

"Now, be nice, boss," Jenkins cautioned.

"No, I mean it. I can't understand why a person who doesn't believe in God wants to go around dressed up like a bishop. With this guy it's Halloween 24/7/365."

Jenkins laughed out loud. The pair reached a locked door. Nichols swiped his ID badge over a prox card reader. When he did, a little light turned green and a magnetic lock released with an audible thunk.

"But hey," he concluded. "I haven't been to the Harvard Divinity School so what the hell do I know?"

2:12

Fuller's Mercedes finally stopped, parking in a reserved space in front of the main Research Building. Situated in a dappled grove of the imported pines, this building was the most spectacular yet, a combination library/laboratory done in the National Parks style of the early 20th century. The Rabbi, however, didn't stop to notice the amenities. He was deep in thought as he followed Fuller out of the car and up to the entrance.

"So we're absolutely sure you got the right man?" he asked.

"Depends on who you talk to," said Fuller, climbing the short cascade of steps. "Most of the theological staff is convinced, yes. But we've still got one or two important players who aren't ready to sign off yet."

"What's the problem?"

"Personally, I think they're just having trouble getting their heads around the man as he really is."

"Meaning?"

"Well, I don't think any of *my* people were expecting him to walk on water. But I guess we were holding out for some kind of fireworks. You know, controversy. Explosive revelations. We even had a camera crew here to get his answers on tape—everything from modern Mid-east politics to abortion."

"And?"

"And...well, he's a bit of a stiff, to tell you the plain truth. Been here three months and hasn't said ten intelligent words the whole time. I'm not sure he's capable."

Fuller opened the front door and both men entered the Complex. They emerged from an entrance foyer into a large sunlit atrium where several hallways branched off in all directions. Right away, it became apparent that this central crossroads was currently the bustling hub of activity for the whole complex. Research assistants were passing by in a steady flow, carrying an endless stream of boxes. A half-dozen young computer techs were disconnecting the multiple workstations arranged at various points of the compass. Whatever work had been going on here, the Rabbi realized, was now winding down dramatically. He also noted, once again, that money had been no object. The décor here in the atrium was a delightful mix of the Arts & Crafts and California rustic styles, and though spring was definitely in the air outside, an inviting fire crackled in a large sandstone fireplace.

"But surely," said Silverberg, regathering his thoughts to the issue at hand, "surely it's a linguistic problem. He doesn't understand you."

"Oh, no," said Fuller, footsteps clicking quietly on the rough stone floor. "He understands perfectly well. Practically the first person I hired for this project was the world's foremost expert on the languages of the ancient Near East."

"McCauley?"

"That's right. He spent four years reconstructing a working 1st century Aramaic for us, out of Mandaic, Turoyo, scraps of Syriac. Several expensive field trips to Iran and southeastern Turkey. Turns out to have been rather a waste of time, though. He understands traditional Hebrew just as well…which, I don't mind telling you, was a matter of great satisfaction to some of our Jewish associates. Our visitor's got an odd accent, to be sure, but otherwise you two should get on famously."

From among the crowd of hustling RAs, two older men suddenly emerged, also academics from the look of them. Fuller hailed them cheerily.

"Gentlemen!"

"Oh, hello, Dr. Fuller"

"I've got someone I'd like you to meet. This is Rabbi Jakob Silverberg of Temple Emmanu-El, Boston. He's going to be taking over as chaplain for a few days."

More cordial handshakes were exchanged. The taller of the two men was a white-haired, barrel-chested gent with a large head and spindly legs; the shorter, a shaggy-headed fellow with Coke-bottle glasses and a distinct Irish lilt in his voice. Both of them looked familiar to Silverberg.

"Rabbi, this is Dr. Kelvin Kent," said Fuller, indicating the tall man. "You know him, I think, as the founder of the *Symposium on the Historic Jesus*."

"Of course," Silverberg nodded. "I've followed your work with great interest, Doctor."

"Thank you," said Dr. Kent, with the lingering traces of a Tennessee accent.

"And you've heard of Professor Breen, I'm sure," Fuller continued. "Georgetown University."

"Of course. A pleasure to finally meet you, sir."

A lady had entered the room a few steps behind. She was an attractive, round-faced woman in her mid-fifties, dressed in a smart conservative suit. She, too, stepped up and extended a hand to the Rabbi.

"Camille Flammerion," she offered. "How do you do?"

Silverberg recognized the lady immediately. "What a joy, Doctor! I just saw you on PBS the other night. The Bill Moyers program, wasn't it?"

"Going over the Gospel of Judas?" she asked.

"That was it. Absolutely fascinating."

"I'm flattered, Rabbi. Thank you for coming."

Fuller turned and, with a wave of his hand, directed Silverberg's attention to the surrounding facility.

"And this is where it all happened, Rabbi—right here in this library. The emphasis will be on the machine, of course, once all this is made public. But this is where the extraction was really accomplished."

"You see," explained Flammerion, "nailing down *where* to go and *when* was as big a challenge as the technological one. Bigger in some ways."

Dr. Breen agreed, glancing at Kent. "Some of us doubted it could be done."

"I admit it, Joe. I didn't think there was enough history in the Gospels to fill a teacup. But there he was, right on schedule." Kent chuckled. "It's enough to turn an old country boy like me back into a fundamentalist." The others joined the laughter.

"The occasion," recalled Breen, "was the fourth night of the Feast of Tabernacles; the 22nd day of the seventh month, Ethanim of Tishri, in the year 29 A.D. of our reckoning."

"St. John's Gospel," added Kent, "the seventh chapter. One of the few passages of Scripture that ties him to a definite place at a definite hour. The trick was which year."

"Amazing," said Silverberg.

Flammerion motioned toward one of the hallways. "We were just headed to lunch, gents. Care to join us?"

"The Commissary?" asked Fuller.

"No, no," said Flammerion. "I've put together a little something here in the staff lounge. Not much—a nice

Caesar and a spinach quiche. We've gotten so tired of that Commissary, haven't you?"

Fuller agreed and the Rabbi seemed more than willing. The group vanished down one of the many halls, leaving the RAs still trucking out boxes, the geeks still hauling their desktops and monitors.

2:13

"Sure you wouldn't like some lunch before you get started?"

Caleb Donophan was pushing Sylvie's wheelchair down the sidewalks of South Street now, headed toward the studios in 'D' Building. A sunlit mountain of cumulus cloud standing on the western horizon gave the impression of a gigantic white dome or temple toward which they were progressing and the trees along the avenue chirped quietly under the influence of a half-dozen hidden blackbirds. Sylvie herself was oblivious, having disappeared into 'Mansfield Park' again.

"Nope," she replied, not looking up. "Just want to get the job done and let you guys get on with your lives."

"You're not very curious, are you? Don't you ask any questions before going out on an assignment like this?"

"As a matter of fact, I do. I ask if the money is green."

"Keeps things simple."

"I'm not a complicated person," said Sylvie, matter-of-factly. "Doesn't mean I don't have my theories."

"I'd be interested to hear one."

"I'm guessing some of MacDonald's tech secrets are walking out the back door."

"Not even close," smiled Caleb.

They reached the main door to 'D' Building. A security camera looked down on them from above as Caleb pressed a doorbell for access. While they waited to be admitted, Donophan noticed that Sylvie, for all her bluster and irony, still wore a tiny silver cross on a chain around her neck—not a big heavy gothic-statement cross, as he might have expected, but something simple, maybe sincere once upon a time. Sylvie happened to look up at just this moment, catching him, as she thought, eyeballing her physique.

"I'm flattered, Professor, but it'd never work out, you know."

"How's that?" Caleb asked, puzzled.

"I just ain't got the equipment anymore. For romance, that is. That's what you were wondering about, isn't it?"

Donophan looked embarrassed, said nothing.

"I can't even go to the bathroom properly these days. But don't worry about it. My ex-fiancé couldn't handle it either."

2:14

"So…you're not disappointed in the work after all?"

Hoping he hadn't hit a sore spot, Rabbi Silverberg asked his question and then put a forkful of salad into his mouth. The large elongated table in the well-lit lounge did become quiet for just a moment, but then the theologian Breen rallied convincingly.

"Oh, not disappointed. Not really. I hope we all knew, going into this, that some re-evaluations would have to be made, some pet theories rejected. That was the whole point, wasn't it?"

"And it's been a bit of both, hasn't it?" said Dr. Flammerion, having just taken her seat.

"Really, it has," agreed Kent.

"I mean, it's clear now," the lady continued, "that I've been crediting the man with an Eastern wisdom he doesn't seem to have been exposed to after all. I've got some books to re-write!"

"Haven't we all?" laughed Breen.

"Bishop Young has fared best in this regard," added Lance Fuller from his end of the table. "Do you know the bishop, Rabbi? I tried to call him over to lunch with us but he was busy elsewhere."

"As a matter of fact, we did meet once—at Château de Bossey, five years ago. Charming man."

"He expects us to get the Nobel Prize just for proving that Jesus ever existed at all! As you probably know, he wasn't at all convinced going in."

"The triumph of low expectations!" laughed Flammerion.

"But honestly," added Kent, drawing a sip of Chardonnay, "even those of us with more conservative ideas have nothing to be ashamed of. After all, we've demonstrated the most important point, haven't we?"

"What was that, Dr. Kent?" asked Silverberg.

"We've proved that Jesus himself is nothing but a figurehead. Someone else built the whole vast edifice of

Christianity in his name, long after the man himself was dead and buried."

"He's right, Rabbi," agreed Fuller, putting down his salad fork. "We built this library with just that thought in mind."

"How so?"

"This facility is probably the single most advanced theological studies center ever created. It was built in hopes of comparing and contrasting the man's every word with digital facsimiles of the whole corpus of surviving manuscript: the Dead Sea Scrolls; all of the Christian apocrypha; the great uncial codices of Scripture..."

"And it was all for nothing," interjected Kent. "He's nothing in the world but a dreamy street corner crank. Sits around and sulks all day. There must have been a hundred like him."

"The best scholars have suspected it for years, of course," said Breen. "But it's not just a theory any longer. We've studied him. We've asked our questions."

"And the verdict is in," continued Kent. "The real Jesus doesn't know any more about the Trinity, or Original Sin, or the Blood Atonement than the man in the moon. He's going to have to be demoted, I'm afraid."

"Incredible," Silverberg concluded. "Who then? Who created the Myth of the Divine Christ?"

"Oh, it took many cooks to spoil that soup," said Kent.

"Parallel tracks, is the best way to describe it," explained Flammerion. "My own specialty was always the Gnostic track. A little dash of Zoroaster, a pinch of Plato—you finish up with Christ as an Eastern sage, preaching self-enlightenment and the sacred feminine. I've filled three best-sellers with the stuff."

"You're too hard on yourself, Camille," said Breen.

"Oh, don't get me wrong," she responded. "It's still an attractive spirituality to my way of thinking. But let's be honest. I was projecting that spirituality *onto* Jesus of Nazareth, not finding it there. We know that now." She paused and took a swallow of wine before continuing. "I mean, God, Joe, you've spent more hours with him than I have. It's like sitting on the creek bank with a farmer. No truly *religious* element to his talk at all. So, yes, I'll stick with the Gnostic Way to God—but it's certainly no more connected to the historic Jesus than the later Roman Orthodoxy which crushed it out."

"The 'Da Vinci' scenario?" asked Silverberg.

"That's the crude, pop form, yes," said Flammerion.

"And we blame the emperor Constantine for that?" the Rabbi inquired.

"Constantine was a central figure, certainly," answered Dr. Breen. "He chose his own favorite strain of Christ-invoking religion and then sponsored it to the exclusion of all others. But most of us here would agree it was Paul of Tarsus who set the ball in motion—just a decade or two after the Crucifixion."

Fuller looked up from his quiche, joking. "Maybe we'll go after him next. Try to broaden his mind a little."

"Point is," said Kent, "that once our befuddled guest goes back to his own time he's destined to become history's great ink blot test. And every man, woman, and child on earth will have the next twenty centuries to create him in their own image. Paul was just the first."

Silverberg pushed himself away from the table. "So this fabulous array of talent has been left with nothing to do but twiddle its thumbs?"

"Far from it, far from it," said Breen, sounding very Irish. "We've switched our focus to developing a plan for breaking the news to the world. As you can imagine, it will need to be handled delicately."

"There's the potential for psychological trauma," added Flammerion. "Civil unrest, even."

The Tennessean seemed impatient with this cautious tone. "Yes, but it has to be done, doesn't it? It's the whole reason a philanthropist like MacDonald got involved to begin with. However it happened, this man Jesus is the central figure of Western Civilization. I can't think of anything more important to the world's future than to settle the issues connected with him once and for all. So that we can all just put the question behind us and move on."

"Well, speaking of moving on," said Fuller, looking at his wristwatch, "God, look at the time. I've got an interview over at 'D' Building in about 20 minutes. And we still haven't got the Rabbi moved into his quarters yet." He rose to his feet. "I don't suppose one of you fine folk would be willing to pinch hit for me the rest of the way?"

Breen spoke up. "Oh, I think I can spare some time, Lance. I'd love a chance to get better acquainted."

"Excellent. We'd like to have him in the Village before sundown, if possible. *Minchah*, you know—afternoon prayer."

Before Fuller could get out the door, Kent called out a final question. "This interview, Lance. It's not what I think it is?"

Fuller paused. "Look, people, I know it's a lot of mumbo jumbo as well as you. It wasn't my idea. But try not to take it so personally."

"How can we do anything else?" demanded Breen. "It's a reflection on everything we've done here, on our professional reputations."

"It's a reflection," said Fuller, lowering his voice markedly, "of Mr. Anson MacDonald's personal issues, is what it is. Nothing more. And it won't be made public whatever the result, as I've already told you. So just—relax. Finish your packing, have a nice afternoon, okay? And let me manage the MacDonald front."

2:15

Rounding a corner, Nichols and Jenkins ran directly into Ross Rocklynne. He was blocking the door to the darkened surveillance monitoring suite, holding a fat manila folder full of paper. Behind him, the younger men could see a bank of brightly lit closed-circuit TVs being closely watched by a trained officer. Apparently, the Master Sergeant had been waiting for them.

"There you are," said Rocklynne. "Got something to show you."

Nichols was still looking past him, his eye fixed by one of the glowing monitors inside—like a restaurant patron who spoils a perfectly good dinner date watching closed-captioned TV commercials on a set over the bar.

"Gee, Rock, can we do it quick? This is a big moment for me."

Rocklynne paused quizzically, then smiled. "That's right," he realized. "You haven't had a look at him yet, have you?"

Nichols bit his lip and held up his arm cast for inspection.

"Well, this won't take a minute," said Rocklynne, handing him the folder. "Initial interviews with the whistle blower. Dolores Mendoza's the name. She cooks his breakfast."

Nichols flipped through some of the pages inside. The first thing he noticed was a black and white photo of a sour-faced Latina wearing a cook's uniform.

"She's seen activity in his house," repeated Nichols, skeptically.

"After hours visitors. Three separate occasions."

"With all the specifics. Dates and times."

"Yep. It's all there."

Nichols glanced at Will Jenkins, who was hanging back but still very much engaged in the discussion. "There's twelve cameras in that house, Will. Twenty-four hour digital recording since January 30th. And we don't have one second of video on this. Is that what we're saying?"

"That's about the size of it."

Nichols flashed a bit of anger, dropping the folder to his side with a snap. "Nobody went to sleep in there?" he asked, indicating the monitoring room.

"That's something we do have video on," said Jenkins. "There's a camera pointed at the monitoring officer. And we oughta give 'em all a raise, Carter. Fantastic job. Watched him like he was the Super Bowl."

Nichols frowned sourly.

"Do you know how it was done, Will?"

"Beats me half to death," said Jenkins, with perfect sincerity.

Nichols turned back to Rocklynne. "This Mendoza lady. She got any motives for yanking our chain on this?"

"We're working on it."

Nichols sighed, resigned for the moment. "Okay. I guess we'll hash it out some more at the meeting tonight."

"We gotta get this, Carter," said Rocklynne, turning stern. "You know what a leak would mean as well as I do. If word got out that Jesus Christ was being held prisoner out in the Nevada desert...?"

"He's not a prisoner," said Nichols. "He's a guest. Fuller says he's had every luxury."

"You know that, I know it. But how do you tell the mobs? The ones with the torches and pitchforks?"

"We'll get it, Rock. Till then, I think I'll have a turn at those cameras myself."

Rocklynne stepped aside, retiring into the larger outer office. Nichols slipped past him into the dim confines of the monitoring room, followed by Jenkins. Once inside, it took fully a minute or more for their eyes to adjust. At least forty color monitors made a bright kaleidoscopic patchwork against one wall, dazzling one's gaze in the small, otherwise unlit chamber. Nichols tapped the current monitoring officer, Banks, on one shoulder.

"Take five, Scott."

Banks turned away from the cameras to respond, taking a second or two to recognize the newcomers.

"Carter! When'd you get in?"

"Morning plane, bud. Nice to see you."

Banks got up from his chair. Nichols took his place and began peering at the monitors in earnest.

"Where's he at?"

"Oh, uh—living room. Camera 14, on the 103 multiplexer."

Nichols pushed a button or two, moving the designated image from one of the smaller sets to the big central monitor. Jenkins was standing to one side in the crowded space so that he saw only his boss's face as he watched. The ghostly glow of the screens gave it an otherworldly look, as if Nichols himself were the visitor come down from heaven. Finally, he spoke.

"So that's meant to be him, is it?"

"In the flesh," said Jenkins.

"What's he doing there? Meditating? Praying?"

"Out of my line," said Jenkins. "Ask the Theos."

"I'll be damned," said Nichols.

"You and me both, if we're not careful."

Nichols was gazing at the screen very intently now, a look of growing wonder on his face. "You know," he said, to no one in particular, "that would be—amazing. If you could really—you know."

Finally, Jenkins saw a little tear form in the corner of one eye which Nichols, after a moment, rubbed out with his thumb.

"Wow," he said softly.

2:16

This Donophan character was a strange bird, Sylvie decided. He bore watching—which was easy to do since he was still close at hand, pouring water from a pitcher into the drinking glass in front of her. Not that he seemed dangerous or anything like that—but his still waters definitely ran deep. She'd thought about touching his hand discreetly as he delivered her to this plush, sound-proof room, with its carpeted walls, its cameras and microphones. And she might have done it, too, if she were going to be here longer or expected to have any kind of ongoing connection to the guy. As it was...well, why bother? Curiosity had killed several of her cats already this year. Caleb finished his pouring and politely pushed her chair a little closer to the table. Finally, the stillness was broken when Lance Fuller burst through the door, full of elaborate bonhomie and acting like a man on a tight schedule.

"Great. You're here already. This room going to be okay?"

"Everything's fine," Sylvie answered.

"Can I get you something? A glass of wine, maybe?"

"No, I'm ready to get started. Let's knock this out."

"Businesslike," said the Administrator. "I love it. No further ado, then."

The reflective side of a two-way mirror could be seen in the large wall opposite; Fuller flashed a "thumbs-up" signal in that direction. In response, a small red light appeared on one of the video cameras.

"Caleb," said Fuller suddenly, "maybe you could just step up to the control booth for now—give us a little more elbow room down here."

Donophan agreed. Sylvie felt disappointed to see him go, though she wasn't sure why. Fuller opened another door on the opposite end of the room and called in two more of the research assistants, young interns dressed in lab coats and white gloves. The big Marine Rocklynne appeared, too, stepping into a back corner right away and slipping almost unconsciously into parade rest. He looked like the guy who stands behind the armored car on payday. Sylvie's curiosity was piqued. What sort of evidence gets the Tiffany's treatment way out here in the desert?

"We've got an interesting case for you today, Sylvie," said the Administrator, brightly. "Let's call it…a missing persons investigation."

One of the interns carried a flat plastic tub into the room; inside was an ordinary gray sweatshirt, clean and neatly folded. She placed the tub on the bare table in front of Sylvie. "This will be your control item," said Fuller. "The man we're trying to identify is known to have worn this shirt less than 48 hours ago."

Sylvie picked up the item and began to examine it.

"In a moment," continued Fuller, "the archivists will start bringing in some additional material. All of these articles are alleged to have belonged to a certain well-known individual—a Middle Eastern man who was involved in some important events in that part of the world some years ago. That man may or may not be the same person who wore the sweatshirt here at the

Compound the day before yesterday. We're hoping you can establish a link."

Sylvie looked up with her red eyes and smiled a crooked, elfish smile. "I'll try anything once," she said with conviction, looking to Fuller as if she already had—some time ago.

2:17

Breen delivered Silverberg to the chaplain's quarters and helped him to unload his bags. It was a nice room, but rather plain and scholarly, like the Abbot's room in an old California Mission. Sun poured pleasantly through a window of wavy glass, adding to the distinct 16th century ambiance.

"Here we are, Rabbi. I think you'll find this comfortable enough for a few days."

"I'm sure I will," said Silverberg. Depositing the bags at the foot of the bed, he stopped suddenly and sniffed at the air. "Someone's been painting."

"Oh…well, yes," said Breen awkwardly. "That's true. They decided to give the place a bit of a going over. After Rabbi Mintz left."

The sun had only begun its dip toward the horizon but Silverberg seemed to feel a sudden breath of chill in the early spring air, as if a cloud had passed over the small freestanding apartment. Breen must have felt it, too, because he turned and shut the door behind them. The resulting stillness was surprisingly complete and quite palpable.

"I don't suppose you could tell me, doctor," asked Silverberg, "what it was that troubled the Rabbi? Mr. Rocklynne didn't say."

Breen looked at the floor. "No, I'm sorry. I don't think I could. Patient confidentiality and all that. You know."

Silverberg pressed. "What about his notes? He left a project log, surely—that goes without saying in so important a case. Might I familiarize myself with that?"

"I will…speak to Dr. Fuller about it."

"Yes, please do. Thank you."

With very little grace, Breen changed the subject abruptly. "Well, I'm sure you're anxious to freshen up a bit after traveling. Shall I just wait in the car?"

"That would be wonderful," said Silverberg. "I won't be a moment."

The Irishman left with an air of relief, pulling the door to behind him. Silverberg hefted one of the bags up onto the bed and, bending over it, unfastened the latch. As he did, he felt the chill again—sharper this time, unmistakable—and then caught the whisper of a voice behind his back, only for an instant. He stood up straight as if shocked by a wire. Was it Breen come inside again after all? No. Looking out the window, Breen could be seen halfway down the walk. But it *had* been a voice, he was certain of it. He could replay it in his mind; muffled, fragmentary, but quite distinct—a sort of caustic snicker in response to an unheard but not very kind jest. The old man shuddered involuntarily, reaching up with his right hand and rubbing the cold prickle in the back of his neck. There *was* someone in the room with him! He looked over his shoulder again, then quickly from side to side. He stepped to the bathroom door, reaching inside and flipping the switch. A small, noisy ventilation fan clattered to life in response, sounding, in contrast to the previous stillness, like the blades of a helicopter, but the room itself, was, of course, quite empty. Just as the Rabbi's reason began to persuade him that he was, indeed, just as alone as he seemed, the presence leapt suddenly into his mind again, so vivid that he felt he could even predict which corner of the room it would be standing in when he swung around to see. He hesitated—and then did swing. And there was nothing.

But then something did catch his eye after all. Something on the wall, close to the floor. A splotch of mold? A spider web? No. It was an unmistakable group of *Hebrew letters* written in magic marker, bleeding through the fresh paint. The Rabbi moved closer, scooting the bed a few inches farther from the wall, dropping to a crouch for a better look. He touched the spot, tried to trace the characters with his index finger. No luck. Standing up again, he moved back to the suitcase. Out of it he quickly produced a bottle of aftershave and unscrewed the top. Pulling an embroidered handkerchief out of his pocket, he soaked it with the fluid and began to rub away the half-dried latex wall paint. It only took a moment for a complete Hebrew word to appear, then another and another. Finally, the Rabbi was able to attempt a hushed translation.

"The ropes of Sheol entangle me, the snares of death..."

It was a quote from the Scriptures—one of the Psalms, as he seemed to recall, or perhaps the book of

Samuel. It was King David, hunted, hounded by the maddened Saul, terrified for his life. Mintz would have known the passage better than he; though the two had never met, Silverberg knew him by reputation—as a Scripture scholar to be sure, but cultured, urbane, no one's idea of orthodox. Definitely not the sort of man who scrawls Bible verses on the wall. Another whisper of wind seemed to waft by, almost imperceptible. Nearby, in the dust behind the chest-of-drawers, Silverberg saw more words bleeding through the paint. He poured more aftershave onto the soiled cloth and set to work again.

2:18

Up in the control booth, Caleb was perched on a high stool, looking down through the two way mirror, watching Sylvie from above. The RAs, handling everything gingerly with their white gloves, were currently presenting her with a small piece of white linen; very old from the look of it, splotchy with dark brown stains, and pressed between two pieces of glass. The two panels opened like the pages of a book and Sylvie was encouraged to touch the delicate fabric. As she did this, Franklin Jones, one of Rocklynne's people and the man running the camera in the booth, turned to Caleb and spoke.

"This chick's a celebrity, you know. Check this out."

He popped a videocassette into a large format VCR, the kind used in television news operations. Within a few seconds the monitor came to life with the familiar face and voice of a well-known cable TV interviewer. *"She has been raped, shot, knifed and strangled. She's had her throat cut and been drowned in a bathtub. She's been inside the minds of murder victims during their last moments of life. She's America's best known and most accurate police psychic and she'll be here for the full hour, answering your questions."*

The video faded to black, then faded back in again.

"Have you ever touched something and gotten an impression – pictures, an idea, or a sense of someone's presence? If so, then you may have what it takes to become a psychometrist. Psychometry is the ability to touch some physical object and gain information about its history…just from holding it in your hand. And it's this rare ability, according to believers, that makes the work of the police psychic possible. Tonight's guest, Sylvia Fortune, has worked on more than 200 homicides and missing persons cases, and has even assisted the Department of Homeland Security in the war on terrorism. She's also known as the only psychic ever to have stumped the experts at New Skeptic magazine – a pretty tough crowd, by all accounts. Welcome to the show, Sylvie."

Caleb couldn't help noticing that Sylvie looked a good deal more respectable on TV than he had seen her so far. She still showed a touch of the gothic, to be sure, but she definitely cleaned up well, reminding him a little of that perky brunette who used to show rock videos when MTV first started up. *"Thank you,"* she said, *"Happy to be here."* The real Sylvie below, some miles down the road and worse for wear and tear, was shaking her head over the splotchy strip, clearly having received no impressions. Fuller ordered it taken away.

"When did you first realize you could do this?" asked the smooth TV pundit. *"Were you born this way?"*

"Actually, no," said the Sylvie on TV. *"For the first twenty-two years of my life I was a totally ordinary girl from La Jolla. In fact, I didn't believe in this kind of thing at all."*

"What happened to change your mind?"

"It started right after the accident that put me into this wheelchair. My sister brought a quilt to the hospital that had been made by my grandmother. And whenever it was placed over me I had the most vivid dreams of Grandma, even though she died when I was four. Turns out the dreams were filled with very accurate details about her – things I never knew."

Turning away from the TV, Caleb focused his attention on the real-life scene in the studio. Two of the archivists had returned together, carrying what Donophan recognized as a heavy brass reliquary—a cross-shaped display stand with a little glass door at the center, such as he had seen in the Catholic churches of his boyhood. They stood it on the table, about three feet tall, directly in front of Sylvie. She looked up at Fuller with a distinct (as it seemed to Caleb) "what in the hell is this all about" look on her face. Using white-gloved hands, one of the archivists opened the glass door and carefully removed a lacy panel to which three tiny black hairs had been affixed.

"How does it work?" continued the TV host. *"I mean, how do you get started?"*

"Um, let's say it's a missing persons case," proposed the taped Sylvie. *"You take hold of something that used to belong to the person you're looking for. And then you touch something else – maybe a bloodied article of clothing found in the woods or something. Most of the time you won't get anything. No connection. But if the two items really are associated in some way you'll get images. Thoughts, symbols, emotions."*

"So it's true then," ventured the interviewer, *"that you, as a psychic, often have to re-live some pretty traumatic events?"*

"Yeah, that's part of it sometimes..."

"You can actually feel their pain?"

"Sometimes. Sometimes I see faces, too."

"Faces of the murderers?"

"Uh huh. It's not so awful during the investigation because you're caught up in the chase, you know? You really want to see these guys get nailed. But after it's all over – well, the bad ones tend to linger."

The panel with the hairs on it was right under Sylvie's nose now; her hands hovered inches above it. Once again, she looked across at Fuller who was wordlessly urging her on. Caleb still heard the newsman asking his questions.

"Do you know why you have this and I don't?"

"No clue. I do think it's a natural power of the mind, though."

"So you don't attribute it to 'spirit guides' or any other occult forces?"

"No, I don't. I realize the stereotypical psychic has got a pocket full of crystals and a Shirley MacLaine book in each hand, but I guess I'm the exception. I'm a bit of a skeptic myself, when it comes right down to it."

"Are you a religious person?"

"No."

"Not at all?"

"No, I've seen too much. Too much to find any, you know, 'overarching plan' in any of this."

"So you approach your gift from – what, a scientific standpoint?"

"Exactly. I think it's more like Savant Syndrome."

"The 'Rain Man' condition?"

"That's right. I think that when my neck broke and I lost control over most of my body, some new area of my brain must have opened up for business. Like the savant that can't even tie his own shoes but who somehow knows the square root of thirty-eight thousand and seventy all of a sudden."

"Kind of like a consolation prize."

"Those wouldn't be my words, but...I guess you might put it that way."

Caleb was watching the real Sylvie very carefully now. Slowly, delicately, she placed two of her fingers on the tiny black hairs, still clutching the gray sweatshirt in her other hand. She closed her eyes tightly...and then opened them. The look on her face was plain; she felt nothing at all. Fuller looked frustrated, then ordered the reliquary removed.

2:19

Nichols was lying in the overhead now, above the security center, his limbs threaded amongst a spider's web of cables and supporting guy wires. He was looking for taps in the system, places where false data might be fed into the wiring in an effort to fool the various surveillance devices. Holding a flashlight between his shoulder and cheek, wallowing in the dust, he was elbow deep and thoroughly in his element. "This is the life for me, Will," he said, speaking to a shadowy head sticking up into the space behind him. "You can really go to work out here. No OSHA, no code inspectors, no unions—just make it happen or get the hell out. And look what we've accomplished. Gives you some idea of how the whole world might look if we could just get government off our backs."

Jenkins was at the top of the ladder below, supplying tools to his boss when called for. "Oh, I don't know," he countered, knowing full well he was opening a can of worms good for the rest of the afternoon. "I really don't mind a little governing if it's just for my own safety."

"Ah, but it's always for your own safety. That's the trouble. You give politicians an inch and they take 20,000 light years." Nichols shifted his weight, sending a little shower of dust raining from the dropped ceiling into the room below. "Unless you've got Anson MacDonald's level of resources," he continued, "they'll just swallow you up eventually. And honestly, I'm not even sure how MacDonald does it. He must be spending a fortune every week just to keep the busybodies out."

"A lot of it passes under the table, I would think," suggested Jenkins.

Nichols grinned. "I wouldn't be a bit surprised."

Jenkins shone his own flashlight into the wiring junction where Nichols was working, trying to provide him some additional light without getting it into his eyes. They collaborated in silence for a moment or two as he tried to dream up a hypothetical stumper. "What if MacDonald had been interested in another branch of physics," Jenkins proposed finally. "Like maybe causing some kind of wacko chain-reaction out here that could destroy the earth. Nuclear fusion run amuck—you know. Even a die-hard like you would want a little government oversight in a case like that, wouldn't he?"

"No," said Nichols flatly.

"Just no?"

"Just no. Getting the government involved only adds a whole new layer of wackiness. What makes you think bureaucrats are more responsible than businessmen? Just let the market fix it."

"The market?" said Jenkins, incredulous. "How does the market stop a nuclear chain-reaction?"

"Well, think about it. Would you stay on a job like this if you thought you were going to get fusioned? Would anybody?"

"I wouldn't, obviously, but somebody might risk it—if the pay was good enough. And MacDonald's got the money, no question."

"C'mon, Will. You can't pay somebody to commit suicide. That's not reality. And all the money in the world couldn't build the thing if nobody was willing to do the work. So once again, enlightened self-interest is the answer."

Jenkins stood breathless again in the presence of such a stunningly one track mind. Nichols was a brilliant guy, no doubt. And he was refreshing to be with most of the time. He was the one political person Jenkins knew who actually bothered to read what the opposition wrote, rather than just relying on straw-man summaries from an approved list of fellow travelers. A *laissez-faire* capitalist who could quote Karl Marx with as much pleasure as Adam Smith, an agnostic with a genuine admiration for C.S. Lewis and Pope John Paul II, Nichols was a talk radio devotee who never dittoed the host. In fact, he seemed to take a kind of abstract pleasure in adopting the opposite side of any argument with which he happened to be presented. In a roomful of complacent liberals he would begin arguing (quite forcefully!) that Herbert Hoover had been the greatest US President; surrounded by smug conservatives he would start championing Clarence Darrow and Hugh Hefner as great 20th century Americans. But Jenkins had watched him long enough to know that it wasn't just a stunt. Nichols was simply aware that a pretty good case could be made for just about any point of view—and he enjoyed watching it done. He wanted to make sure you didn't get away without becoming aware of it, too. Because of this, lots of people found him annoying; Nichols made you think too hard. Jenkins, on the other hand, liked the treatment most of the time. But the man's one dogma was this matter of the market—of letting nature take its course in any and all situations. It seemed related to his notion of ultimate truth somehow; just let everything play out to the end, chips falling where they may, and Evolution (or somebody) would eventually publish the answer by leaving you (or somebody else!) the Last Man Standing. No one, at any rate, had a right to interfere with the process by forcing someone else to follow their idea of "the rules"—not even if it meant risking nuclear holocaust! It was this thought which at last prompted Jenkins to sum up his reaction by saying, "You're a man of faith, boss. I've gotta hand you that. You've got your story and you're sticking to it."

"It doesn't take faith to see the truth here, Will. Lawyers are killing this country—and don't forget, most of the political class started out as lawyers." Uh oh. This was another favorite theme. Nichols had stumbled into a stupid weekend affair a few years back and his wife, like Queen Victoria, had not been amused. She instantly sicced a divorce lawyer on him, one of the nastiest on the planet. Nichols was a code writer at the time for one of the big security software firms, doing very well, but before it was over she hadn't even left him car fare. She then moved to the opposite coast, taking two daughters that Nichols positively worshipped, and began to pretend he had never existed at all. He had to start completely over; that was when he founded Tech Services and, a few months later, hired Jenkins himself. Lawyers, therefore, as Jenkins now heard him summarizing, were responsible for all of the world's ills, from the Spanish Inquisition to allergies in the springtime. "To paraphrase Jefferson," he concluded, "'Lawyers add just so much to the health of the nation as sores do to strength of the human body.'" Nichols paused triumphantly, then crowned this pronouncement with "Wouldja send me up a 5/8ths socket?"

"You're opening the manufacturer's box?"

"Yup."

"All of them?"

"Uh huh."

"The other buildings, too?"

"You bet. We're not going to find anything, of course—I'm with you, it's some kind of bug in the software if it's anything. But when Fuller asks me if I did all this, the answer's gonna be yes. Hell, yes. If we have to root around up here all night."

Will Jenkins sighed, feeling certain that they would be doing just that.

2:20

Still Sylvie had felt nothing. Five or six of these crazy religious antiques in a row and nary a tingle. Her mind raced, scrambling for a theory. Perhaps MacDonald collected junk like this—antiquities, as they called them in high-toned circles, acquired at auction houses like Sotheby's or Christie's. Maybe he spent a bunch of money on this stuff and now he's worried about fakes. That must be what Rocklynne was here for—hell, this whole dusty garage sale must be worth millions. But what about the sweatshirt? What was the connection there? Had it belonged to a smuggler, perhaps? One of MacDonald's own people working an inside job? Surely Fuller knew that not everyone who ever touched one of these things would have left discernable impressions. She'd told them as much over the phone. There had to be strong, lasting psychic bonds—the kind created by powerful trauma, intense emotion. Damn. These people were going to be pissed if she had to tell them this whole outing had been a wild goose chase. They might even try to weasel out of paying her. Dammit.

"Okay, Sylvie," said Fuller, interrupting her speculations. "Just a few more moments." One of the archivists returned carrying a final article: a jewel-encrusted casket, about the size of a shoebox, with a Byzantine icon of Christ on the lid. It was brought solemnly to the table and set before Sylvie.

"This last is a very interesting item," said Fuller. "One of three, I believe." He stepped up and opened the box himself. Inside was a long black nail made of iron, sharp on one end and rounded at the top. The instant it was exposed Sylvie felt as if she had been kicked in the head by a horse. Both hands flew up to her temples and she slammed her eyes tightly shut. The pale fluorescent lights of the studio felt like the third degree now, like the morning after an all-night frat house binge. She groaned once—and then began to see images. Clear, cold, remote images and yet somehow utterly real, from some wavelength she had never before visited.

She was looking down into a church, as if she herself were standing where the preacher usually stands (at least in the churches Sylvie knew). The walls on either side were a spangled explosion of multicolored tile, rainbow spatters of topaz and aquamarine which resolved themselves slowly, as Sylvie watched, into stern-looking saints, a sorrowful Virgin Mary. The strong, sweet aroma of incense was everywhere. On the steps immediately below Sylvie shuddered to see a dead body; a Greek priest or monk, as it seemed to her, his face pressed against the cold marble floor, his black bushy beard trying to absorb the widening pool of his own blood. Several more bodies were scattered nearby and from the pattern Sylvie could see that they had been trying to deny someone access to the altar area. One young man, no more than twenty, was sprawled across the floor to her left with a piece of dirty brown rope garroted around his neck. His eyes were popped out absurdly; if Sylvie had seen the same effect in a horror movie she'd have thought it overdone, unrealistic. Outside, she heard the flat, mechanical clatter of a Tommy-gun. Finally, Lance Fuller's voice cut through the imagery and brought her back to the here and now.

"It was stolen by the communists," he said, indicating the nail box with a smooth gesture. "From an Orthodox cathedral in Bulgaria, 1922. It spent most of the last eighty-plus years locked in a vault at KGB headquarters in Moscow. Mr. MacDonald acquired it on the Russian black market—for a very great sum of money, I should add." Sylvie scanned the man's face wildly, then turned her gaze back upon the cruel iron shard. Ever so tentatively, she lifted one hand as if to touch the thing. This mere act produced another wave of headache and dizziness—and another intensely powerful vision.

Sylvie was in a different room now, a fortress or a castle perhaps, but standing once more against a wall, looking down as if on a raised dais. All around her were dozens of strange figures, bowing, prostrating themselves in front of her, crossing themselves and murmuring Latin prayers. Nearly all were dressed in the armor of 12th century knights, such as Sylvie had seen in old films about the Crusades. They were exactly like that—only they weren't. Not at all. There was a particularity, a sharp tang of reality that no Hollywood costume designer could hope to match, no matter how careful his research. The faces weren't those of actors either—not even actors hired by a producer striving for realism. She couldn't have explained how, but it was just like on TV, where the difference between an actor pretending to be a satisfied customer and a real satisfied customer sticks out like a sore thumb. Yet these were also faces that managed, in spite of all that, to communicate an alien mind—ways of thinking and feeling that would have rendered these men, to Sylvie, as different as men from Mars. Piled on the floor between her and them: a huge heap of oriental swords and shields. Through a dazzling stone arch at the rear of the hall the turrets and minarets of an ancient city were visible, sparkling under an unfiltered Levantine sun. And then Fuller spoke again, rousing her a second time.

"Go ahead. Touch it. It won't hurt you."

Though her eyes were now filled with dread, Sylvie did seem drawn to finish the job somehow. Trembling, she put her hand forward and then delicately touched the rough black surface with the tip of her right index finger. And when she did, the world simply ended. She was in hell.

The pain was beyond anything she had ever dreamed possible. Every inch of her body was aflame with agony, as if she had just spent the morning wallowing in a dumpster full of broken liquor bottles. She looked around in mad panic, desperate to get her bearings, to find help somewhere, anywhere. She found that she couldn't move. She was pinned, like a butterfly on a card. And perched aloft for some reason, tied to a telephone pole or, or…her mind reeled. She saw drops of blood and sweat falling from her own face, dropping some distance through the air, then spattering onto a group of weeping figures huddled below. And then all rational thought was extinguished as her outraged brain activated a thousand jangling alarm bells at once. Her lungs were demanding air and could get none. Filling them instead she felt a gurgling reservoir of accumulated pulmonary fluid. She was drowning, plain and simple. She tried pushing up with her legs in a vain attempt to wrest one more breath out of the atmosphere. When she did she felt the tearing of flesh in her feet, and the grinding of bone against iron. She was going to die. Immediately, within the next few minutes. How could this be happening? What kind of a world—where a person can be expected to bear such anguish, such terror, with no comfort, for no reason? And all alone. God, so totally alone! She rebelled. She protested. She had to spit something out in anger, fling some burning accusation at someone, or go insane. Words sprang to mind; bizarre, alien words, in a tongue she had never learned. She let them out anyway, neither knowing nor caring what they meant. She knew what they meant to her.

"Eloi, eloi, lama sabachthani?"

She heard herself speak, but the voice sounded like a man's.

Simultaneously, the Sylvie in the studio ripped her voice hoarse in a scream which frightened even the hard-boiled ex-Marine. Then she collapsed heavily across the table and was, blessedly, swallowed by velvety unconsciousness.

2:21

Caleb rose to his feet in alarm. Down in the studio he saw Sylvie crumpled in her wheelchair, saw Fuller and the archivists rushing to revive her. Rocklynne picked up the telephone on the wall and started punching buttons—summoning the med staff, no doubt. All the while he heard the interviewer continuing to question the girl on TV.

"How do you deal with doubters, Sylvie?"

"I don't deal with them. I don't care what they think."

"Well, what about those who say it's really a person's own belief system that predisposes them to accept what you're doing?"

"Honestly, I don't go tit for tat with these guys. I mean, there's such a thing as an 'unbelief system' too, you know?

2:22

The sun was low in the heavens. Palm trees stood against a cloudless sky and a rosy light illuminated a low Mediterranean house of the type seen in Bible movies. One of the Unit 16 vehicles pulled up slowly in front, then parked and discharged both driver and passenger. They stood next to the car for a moment, Breen and Silverberg, and exchanged a few words.

"You know," said the Rabbi, smiling nervously, "I used to beg my parents to let us put up a tree at Christmas. Couldn't understand why we were the only family on our street not allowed to have one." He opened what looked like an old fashioned leather doctor bag and took out a white prayer shawl with blue trim. He draped it across his shoulders. Breen, watching, said nothing. Also inside the bag, though not visible to the Irishman, were all the ingredients for a traditional Haggadah tomorrow night: a bottle of wine for the four cups, a shank bone, matzoh, bitter herbs, a brown roasted egg. All the things that most strongly emphasized, for Silverberg, the gulf between himself and his Gentile hosts.

"This is...difficult," said Silverberg quietly. "Unexpectedly difficult. You have to imagine, oh, how a Catholic priest might feel if called upon to pray with Martin Luther."

Breen smiled wryly. "It happened, you know. Luther had a Catholic chaplain during his own imprisonment."

Silverberg seemed driven to say more. "I've heard this man blamed, Dr. Breen. For many things."

"You'll do fine, Rabbi," said Breen in reassuring tones. "Whatever else he may be, the old stories were right about one thing."

"What was that?"

"He's gentle. And kind."

Breen got back behind the wheel of the Jeep and closed the door. He started the engine and drove quietly away. Silverberg, carrying his bag of religious articles, walked slowly to the front door, opened it, and disappeared inside.

E P I P H A N Y

"For even God lacks this one thing alone, to make a deed that has been done undone."

Aristotle

3:1

Sylvie's snow globe sat on the dashboard of a shabby red Ford—a 1963 Galaxie, to be exact— mercilessly pounded by a million watts of Mississippi sunshine. How it got to Mississippi, who had brought it there from La Jolla, California (or from Hot Springs, Arkansas, for that matter) was a complete, unfathomable mystery. The car was sitting in a dusty gravel lot outside a white clapboard church and pouring out of this building Sylvie could hear one of most distinctive and musical noises ever born on the North American continent: the rolling thunder of a traditional black gospel preacher well into his rhythm. Earnest, impassioned, pausing at dramatic intervals to wipe the sweat from his brow, his appreciative congregation supplied the steady stream of 'Amens' which are such a vital accompaniment to that music. The Preacher's theme for this particular Sunday, with all of its powerful subtext for Mississippi blacks, appeared to be that of Moses leading the Israelites out of bondage to Egypt, all the way to the shores of the forbidding Red Sea.

Sylvie's point of view seemed to change. The oven-like insides of the tiny church slowly became visible—sweaty, stuffed with humanity, restless with the waving of funeral home fans—and on the front row Sylvie recognized what must surely have been the pastor's large, immaculately dressed family. There was a care-worn matron in white gloves, a pink dress, and a pillbox hat; several small, well-behaved youngsters; and two handsome teens, a boy and a girl. With an open Bible spread across his lap, the teenage boy could be seen following the sermon with sparkling eyes, eager attention. His eldest sister listened with a darker, more conflicted look on her face.

Soon, sundown fell upon this long-ago Sunday. The buzz of the evening cicadas was deafening, the humidity smothering, the temperature still hovering close to 100 degrees. In the waning light, Sylvie saw the boy himself preaching now, preaching to the chickens and the hogs, like St. Francis converting the sparrows. Holding the leathery Bible aloft in one hand and clearly imitating the distinctive cadences of his father's style, this would-be shepherd of souls, a black silhouette against the crimson sky, wandered aimlessly toward a ramshackle barn on the back end of the family homestead, lost in the rhythms of the sacred word. *"And the Lord said unto Moses,"* he solemnly intoned, *"Wherefore criest thou unto me?—lift thou up thy rod, and stretch out thine hand over the sea, and divide it: and the children of Israel shall go on dry ground!"* A great sternness came over the boy's features, a fierceness into his voice. *"And so Moses said unto the people, Fear ye not, stand still, and see the salvation of the LORD, which he will shew to you today: for the Egyptians whom ye have seen today, ye shall see them again no more for ever. The LORD shall fight for you, and ye shall hold your peace!"* There was no mistaking it,

Sylvie thought: the youth really was quite good and he certainly seemed to have a promising future ahead of him, following in his father's footsteps.

Pausing to catch his breath, the teen's ears pricked up suddenly at the barest scrap of a girl's muffled whimper. Stepping quietly over to the barn, he pushed the door open a crack and peered into the gloom. A sliver of light from the opening fell onto a haystack inside—and onto a man's naked backside. The Preacher was bent over his teenage daughter, pants down around his knees. The girl's face was blank, zombie-like. She continued to lie still. Then the boy's father looked up suddenly...and Sylvie stopped breathing.

"Come in here, boy."

A moment later the Preacher was dressed, on his feet, and rummaging around in the dark corners of the old barn. "I ain't hurt your sister, son," he said as he went. "You ask her. I ain't never hurt her a bit."

The boy stood wide-eyed, silent.

"Mens is made of flesh," his father continued. "Flesh is weak. Jesus hisself done said it. He don't expect much from flesh. Jesus forgives."

The Preacher came up with a thick pine axe-handle.

"I'm gon' forgive, too. Right after this ass-whippin' I'm 'bout to lay down. But as soon as you heal up, I want you off this property for good. And if I ever gets word you tole what you seen...I'll kill you dead, son. I'll put you in the ground. Don't think I won't."

The axe-handle came down with a terrifying crack—and Sylvie screamed like a child. She felt the blow as truly as if it were on her own back, but in reality she was lying in a hospital bed, covered in sweat. Caleb Donophan had been dozing in a chair nearby. At the sound of the scream he rose quickly and came to her bedside. Sylvie surprised him by taking his hand instinctively and clutching it in terror.

"It's alright, Sylvie," he said. "You're okay. I'm right here."

The girl looked around, still wide-eyed, wondering where she was now and what new horrors this particular tiny, dark chamber might have in store. Her wet blue eyes soon darted, however, across the face of the hovering scientist, looking concerned and fatherly, and there they came to rest. Caleb, who still thought of himself internally as a rather long-lived twenty-two year old, would not have liked being thought of thusly but would not probably have complained under the circumstances. Sylvie, meanwhile, still feeling the heat of the Mississippi twilight, still smelling the mud around Reverend Rocklynne's barn, was trying to reconcile these sensations with the new input coming in through her eyes. In this condition she did something she'd have been embarrassed about normally; she allowed herself to relish the father figure for a moment, even noticing that the cigarette pack now visible in Donophan's shirt pocket was of the same brand her own real father had used. Caleb watched her closely as her disoriented expression began to fade and as the trembling fit slowly abated.

"More visions?" he finally asked.

Sylvie rallied sharply at the mention of her peculiar vulnerability and, though still weak and a little weepy, managed a testy reply.

"Just another in-flight movie," she avowed. "I don't give a shit anymore." She dropped Donophan's hand shortly thereafter.

Caleb stood and raised the bed to a sitting position, then lifted the blinds to let in more sun. In the improved light, Sylvie gradually noticed that she'd been clutching something in her other hand as well: a man's pocket handkerchief, balled into a tight little wad. She unballed it with both hands now, then held it to her face and sniffed at it, almost like an animal.

"How long have *you* been in here?" she asked at length.

"Just an hour or so. Rocklynne needed a break."

Rocklynne, then. The big marine. The handkerchief belong to him.

"How long was I out?"

"Twenty-two hours. I'm afraid it's afternoon again."

Looking past the sweat-soaked rag in her fist, Sylvie saw an IV tube penetrating the inside of her left elbow. She was wearing a short-sleeved hospital gown now and it had become quite glaringly obvious, she realized, that both of her arms were covered in ugly heroin tracks. Snapping upward, her fiery eyes met those of Donophan again who had, of course, already noticed her condition. Before either of them could say anything more, the door of the room sung open and a nurse rushed in, followed immediately by the Administrator, Lance Fuller.

"What happened? Is she all right?"

"I'm okay," said Sylvie shortly. "I was just about to explain drug addiction to the Marshal here. I don't guess you get many skanky little degenerates like me out here in Red State America."

Fuller laughed out loud. In fact, it took him a moment to stop.

"What's so funny?" asked Sylvie.

"You are," said Fuller. "Ever hear of Woodstock? Haight-Ashbury?"

" 'Course I did," said Sylvie, defensively.

"Well, Caleb Donophan was at ground zero for all that. He was dropping acid with Timothy Leary when your mother was in diapers." Sylvie looked at the scientist differently; his piercing gray eyes were neither angry nor smug, just bright and slightly amused. "He gave it all up for theoretical physics," continued Fuller, "or none of us would be out here at all."

"Better than acid," added Donophan, suppressing a wry smile. "And it uses the same parts of your brain."

Sylvie didn't know what to say. She did, however, start suddenly; and then she began scanning the room in something of a small panic, as if searching for a misplaced treasure. "Where's my bag?" she at last demanded.

"We threw it out," said Fuller. "You won't need it anymore."

Sylvie closed her eyes with a look of complete despair, then slowly opened them again as if pleasantly surprised.

"No cravings at all, are there?" asked Fuller. "I came in last night and introduced a shot of something better—right there." He indicated the IV port.

"Better?" asked Sylvie.

"Call it Vitamin X. Everything you like about heroin and half the calories. That nasty shit you brought with you was mostly quinine, did you know it?"

Sylvie stared at Fuller as if he had just grown a third eye.

"Lance is a medical doctor in real life," Caleb explained. "A neurophysiologist."

"So there's no needed to rush off, young lady," said Fuller. "Just come up to my office. 'E' Building, right down the street. Anytime the Spirit moves..."

Sylvie looked more flummoxed than ever. "Well, that's a new one, I've gotta say. I've injected it, I've smoked it, I've stuck it up my ass, but I'm pretty sure this is the first time I've ever had it administered by someone with actual medical credentials. Just who are you people, anyway?"

Fuller smiled condescendingly.

"I mean, the only reason I took this job," Sylvie continued, "the only reason I take any of them anymore, is to get money for drugs. Now you tell me it's all you can eat out here and everything's on the house. Not to be rude, but normal people don't talk that way."

"Normal people?" asked Fuller, with a raised eyebrow. The point was taken. Sylvie had no reply.

"I'm wondering, Sylvie," he continued. "Would you like to tell us what you saw when you touched the nail? Or maybe you felt something?"

Sylvie broke eye contact. The memory of the moment came rushing back. She found it impossible to speak.

"Well?"

"None of your damn business," she finally managed.

"Now there you're wrong. It is my business." Fuller switched to a hushed tone of voice. "He's *here,* Sylvie. At this facility."

"What are you talking about?"

"You know very well who I'm talking about. He's staying in a little adobe house about 400 yards from this very spot."

Sylvie honestly looked like she had been tranquilized. She sat there listening but not responding at all. At last, Caleb pitched in.

"It's true, Sylvie. Hard as it may be to grasp, this is a time travel experiment…"

"Mr. MacDonald calls it the 'Christus Experiment'," Fuller interjected.

"…and you've been helping us with verification," concluded Donophan.

"And I thought I was the only one on drugs around here."

Fuller laughed again. "Don't believe us, eh?"

" 'Course not. Would you?"

"Let me get this straight," said Fuller. "The lady who sees dead people can't imagine that a little touch of *chronokinesis* might be possible in this wide world of ours? That's a tad dogmatic, don't you think?"

Sylvie was speechless again. Her eyes shot back and forth between the two men, hoping one of them would break down and start talking sense. "I can't…you don't mean…Christ, you don't aim at the top, do you? I mean, couldn't you have started out with George Washington or somebody? Gandhi?"

"You've decided to play the role of Doubting Thomas, then?" worried Fuller. "I hope not because I've already got one skeptic to convince."

"Skeptic?"

"Mr. MacDonald. He's been a little disappointed in our man, to be honest, and, in the absence of a birth certificate or what not, he's been slow to accept our results. But I called him last night after you collapsed, told him your story. He's very excited about meeting you and he'll be here tomorrow morning."

Sylvie's thoughts were crashing through her brain like a rodeo bull. Did they really expect her to believe a bullshit story like this? And yet she did believe it somehow. She had believed it immediately, she realized. It seemed cut from precisely the same cloth as her recent visions. She had *been* to those places! The church, the castle—and to, well, that pole or whatever. And all of her visions, ever since the accident, had always had this element to one degree or another. Once she had worked a cold case file that dated from 1961. She could still taste the chili fries the chick had eaten in Pasadena an hour or so before she got her throat cut. So how different was that from what Fuller was saying? Yes, these guys were talking about a machine, a mechanical apparatus. But then what is the brain but a complex machine? Her own mind was a time machine then, and she had been traveling for years.

"I don't know what to say," Sylvie managed at last.

"Then maybe we'd better show you," said Donophan.

"Excellent idea, Caleb," proclaimed Fuller. "Seeing is believing, as they say. How about a look at the world's first working time machine?"

"I'm not sure she should be exerting herself just yet," said the nurse.

Sylvie rose to her elbows without hesitation. "Tell you what, then," she responded. "If you'll just push me up that wheelchair over there I promise not to take a step. Scout's honor."

3:2

The tunnel opening reminded Sylvie of the entrance to Carlsbad Caverns. She'd visited it once with her family and could still remember this same odor of wet limestone. She half expected to see a cloud of bats come pouring out. Instead, there was a man at a security checkpoint who waived them through with little delay and soon Fuller was leading the way down a long sloping passage, with Caleb pushing Sylvie's wheelchair behind. She'd much rather have had her own electric model from home but had reluctantly agreed to leave it behind when told it was too cumbersome to be loaded onto the jet. As the trio progressed deeper and deeper into the earth, the daylight began to disappear at the far end of the tunnel.

"It all comes out of the nuclear weapons industry," Sylvie heard Fuller explain as they walked. "The 1992 test ban forced the government to come up with alternative ways of making sure their atomic bombs actually work. One of the ways of doing this is to simulate certain aspects of a nuclear detonation with powerful pulses of electricity."

"Lets you study fluid-flow interactions," Caleb added, "with macroscopic objects in complex geometries."

"If you say so."

"So back in 2002," continued Fuller, "the Department of Energy built this enormous pulsed-power device called the *Titan*. Down at Los Alamos, in New Mexico."

"Incredible machine," said Caleb. "It works like a giant power multiplier. Stores up electricity over a long period of time and then discharges it all at once. Ka-bang."

"Almost 40 million amps," Fuller said.

"Only operates for a few nanoseconds but while it does it puts out four times more power than all the rest of the electricity on earth."

"Holy shit," said Sylvie.

Reaching the end of the tunnel, the group stopped at an elevator. Fuller swiped his prox card and the door opened with a soft ding. The group boarded the elevator and began a short downward descent.

"Well, it turns out that the *Titan* was capable of a lot more than that. In October of 2004 they had an overload during one of the tests and it happened to trip the safety breakers at just the right moment. The sudden collapse caused a field surge..."

"A helluva field surge," enthused Donophan, "like nothing you've ever seen."

"...and it created a temporal displacement. The first in history, as far as anybody knows."

"'Temporal displacement?'"

"An anomaly. A little tube of hyperspace linking two otherwise discrete points on the continuum. One end of it was there at Los Alamos, the other end was in the parking lot outside—but nine days earlier. It only survived for about eleven seconds before it rotated itself out of existence but it was real enough while it lasted. The data recorders captured everything."

The elevator opened again and a new tunnel appeared, its walls lined with pipes and conduit. A bright circle could be seen at the other end, some fifty yards below.

"But how is that possible?"

"Well," said Caleb, "one of the biggest scandals in 20th century physics was the fact that none of the known laws of science actually *outlawed* time travel to the past. Certainly Einstein's general theory didn't—Kurt Gödel proved that as far back as 1949. Some of what we were learning, in fact, strongly suggested that time travel could be real."

"The *Titan* accident just proved it experimentally," said Fuller. "Caleb was already doing the math at MIT when the report was published."

"You don't mean they released something like that to the public?" said Sylvie. "That's not the Uncle Sam I know. They'd lock it up in Area 51 or something."

"They didn't understand what happened," explained Caleb. "They didn't know it was a time anomaly. They didn't know *what* it was."

"Caleb's been at this since the early Eighties, Sylvie—Mr. Time Travel, they call him in the physics journals. While Hawking and the rest were scrambling around trying to find the new physics that would affirm their prejudice against the idea, Caleb had been taking the opposite tack. So he was the only person on earth who knew how to interpret the numbers that came out of Los Alamos."

"Basically," said Caleb, "the DOE didn't want to pay for the follow-up research. So they outsourced it."

"Can you blame them?" Fuller asked. "Without knowing at lot more than they did they could never have justified this level of spending."

"Which is where Anson MacDonald came in," Sylvie realized.

"Exactly."

The trio came at last to the time cavern proper—a huge circular chamber that looked to have been hewn out of solid basalt. The ceiling was a brightly lit latticework of corrugated metal, painted white, like the ceiling of a large warehouse. Below this ceiling was the time machine itself, Sylvie supposed, spread across eighty feet of floor space and shaped like a wagon wheel. The hub of this wheel resembled an open well sunk into the ground: twenty feet wide, a dark beckoning pit, almost like an empty elevator shaft. And like all the rest of the Compound, this room too was abuzz with activity, but no one here seemed to be packing out. Everywhere electricians wearing hardhats and eccentric young techies were monitoring readouts and making adjustments to the equipment.

"And here we are," announced Fuller. "I won't tell you the final price tag on account of your recent neurological trauma."

"Bloody hell," said Sylvie, putting on, under the circumstances, a very creditable punk rock London accent.

"That barrel-shaped shaft down there is called the cryostat," Donophan said. "The rings around it have to be cooled down to 4.6 degrees Kelvin for superconductivity. And those spokes you see are banks of capacitors. We buy the power from Sierra Pacific and store it up there. It takes three full months to build up the necessary amperage so we've been at it since right after the first trip was completed."

"And all of these people are doing—what?"

"Prepping the machine for the Savior's return trip," said Fuller. "The day after tomorrow."

Sylvie looked him full in the face. "This is completely bugnuts crazy, you know that, don't you? Who the hell thought this up? MacDonald?"

"In part."

"And nobody stopped to wonder whether it was really such a good idea—to bend Mother Nature over like this and rape her half to death? I mean, God, isn't your famous Guinea Pig going to be altered beyond all recognition after a trip like this?"

Caleb pitched in here. "We'll be returning him to his own time just seconds after the point at which he was taken. So he'll most likely interpret the whole experience as a dream or a religious vision."

"Most likely?" said Sylvie. "And that works for you? You're not worried about changing the past? I mean, hell, I've read a science fiction book or two in my life. You could wipe out our whole timeline with this, couldn't you?"

"Can't happen," said Caleb flatly.

"Why not?"

"The past can't be changed."

"Sure it can! You went and got him, didn't you?"

"What makes you think that episode hasn't been part of the Life of Christ all along?" asked Fuller. "Surely you don't think the Bible records everything that ever happened to him?"

"Oh, come on," said Sylvie impatiently.

"No, you come on. Did you ever stop to think that maybe this is the world from which Jesus *was* removed? Maybe he simply vanished from Palestine one day. Maybe the whole history of Christianity since then, with its fancy stories about empty tombs and ascensions, is just one big tall-tale to explain the results of the temporal extraction accomplished by Master Sergeant Rocklynne."

"Well—dammit, what if we sent Rocklynne back a second time?" exclaimed Sylvie. "To Bethlehem, maybe. Have him tie those swaddling clothes around the baby's neck good 'n tight. That'd change the past, wouldn't it?"

Caleb smiled. "I like this girl, Lance. She knows which questions to ask."

"Well, what about it?" demanded Sylvie.

"Couldn't happen," said Caleb. "We've got a fully grown Jesus with us right now to prove it couldn't happen."

"But what would prevent him from doing it? An invisible wall or something?"

"Something more powerful still," answered Fuller. "Fate. Rocklynne would kill the wrong baby. Or he'd miss the last camel train to Bethlehem. Could be anything."

"So much for free will," said Sylvie sullenly.

"Not at all," continued Fuller. "Rocklynne would still be perfectly free. It's just that whatever free choices he makes will turn out to be exactly the ones that were needed to create the world we know."

Sylvie frowned, visibly wrestling with the difficult concept. Caleb tried to clarify. "You're falling into the common trap of imagining two 29 ADs—one without Rocklynne in it, and a subsequent one with him present. But it's not like that. There's only one 29 AD. There's never been anything but one. And since we know for a fact that Rocklynne *was* part of it, then he always was part of it."

"Even before you sent him back?" asked Sylvie.

"Even before he was born. I know it's hard to imagine, but that's just how it works."

"So nothing he did back there affected things at all?"

"Oh, no," said Fuller. "Of course he affected things, but *affecting* the past isn't the same thing as changing it."

"It isn't?"

"No. Let's say you tried to go back and prevent the Great Chicago Fire of 1871. You'd fail, of course, since we know that Chicago did, in fact, burn in 1871. But you just might find out that you, yourself, were the *cause* of the fire. Perhaps the sudden sound of your arrival is what startled Mrs. O'Leary's cow. You made a noise, Bossy kicked over the lamp, and there you go—you have affected the past. But you certainly haven't changed it. The past can't be changed."

Sylvie seemed to follow this line of reasoning, but the look on her face told Caleb she still had a thousand questions. "Listen, Sylvie," he said, trying to sum up, "if there's one thing the best thinkers in the field agree on, it's this: whatever happened 2,000 years ago already happened. And once a thing has truly happened not even God himself could ever make it unhappen. Ask Thomas Aquinas."

"It's the great safeguard on everything we've done," added Fuller. "We'd never have gone ahead without it."

"Then, if that's true," asked Sylvie, "why bother to send Jesus back at all?"

Donophan went completely silent. Fuller hesitated, but then spoke dismissively. "Oh, none of what we've said gives anyone a license to behave unethically. Of course we're sending him back. We're not kidnappers."

3:3

The reading room in the lavish Research Center was well-lit but Rabbi Silverberg had fallen asleep at his desk just the same, surrounded on all sides by stacks of old books. The late afternoon sun fell through one of the picture windows casting a complex chiaroscuro of pine bough shadows across his slumping shoulders. Rocklynne approached gently from behind, trying not to startle the old man. Stepping alongside, he saw that the Rabbi had completely filled a big yellow legal pad with Greek phrases, weird geometrical diagrams, and complex mathematical equations. Flipping the pages, the Security Chief puzzled over these images for several minutes before Silverberg finally woke.

"Oh. Hello. I must have dozed."

"You missed the time tour."

The Rabbi sat up, blinking. "I didn't sleep well last night."

"Right—your debut," guessed Rocklynne. "Well, what'd you think of him? Jesus I mean. He's a big letdown to most people."

Silverberg paused for a moment. "He's a Jew. I knew it, of course—I mean, that's what I'm here for. But, my God, he reminds me of my nephew Haim."

Rocklynne smiled and began examining the books. "*Hebrew Numerology, Principles of Kabbalah, Commentaries on the Zofar*—you workin' a puzzle or something?"

"No," said Silverberg, "I'm just, ah, taking advantage of this excellent library while I've got the opportunity."

Rocklynne picked up one of the weightier volumes—*Patristic Commentary on the Book of Jonah*—and began leafing through the pages.

"How is the young lady?" Silverberg asked. "You were sitting up with her, were you not?"

"She's awake now, if that's what you mean."

"There's permanent damage, then?"

Rocklynne did not look up from the book. "You could say that. We found out she's a hopeless drug addict. Fuller says she can't live more than a year or two."

"No," groaned the Rabbi, with genuine compassion.

"Heroin's not good for anybody, of course, but it's deadly for a paraplegic. She won't be able to keep up with herself. She'll get an infection someday—all paraplegics get 'em—starting in her urinary tract and creeping up from there. She'll be too knocked out to care. After that, systemic sepsis and heart failure."

"How terrible."

Rocklynne closed the book and placed it back on the desk. "Say, Colonel," he said, coolly switching topics, "I couldn't help noticing you got a lot of books on Jonah laid out here. Why the sudden interest in that particular prophet—if you don't mind me asking?"

Silverberg faltered a moment. He seemed to be searching Rocklynne's face, questioning his motivation. He tried to recover finally, with a weak joke. "Oh, I'm a bit of a sportsman. I always did like a good fish story."

Rocklynne didn't smile. "There's a lot more in Jonah than just a fish story, Colonel."

"You know the book?"

"You might be surprised what a security guard knows. I picked up my biblical expertise in Mississippi. Bible belt, they call it. I got belted with it real good."

"I didn't mean to imply..."

"Relax, Colonel. No offense taken. But yeah, I know Jonah." Rocklynne paused, and then slipped almost unconsciously into his King James tone of voice. *"'And Jonah cried, and said, Yet forty days, and Nineveh shall be overthrown...but God saw their works, that they turned from their evil way; and God repented of the evil that he had said he would do unto them; and he did it not."*

Silverberg was scanning his dark, inscrutable face more closely than ever. He almost seemed to be trying to read Rocklynne's mind. At last, the Rabbi opened his mouth and said only one word. "Well?"

"Well what?"

"What do you think?"

Rocklynne smiled patiently and began gathering up the books. "I think you'd better let me give these back to the librarian. She asked me to come and get them. They're trying to get packed out by Saturday. You know how it is."

"The librarian called you?"

"That's right."

Silverberg's hackles were raised now. His eyes narrowed and his voice took on an edge Rocklynne hadn't heard yet. "And can I expect my every move to be reported as long as I'm here?"

"Yeah, Rabbi," said Rocklynne, "I'm afraid that's exactly what you can expect."

Silverberg was taken aback.

"Look, you understand all this, Colonel—a military man like yourself. It's a top secret site! You signed a stack of waivers an inch thick."

This seemed to calm Silverberg down again.

"I'm not sure you appreciate the kind of security risk we're running out here," the big Marine continued. "This thing could create an international incident. I mean, think about it. Every nation on earth considers him their own. Even the Muslim jihadists. I don't need to remind you—Jesus is a prophet in Islam, too. The greatest besides Muhammad himself."

"'The righteous prophet Isa Al Masih' they call him," said Silverberg, completing Rocklynne's train of thought. " 'The Apostle of Allah'."

"That'd make quite a headline for Al Jazeera, wouldn't it? *'American Infidels Holding Righteous Prophet at Desert Fortress.'*"

Silverberg saw the point.

"And anyway," continued Rocklynne, still gathering the books, "don't you have a Seder to conduct here in an hour or two?"

Silverberg glanced at his watch, his tone turning apologetic. "You're right, of course. Let me help you with those."

The two men gathered the books silently for a minute or two, before the Rabbi spoke again. "Oh, I do have one more small request, Gunny."

"What's that, Colonel?"

"Is there some kind of concierge or something at the dormitory?"

Rocklynne smiled. "What'd you forget your toothbrush?"

"Aftershave lotion, actually. I, um, spilled mine."

3:4

The tour group reached the opposite side of the wheel, where an elaborate control station stood. A broad panel with at least 200 sliding bars faced the center of the hub. Caleb piloted Sylvie's chair right up against it, almost as if she herself might be operating the controls someday.

"And this is stabilization control," said Fuller proudly. "You see, just creating the anomaly isn't the hard part. The hard part is keeping it stable."

"Looks like a mixer board for somebody's garage band," said Sylvie.

"Funny you should say that," continued the Administrator. "Once the hole is open there's a real art to keeping it contained. It's more like music than science. Caleb here's the only one who's any good at it."

"A spinning singularity will always try to radiate its angular momentum away," a modest Donophan explained. "You have to compensate moment by moment or the rotation will slow to the point that closed time-like curves aren't being generated anymore. Vacuum fluctuations in the quantum fields will just choke them off."

One of the techies approached the group at this point, an overweight redheaded guy with a clipboard in his hands. "Yo, Caleb," he said cheerily. "I was just about to call you. We're not finished with the cryo yet but I do have those deformation reports you asked about."

"Great," said Donophan. "How long on the cryo?"

"Three hours, maybe."

Caleb took the clipboard to a nearby workstation and sat down with it. As he reached into his shirt pocket for a pair of reading glasses, his long sleeves drew back a couple of inches, exposing his wrists. When this happened, Sylvie noticed something she hadn't before: both of the wrists were marked with very old, but quite noticeable *scars*—the unmistakable signs of some past suicide attempt. She puzzled over them silently as Fuller continued to talk.

"This is Caleb's right hand man, Sylvie. He was actually on the *Titan* project before we lured him away. We call him Spaz around here."

Sylvie turned away from Caleb's scars and began to process what she'd just been told. Finally, she said to Fuller, "I'm cool with it if he is."

"Pleasure," said Spaz, extending a freckled hand. Sylvie took it, trying to seem polite, but went quickly back to Lance Fuller and the topic at hand.

"Um, what happens if it does go out of whack? Your 'singularity', I mean."

"Aye, well there's the rub."

Caleb didn't look up from his papers, but he did rejoin the conversation. "Usually it'll just fold back in on itself. No harm done. You're just out 26 million dollars for the electricity."

"But…?"

"Sometimes, every now and then, it takes that famous left turn at Albuquerque. Becomes a runaway."

Fuller grinned strangely. "A Hellmouth, as we refer to them around here."

"Christ," exclaimed Sylvie. "Who came up with that?"

"I did actually," Fuller continued. "The Hellmouth was an old stage convention in the miracle plays of the Middle Ages. You could always count on a good shudder from the groundlings when the devils came out at the end and dragged Judas Iscariot into the Hellmouth."

"And the point would be," asked Sylvie, "in this context?"

"Here. Let me show you."

Fuller pressed a few buttons and pulled up a video simulation on a nearby screen. Computer graphics depicted a tornado-like whatzit emerging from the center of the hub, slowly expanding, eating up everything it touched, pulling the time lab into itself at last, like water down a bathtub drain. As it played, Caleb came out of his clipboard to explain what Sylvie was seeing.

"A runaway anomaly could tear a hole in the spacetime continuum. Failure of the normal quantum gravity cut-off, as we would say. Without any way to stop it the tear would keep growing and growing. Maybe forever. And it would swallow up whatever it touched."

"Sort of like the Big Bang in reverse," added Fuller.

"You gotta be kidding me," said Sylvie. "What would happen to a person who got swallowed up?" Sylvie asked.

"Oh, don't let him scare you, Sylvie," interrupted Caleb. "You'd never get in. The tidal forces around the event horizon would likely tear you to pieces long before it came to that."

"Which is *better* than being swallowed?" asked Sylvie, aghast.

"Oh, much better," said Fuller. "You see, a runaway anomaly isn't a doorway to anyplace. It's a way out of time and space altogether. You'd still be you, of course, with all your thoughts and dreams. But you'd be lost in perpetual darkness, totally alone, closed up inside your own mind for all eternity. Which was, I think, a favorite image for hell itself with one popular school of Christian writers." There was total silence for a moment or two as Fuller, ever the showman, allowed this horrific thought to sink completely in. He then resumed with a coda. "But Caleb's right. Ten to one you'd be killed before you got through the eyewall."

"You guys really are brainsick," said Sylvie at last.

Caleb spoke up again, clearly annoyed by Fuller's theatrics. "There's a failsafe, of course. You don't think we'd build something like this without one?"

"The ring you saw from the plane," said Fuller. "It acts as an automatic dampener."

"The time machine and the ring are linked," Donophan explained, "so that you can't operate the one without the other. Any potential runaway might expand out to that perimeter, but no further." He pointed to the video monitor, where the simulation could be seen illustrating this concept. The wall of the tornado, sure enough, collided finally with the ring wall and fizzled out in a tremendous anti-climax.

"The ring generates a counter-rotating field that would smother it like a wet blanket."

"How does that help us poor schmucks in here?" asked Sylvie, wide-eyed.

"The Hellmouth doesn't spread that quickly," said Fuller. "Anyone inside the ring would have at least 13 minutes to reach the perimeter, open one of the egress doors, and then step outside to safety. We made the keycode easy to remember: just punch 911."

Fuller's walkie-talkie chirped suddenly. Pushing back his sport-coat, he took it from off his belt and answered in his usual all-business tone. "Go ahead…yes…no… you're kidding…he's ready now?...okay, we'll be right there." Hanging up, he spoke to the group again. "Now we're getting somewhere. Nichols has found a worm in the surveillance software."

"No kidding," said an awestruck Spaz, still standing nearby. "And I was chalking the whole thing up to Acapulco Gold."

Fuller ignored the outburst. "He wants us all to come over for a demonstration," he announced softly.

3:5

"Cleverest thing I've ever seen," said Carter Nichols, sitting at the monitoring console again. Caleb, Fuller, and the Reverend Kent were all crowded in behind him, peering over his shoulder. "The software patch is absolutely brilliant," he continued. "Elegant, even."

Sylvie watched from the larger office outside. There hadn't been room for her wheelchair in the tiny alcove, so Rocklynne had tried to position it at an angle that would afford her at least an oblique look at the main screen. While they waited for Carter to begin his demonstration, she produced the Security Chief's crumpled handkerchief and offered it to him quietly.

"This yours?" Sylvie asked.

"I guess it is," said Rocklynne, his expression neither hard nor particularly sympathetic. "You were really sweating it out last night. I used it to wipe your face."

"Thank you," she said simply. He took the cloth from her and for just an instant their hands met, making quite an image—Rocklynne's calloused, powerful, and black; Sylvie's lithe, painted at the tips, and snow white. Both noted the visual poetry of the thing but said, of course, nothing at all.

Carter had his own personal laptop open, sitting on the desk and connected to the main system via a network cable. As he tapped at his keyboard the video on the main screen went black. When it came back again it began to mirror the images on the smaller screen below.

"Here is what we've been getting out of his bedroom," Carter began. "Every night for the last three months."

The image of an ordinary back bedroom came up, with the shadowy figure of a man asleep in bed. The man's face was not visible.

"And this," he said, tapping buttons again, "is what's coming from the living room right now."

The view switched to a spacious suburban living room, again in the Mediterranean style, completely still and empty. A couch, a fireplace, several low leather chairs, a table with a bowl of flowers.

"Now," said Carter, "I'm going to switch to the same room, without the little software detour, live feed. In three, two, one..."

A totally new image came up on the screen. A stout Hispanic man in his fifties was sitting at the table now, playing checkers. His opponent was younger, dark-haired, olive-skinned, plainly of Middle Eastern origin—but though Sylvie craned her neck trying to see him better not much more could be distinguished in the low-res profile shot coming from the ceiling camera. It could have been anyone, really—though who it was alleged to be Sylvie knew perfectly well. Adding immeasurably to the surreal quality of the scene was the lively Mariachi music spilling out of a boombox on the mantelpiece.

"That's him?" Sylvie said, finally.

"Live and in person," said Carter, turning to face her. "Not what you expected?"

"He looks like a Palestinian."

"He is a Palestinian!"

"You know what I mean," said the exasperated Sylvie. "He looks like he ought to be on CNN, burning an American flag or something. Who's the other guy?"

"One of the gardeners," said Fuller.

"Reynoso, looks like," added Rocklynne.

Fuller throttled the back of Carter's chair with both hands. "Dammit!"

"We've been watching a fake prophet all this time," Rocklynne concluded grimly.

"Actually, no," Carter corrected. "The image isn't synthetic or anything. It's just a loop back to some earlier data, made a few days after the original extraction. A touch of *digital* time travel, shall we say."

Suddenly, voices could be heard. Jesus and Reynoso began to exchange a few words about the game…in Spanish.

"That's Spanish!" cried Fuller. "He spoke Spanish!"

Kent was incredulous. "He's never attempted any modern language before. Not that we've ever heard."

"What did he say?" asked Fuller. "Anybody?"

Sylvie was a bit dazed, but eventually replied. "He, um, wants the Mexican guy to crown him. You know—the checkers."

"Oh my God," said Kent.

Fuller turned and looked out at Rocklynne. "It's what we always feared. This is a breach, Rock. A bad one."

Rocklynne was silent, stoic, but clearly he wasn't happy either.

"How the hell did he learn to speak Spanish?" the seething Fuller wondered aloud. "He won't even look at a frickin' English book!"

"He's picking it up from the help," said Rocklynne. "This has probably been going on since the first week."

"Then why hasn't he picked anything up from us?" asked Kent. "We've been grilling him for hours every day! Even getting a few words of Hebrew has been like pulling teeth."

"Why don't we just ask him ourselves?" asked Carter suddenly.

"What are you suggesting?"

"According to your whistleblower there's some kind of meeting on for later tonight. Let's just crash the party."

Kent looked around in near-panic. "We're just throwing all the protocols out the window now? These are very clean, controlled encounters we've been having with him, Mr. Nichols."

"Not, it would seem, as clean as you'd hoped, Reverend. I figure you've got nothing to lose at this point."

Fuller went silent, furrowing his brow for a while. Sylvie just kept staring at the screen from a distance.

"All right," said Fuller at last. "Nichols is right. We'll show up unannounced and get the unvarnished truth. I mean, he can't very well pretend he doesn't understand us anymore, can he? Anyone here *habla* a little *Español?*"

Kent deferred. "Mine's high school level, I fear."

No one else replied.

"I could get the foreman in," offered Rocklynne.

"No," said Fuller, "let's not get any more people involved in this than we have to. Are you willing to stick with us a little longer, Sylvie?"

The girl had gone quiet as she watched, her eyes unfocused. Fuller's question roused her from some distant place.

"Oh," she said. "Right. Well, um, look. I don't really think that I, you know, need to be involved too deep myself."

"Why not?" asked Caleb.

"Well, it's obvious, isn't it? I mean, I don't really believe in him, you know?"

"What do you mean you don't believe in him?" asked Carter. "There he sits."

"You know what I mean," said Sylvie crossly.

"What about your vision?" asked Caleb.

"I saw—I felt—a man dying, okay? Your man, I guess. Doesn't mean I'm ready to start drinking the purple Kool-Aid again."

There was a long pregnant pause. Finally, Kent spoke up.

"I think possibly you've gotten a mistaken impression of what we're after here, Miss."

"We're not asking you to kiss his feet, Sylvie," said Fuller. "We just need an interpreter."

3:6

The sun had been down perhaps an hour. The western horizon still a bright, vibrant azure and the chill of the desert was beginning to make itself felt. As the group left the security building Caleb Donophan moved to resume his duties behind Sylvie's wheelchair. Carter, however, tapped him on the shoulder, cutting in, as Caleb thought, like a dancer on Prom Night. Under different circumstances Sylvie might have thought this was cute, might even have responded. As it was, she didn't even notice. She was shifting in her seat, biting her fingernails, and messing around (for no apparent reason) with the folds of the plaid blanket that was once again spread across her lap. She spoke not a word the whole trip.

They came shortly to a high steel fence with a gate on rollers, almost like the entrance to a gated housing development. Fuller entered a series of numbers into a keypad and the fence rumbled slowly open. Donophan, Kent, Rocklynne, and Nichols followed him inside, Carter piloting Sylvie's chair with great judiciousness. Doctors Breen and Flammerion had been summoned as well; Bishop Young, who would normally have been present, too, had finished packing out earlier in the day. Hearing that the Gulfstream was being sent to New York to pick up Anson MacDonald, the cleric had hitched a ride on the outbound trip, anxious to begin preparing the UN address he hoped to make, the inevitable TV documentary in which he hoped to star.

As soon as the gate shut behind them, Sylvie found herself, for all intents and purposes, back in Bible Times. From the inside, Fuller's gate looked like the archway of a walled city; looking ahead, she saw narrow, intriguing little streets branching off in all directions, lined with date palms and lit by flickering gaslight. The aroma of some heady eastern spice filled the air. This whole section of the site had, apparently, been sealed off from the rest and elaborately imagineered into somebody's idea of Jesus World. Sylvie looked up at Fuller with a dull, dazed expression, completely gobsmacked.

"Where are we now? Disneyland?"

Fuller laughed. "No, we call this the Palestinian Village. It's another of Mr. MacDonald's notions. The idea was to make our guest feel more at home. Lessen the culture shock."

"Do people really live in these other houses?" Sylvie asked.

"They do, as a matter of fact. All the gardeners, maintenance men, and so forth. Families, too."

"Actually, it feels rather deserted right now," observed Caleb. "Half of them have moved out already. The rest will go out on a bus tomorrow morning."

"Provided, that is," said Fuller, "we can get to the bottom of this mess tonight."

Following Fuller's lead, the team started down one of the twisting streets. The stones under their feet might really have been ancient; each and every doorpost was adorned with its mezuzah, silently calling out the Shema Yizrael.

"I thought you were trying to keep people away from him?" asked Sylvie, presently.

"We were," said Caleb. "His house is fenced off from the others."

"But some limited contact was thought to be psychologically helpful," Fuller continued. "Carefully supervised, of course."

Breen piped up here. "He goes walking out here with us twice a day."

Another corner was rounded. A picturesque square, modeled around a romanticized replica of Jacob's Well, sparkled in the light of the rising moon.

"What did you tell the workers about him?" inquired Sylvie.

"We told them the truth," said Flammerion, keeping up well in her sensible shoes. "We told them that their neighbor is a visiting teacher from Israel. Who needs peace and quiet."

"And wasn't to be disturbed," added a grumpy Kelvin Kent.

"We deliberately chose people with little or no religious background," Flammerion continued. "We didn't want anything he might overhear in the Village to affect the experiment."

Turning off of the square, the group encountered another tall fence. The gate here, however, was standing wide open.

"This is supposed to stay locked after hours!" exclaimed Kent.

Fuller's tone was accusatory. "Mr. Nichols?"

Carter stepped up to the keypad and pulled a voltage tester out of his back pocket. The bulb on it stayed unlit. "Dead as Caesar," he said glumly. "Somebody's killed the power to the mag locks."

Rocklynne was scanning the surrounding area anxiously. "This oughta have bells ringing all over the place."

The group passed through the second gateway. Jesus' house now came into view—ablaze with lights. Many cheery voices could be heard through the open windows, all of them speaking Spanish. Carter, astonished, scanned the area, looking around at rooftops, poles, palm trees—there were cameras everywhere. He spoke quietly to Rocklynne. "This is no amateur hour, Rock. Somebody went to a lot of trouble to get some privacy down here."

Fuller's eyes were fixed on the house now, but he too spoke to Rocklynne. "Bring the girl down here."

The little knot of outsiders headed down this last street, the final few yards to the house. Caleb noticed that Sylvie was not looking well. Even so, she did manage to speak to Flammerion walking nearby.

"He's really down there?"

"Looks like it."

"What should we—I mean, how should I address him? Rabbi? Sir?"

Carter piped up. "'Lord' is customary in some circles, I think. 'Master' works, too."

Sylvie's eyes widened just a bit more.

"Don't worry," said Kent. "You won't hear choirs or anything. And if he ever had a halo he lost it before he came to us."

"Mainly," added Breen, "you'll notice that he's a foreigner. He smells differently than we do. I don't know why, but even I found that surprising at first. I suppose none of us has escaped the conditioning, really."

"Since you're a woman," said Flammerion, "he probably won't even speak to you. But don't take it personally—he comes from a very sexist, patriarchal culture."

Fuller entered first, walking in on a houseful of Mexicans: twenty-five or thirty people, practically the whole remaining support staff. Tortilla crumbs and empty wine bottles were scattered across almost every horizontal surface, the remnants of a big Mexican supper. Little groups of excited women stood around laughing and talking; one of them had the top of her peasant-type dress rolled down, shamelessly (to Anglo eyes) breastfeeding a six month old infant. A young man nearby, little more than a teen, was playing guitar, one foot propped on the coffee table. Carter couldn't help smiling. The whole scene was cheery, earthy, rural, and spontaneous—all the things most likely to offend the very anal Lance Fuller. One by one, the Mexicans began to notice the presence of said Administrator, and gradually the happy crowd fell silent. The women looked at Fuller as if they expected him to literally explode.

And then Sylvie and Carter saw Jesus himself for the first time. He was standing next to the fireplace, talking privately with a smaller group of men. He did indeed look quite foreign, nothing at all like the stained-glass Savior of European imagination. His eyes were so brown they were almost black. His thick shoulder-length hair ended in a cascade of ringlets. He had a dark, wiry beard which gave him a distinct rabbinical quality. His attire was also a surprise. No robes or sandals—Jesus was wearing a pair of clean blue jeans and a simple gray warm-up jacket, with white dock shoes on his feet. He really did look like a typical young Israeli Jew, the kind of person who might be a regular at the Tel Aviv branch of Starbucks coffee house. Noticing the sudden quiet, he and his group also turned their faces toward the newcomers. Finally, one of the men who had been conversing with Jesus broke away and strode toward the door. He walked directly up to Fuller and said, with a heavy Mexican accent, "We were just coming to see you, sir."

Fuller seethed. "You were just—well, I'm very glad to hear that, pardner! We've got a lot to talk about, it would seem! You speak English, I see. What's your name?"

"Santiago Ramirez."

"Well, Mr. Ramirez, I'm interested to hear how you're going to justify all this—given the fact that every one of you signed, when you took these jobs, a strict agreement *not* to molest our visitor and *not* to interfere with him in any way!"

"We're not molesting him, sir. He invited us."

Several of the other men from Jesus' group stepped up to join Ramirez, giving the impression they were trying to demonstrate a united front.

"Get out," Fuller said, with barely controlled anger. "All of you. Finish packing your things. We're not going to wait till morning. I want you off this property tonight."

Now Jesus himself called out from across the room—speaking Hebrew, which only Fuller and the academics could understand. "This house was to be called mine, was it not?"

Fuller seemed to get hold of himself, turning slowly to face the Visitor. "It is yours to live in, yes." He, too, spoke Hebrew.

"If it is mine," said Jesus, "then I am the master of it until it is not mine. And it is my will that these should remain."

Fuller had no answer. He paused and then responded with a question of his own. "How did you learn to speak their language?"

"They are my friends. I needed it for their sakes."

Ramirez had not been able to follow the exchange but he joined in now, speaking English. "We have done nothing, sir. He sings with us. He talks with us. He drinks our wine. Nothing more."

There was another moment of uncomfortable silence. Carter looked at Sylvie, who had an expression of bewildered wonderment on her face. Rocklynne, meanwhile, had been prowling around in the back of the room, plying his trade. He'd discovered a thick, black book on an end table next to the sofa, two words only on the cover: *Santa Biblia.*

Kent, who had moved up and was standing next to Fuller, questioned Ramirez himself. "Do you know who this man is?" he asked portentously.

"Yes," said the Mexican. "We know."

"Who then?"

"He has told us his name is *Josue*."

The Theos exchanged puzzled looks for a moment, then a bulb seemed to go off over Flammerion's head.

"Obviously!" she said to Kent and the rest. "His real name in Aramaic is *Yeshua.* A straight transliteration of that into English would be Joshua, just like Moses' lieutenant in the Old Testament."

"And in Spanish, *Josue,*" said Sylvie, in low tones. "But where did we get *Jesus* from?"

"It's a holdover from the Vulgate—the Latin Bible," said Breen. "His common Spanish name comes from there as well."

Kent turned back to the Mexicans again. "Then you don't—uh, know anything more? More than that?"

"We do know more, Señor. That is why we were coming to see you."

The Theos exchanged a series of timorous, agitated glances. Rocklynne stepped up to Fuller's side to receive instructions.

"Have Jimmy bring the bus around," the Administrator said. "I want all these men taken down to 'F' building for debriefing." Turning to Ramirez he said, "Send the women back to their quarters."

Ramirez hesitated but spoke at last. "We will do as he asks," he told the others in Spanish. "Go back to your rooms. The brothers and I will address you in the morning." The crowd began reluctantly to comply.

Fuller, Donophan, and the Theos turned and headed toward the door as well. But as they went, Jesus called out again, this time in perfect Spanish. "I would speak with the young woman."

Sylvie froze in her seat, her face a mixture of astonishment and terror. His was unreadable, impassive. When he spoke again, it was directly to Sylvie, also in

Spanish. "I have something to say to you, daughter." Sylvie seemed incapable of making any sound in reply. "Will you talk with me on the terrace?" he asked, in a voice neither frightening nor reassuring.

Carter looked at Sylvie who finally, with a stiff, almost imperceptible nod, gave him her permission. Nichols stepped behind the chair again and pushed her forward. Meeting him halfway, Jesus took control of the chair himself, turned, and wheeled Sylvie through an open set of bay doors on the back side of the house. Fuller and the others watched helplessly, not knowing quite how to intervene even if they had determined to do so. This being the case, they simply turned and departed, almost in unison, leaving the girl alone on the vacated property with Jesus of Nazareth, who is called the Christ.

3:6

Sylvie was grateful for the cold night air which embraced her when the man first pushed the chair outside. She'd been overheating in the stuffy living room, getting irritated, with too many people around, too much to think about all at once. It felt very good to pull some of the arid, invigorating coolness into her fluttering, unsettled diaphragm. There was a magnificent moon overhead, just past full, reflected in the lake nearby. The flat plain to the east was a desolate monochrome, looking very much the way Sylvie imagined the ancient Middle East to have looked. The whole scene, in fact, might have been from 2,000 years ago—except that the fancy redwood deck from which she observed it was well-appointed, with a modern gas grill and spacious hot tub.

The man was apparently concerned that it had gotten too cool; he took a folded Navajo blanket off a nearby patio chair and draped it carefully over Sylvie's shoulders. She felt a strange, almost sickening thrill at the brief pressure of one of his hands against her back. He then stepped around in front again, feeling the chill himself and raising the hood of his own grey warm-up jacket. This suddenly made him look much more like the Jesus Sylvie had expected. His face was framed in the hood, as if peering from beneath a set of first century robes, and it reminded her of the serene, remote Christ she'd seen on TV in one of the old deluxe Bible epics out of the 1960's. Her emotions were all over the map. She noticed first (and it troubled her) that he was a manly, attractive member of the opposite sex. Seconds later, an old hymn rushed into her mind—one of dozens she still knew by heart—extolling his praises as King of Kings, Mighty God, Prince of Peace. Plainly, the man was only a few years older than she—or was it 2,000 years older? The process shorted out finally, leaving her exhausted, overcome, still and quiet. Even so, it was Sylvie herself who broke the silence at last.

"My name's Sylvie," she said suddenly, talking in Spanish. "Sylvia Fortune. I'm from California."

It was a ridiculous beginning, of course. She felt embarrassed to have said it. But what words would have been better? She felt even more foolish as the man failed to respond immediately. She tried again, still in *Español*. "I don't know if you can understand me or not. Or how this can even be happening, you know? I don't even know who you are..." She broke off in frustration, switching back to English. "Jesus, I don't even know if I'm in my right mind!" She looked up into his face miserably, realizing right away that she had just used his name as an expletive. She cowered, awaiting his reaction. There wasn't any. He simply continued to watch her, his features unreadable. He was thinking, probably, that she must be a complete freaking idiot...which, in fact, was exactly how she felt.

Finally, Jesus did speak. The words were in Spanish, but the meaning was "Shall I apologize to you, Sylvie?"

"Apologize?"

"We were friends once. I think I must have done something to drive you away."

Sylvie caught her breath with a sharp gasp.

"We used to pray the Psalm together, remember? When you were a girl. You had a little printed card tacked to the underside of the top bunk."

Sylvie peered directly into his eyes in dumb, stupefied shock. A wave of something like terror swept over her. Her eyes began to well up with tears. Jesus spoke again, still referencing the little Bible card she'd been given by her fourth grade Sunday School teacher. He actually quoted it now—*in English*—though with a distinct Hebraic accent.

"'Let the words of my mouth, and the meditation of my heart, be acceptable in thy sight, O Lord, my strength and my redeemer.'"

"This isn't possible," said Sylvie. "I'm asleep."

The girl began to shiver visibly. Jesus reverted back to Spanish, speaking very tenderly. "So tell me, Sylvie.

For what must I apologize? Tell me, so that we may be friends again."

Sylvie's trembling now gave way to a violent coughing spell, and finally to a hard retch. She hung her head over the edge of the chair and vomited onto the floor. Jesus took a clean towel from a rack next to the hot tub. Moving directly alongside the wheelchair, he placed his right hand on the arm of it and bent to his knees. With the towel in his left hand he began to clean up the mess.

Sylvie opened a bleary pair of eyes. She used the sleeve of her bathrobe to wipe the tears off her face, the vomitus off her mouth. Looking down, she saw Jesus' hand gripping the armrest. He was very close now, his dark hair only a foot or so from her face. Almost without thinking, she reached out and began to gingerly stroke the top of his head with her fingers. When she did, she experienced another brief flash of psychic insight—a vision of that same head ringed with a crown of bloody thorns. It was only an image, almost like the flashing of a photographic bulb, and it was over as soon as it began. But when it ended, Sylvie broke down completely. Abruptly, even explosively, she grabbed Jesus around the neck and buried her face into his shoulder. Every ounce of bottled up grief and anguish seemed to come out all at once and she was wracked by a series of hard, convulsive sobs. Jesus made no attempt to free himself.

3:7

The rhythmic creak of an old-fashioned porch swing betrayed the nervousness of Carter Nichols. He was rocking back and forth on the front veranda waiting for

Sylvie to come out. Caleb was standing on the steps nearby, smoking and talking with Fuller. After a few minutes, an airport-style bus pulled up and Rocklynne began loading the Mexican men into the back. Fuller left the front of the house to join him.

"What happened to your friend Silverberg?" he asked.

"Looks like he's AWOL," the Marine replied.

"Then what's he even here for?" asked Fuller in frustration. "He's not in the library cracking codes again?"

Rocklynne said nothing.

"Find him," said Fuller severely.

Most of the Theos were huddled under a gas lamppost nearby, deep in an agitated conversation. Fuller turned away from the bus and joined the debate already in progress.

"There you are, Lance," said the red-faced Kent. "Have you seen this?" He handed Fuller the Spanish Bible. "Rocklynne found it in there."

"Not surprised," said Fuller, looking grim. "Any idea where it came from?"

"One of the women gave it to him. They've got some notion he's a prisoner or something."

"So he can read Spanish now, as well as speak it," said the Administrator. "How is that possible?"

"We were just discussing that point," said the Irishman Breen, with a touch of enthusiasm in his voice. "Dr. Flammerion has quite an interesting theory. Doctor?"

"It's just this," said the lone woman of the group. "Perhaps this man isn't as ordinary as we thought."

"Go on."

"Perhaps his ability to learn languages marks him as a genius, a prodigy."

"After all," added Breen, "Mozart composed his first symphony when he was seven years old. Jesus has certainly had a similar impact on the world."

"So perhaps this is another incidence of the same phenomenon," continued Flammerion. "Maybe it's an evolutionary mechanism. Maybe nature tosses one of these genetic enormities into the mix every few centuries—to move us along. The next leap forward, if you will."

It's possible that the Theos expected Fuller to be flattered by this idea; certainly they were aware that he himself had finished high school at age eleven, graduated the Harvard Medical School the day after his nineteenth birthday. If so, they were disappointed. When the driver beeped his horn signaling a readiness to depart, Fuller moved toward the bus, tossing one final question over his shoulder as he went.

"And the cameras? I suppose evolution shut the surveillance system down as well?"

Fuller stepped up into the passenger seat and the bus roared away.

At roughly the same moment, the front door of the house opened again. Carter and Caleb turned to see Sylvie Fortune emerging from inside, wheeling her own chair. Jesus was nowhere to be seen. The girl was quiet now, even tranquil, but she had plainly been crying. Carter ventured a question. "Well?"

"Well what?"

"What happened?"

Sylvie managed a weak laugh. "For somebody who's supposed to be an atheist I just made a complete blubbering ass of myself."

"What did he say?" asked Caleb.

"Look, I'm sorry," said Sylvie, "I just don't think I can talk about it right now."

"Why not?" Carter persisted.

Sylvie stopped, then hitched herself up with another short laugh and a look of wonder on her face. "I think it's him, Carter."

"So does Fuller."

"No, I mean *Him*. He spoke to me in English for a moment. *English,* this time."

There was a short silence. Carter had a look of concern on his face. "Listen, Sylvie, I wouldn't stick my neck out too far on this thing if I were you. Why don't you get some sleep? I'm sure it will all make more sense in the light of day."

Sylvie surprised him by snapping back with anger in her voice. "I haven't slept the night through in eight years, Carter. I dread turning out the lights like you dread an effing root canal. If this man, whoever he is, could give me just one good night's sleep, just one night without the blood and the knives and the pleas for mercy—I'd join the Mormon Tabernacle Choir."

Carter and Caleb were taken aback, as if realizing for the first time just how haunted Sylvie really was.

"I'm going to try it out tonight," the girl continued. "Scientifically. 'Now I lay me down to sleep'—the whole nine yards. My own little private 'Christus Experiment' so to speak. I'll give you a full report in the morning."

She rolled herself down the ADA ramp at the opposite end of the porch, and then started off toward the village gate under her own steam.

3:8

With the sound of a jingling key ring, the door to Silverberg's room came open. As soon as Rocklynne stepped in and turned on the lights he was hit full in the face by strong fumes and began fanning them away with his hand. It didn't take long to find the empty bottles of aftershave, cologne, and Listerine sitting in the window sill, the wadded paper towels strewn everywhere. The Rabbi himself was absent, his bed not slept in.

Standing back, Rocklynne surveyed the largest wall in the room completely stripped of paint, secrets fully revealed. It was covered from top to bottom in what could only be described as the fevered scrawls of a madman—the same kind of Hebrew lettering, geometrical patterns, and cabalistic symbols that had crept across Silverberg's pad in the library. One phrase in particular stood out, the only words written in English:

"Now, I am become Death, the Destroyer of worlds."

The security chief did not pause to puzzle over the messages. He stepped outside, closed the door quickly, and locked it again. He got back in the Security Jeep and went looking for the Rabbi.

3:9

Fuller and the Theos sat around one end of a huge conference table, looking very much like the board members of a big corporation. Three of the Mexicans occupied the opposite end, looking like precisely what they were—a gardener, a plumber, and a cook. The cook was Dominguez, the teenager who'd been happily playing his guitar for Jesus just a few hours before. The gardener was Reynoso, the heavier, square-faced man who'd been beating that same Nazarene at checkers a couple hours before that.

Santiago Ramirez, still spokesman for the group since he was the only one with a decent command of English, was a plumber by trade.

"Perhaps I'm going deaf, Mr. Ramirez," said Fuller, doing a good job of trying to sound shocked, "but I could have sworn you just said Jesus Christ."

"Yes, sir."

"Jesus Christ," he repeated. "Of Nazareth. The one who died 2,000 years ago?"

"Oh, no, Señor. I mean..."

Ramirez was interrupted by the teenager, Dominguez. "Si, si! Jesucristo el Señor!"

"Well?" demanded Dr. Kent. "Which is it? Yes or no?"

"He means to say," continued Ramirez, "*Regresso del Señor*. Um, how you say in Inglés?—the Second Coming."

The Theos sat flabbergasted at this phrase. Breen looked like he was going to have a stroke. Flammerion seemed embarrassed, as if the remark were in bad taste. Kent, finally, broke into an odd-looking smile.

"You're saying," he began patiently, "that you believe our friend Joshua—Josue, as you say—is the Second Coming of Jesus Christ?"

"Yes, sir."

Dr. Breen hissed in Fuller's ear. "I thought we'd screened these people, Lance! Non-religious types, remember?"

Fuller turned away and spoke to Ramirez directly. "How would you know about any Second Coming of Christ?"

"Oscar, here" he said, indicating Dominguez, "he told us. Oscar knows about such things."

"And where, pray tell," asked Flammerion, "did Oscar acquire his theological education?"

Ramirez leaned across to Dominguez. The two exchanged a few private words in Spanish. Presently, Ramirez said, "He saw a film about it once."

"What was the name of the film?"

Dominguez looked Fuller in the eye and surprised him by answering in English, with, admittedly, an overpowering Mexican accent.

"*The Omen*."

Fuller threw up his hands. "And this is the theologian of the group?"

"Also," continued the plumber, "his brother Carlos is a tongues talker. He speaks in tongues. *Iglesia Pentecostal*."

All of the Theos sunk their heads into their hands in despair. Flammerion, finally, regained her composure and spoke again.

"Would you tell us, please, Señor Ramirez, how you came to such a startling conclusion?"

"From listening," said Ramirez. "From watching him. He does what no man can do."

"For instance?"

"Maravillas. How you say—miracles."

This thought seemed to take the air out of the room. Kent's eyes narrowed for a moment, but by the time he spoke again it was with a condescending smile and in a paternalistic tone of voice.

"Such as?"

"Juanito Cuaron. A boy, ocho años. He wear very big, thick anteojos when he come here. Spectacles. Josue made him see again."

"What else?" asked Flammerion.

"Alfredo Sanchez. A mechanic. He is a very bad man when he come to this place—a bad spirit was over him. Always fighting, cursing. Now he is free. Josue freed him."

"That's it?" chuckled Kent. "No raising of the dead? No calming of the storm with a single command?"

"He gave little Maria Rosa her hand back," said Ramirez.

"What's that?" asked Flammerion.

"Maria Rosa. A little girl from San Luis Potosi."

Recognition seemed to come into Flammerion's eyes. "I remember seeing her in the village. She lost a hand in a road accident when she was a toddler."

"Josue gave it back," said Ramirez. "She has two hands now."

There was another strange pause. Kent harrumphed finally and said, "Ridiculous. Two hands."

"I will introduce you to her in the morning," said Ramirez.

3:10

It was well past midnight when Rocklynne returned to the Research Complex. The building was darkened but already he could see Silverberg inside the atrium, illuminated by the glow of the lone remaining computer monitor before which he was seated. He had another stack of old books at his elbow. Punching in a key code, the Security Chief entered the building.

Without looking away from his work, Silverberg heard Rocklynne approaching and spoke. "I gather that Rabbi Mintz' illness was…psychiatric in nature."

"Classic delusional paranoid," said Rocklynne, no longer hiding anything. "Got worse and worse the longer he was here. Fuller says it was the time travel—boggled his mind eventually."

"And what were the delusions? Specifically?"

Rocklynne hesitated, then answered straight up. "The devil was after him. Satan himself. There's a doorway to hell right in this very Compound. Or didn't you know?"

"There was a word or two to that effect, yes."

Rocklynne drew up a rolling desk chair and sat in it backwards, with his arms folded across the seatback. "How'd you get in here?" he asked pointedly.

"Oh, the Rabbi wrote some of the door codes on the wall. Among other things."

"And Passover? How'd that go?"

"I wouldn't know. I didn't attend."

"Why not?"

"Not invited, I suppose. He seems to have done it himself, with our Mexican friends."

"You know they've been meeting with him for weeks. Was it Mintz that let 'em in?"

"No, it wasn't. But he knew about it, right from the beginning."

"Why didn't he report it?"

"He worried about what would happen to them."

Rocklynne frowned. "What're you talking about?"

Silverberg stood up, closed one of the big books and stacked it on top of the others. "They're all unregistered, aren't they?" he said at last. "Illegals."

"So what?"

"Rabbi Mintz became convinced they would be in danger if they ever tried to leave—that you wouldn't allow it."

"I told you before, Mintz was paranoid. We kept the help away from Jesus to avoid tainting the Experiment."

"And if they *had* insisted on leaving? After spending three months with your special visitor?"

"We'd have let 'em go, of course. I mean, come on—a group of peasants walks out of the desert, claiming to have seen Jesus Christ? That's not gonna make any headlines."

"You're right. No one would believe it. Unless one of them happened to mention the name Caleb Donophan. To the right person."

Rocklynne went silent for a moment. Finally, he said, "Why don't you just come to the point, Colonel?"

Silverberg paused, then turned his computer monitor on its base so that the screen could be seen by

Rocklynne. Displayed on it was an old black and white photo of a somber, pipe-smoking scientist.

"You're a military man, Gunny," the Rabbi said. "Recognize this fellow?"

"Vaguely familiar."

"That's J. Robert Oppenheimer, the physicist. He headed up the team that invented the atomic bomb. After the first successful test, they asked him how he felt. It's a famous quote, actually—he cited the *Bhagavad-Gita,* the Hindu scriptures: *'Now I am become Death, the destroyer of worlds....'* "

Rocklynne said nothing. He just looked at the picture silently.

"I'll be honest with you, my friend," said Silverberg with a growing earnestness. "I don't think Dr. Fuller is all that concerned about fanatics, jihadists, whatever. I think he's worried that our own United States Government will come and take all this away from him."

"For what purpose?" Rocklynne asked.

"Well, that's the mind-boggling part, isn't it?" The Rabbi hesitated, as if he himself were startled at what he was about to say. "I'm not sure I'd have worked it out for myself. But Rabbi Mintz did." Silverberg leaned forward, his voice taking on an awed, even reverent tone. *"It's another bomb, Gunny.* The Time Bomb. And it makes this little adventure with your Palestinian street prophet seem like small potatoes."

3:11

Jesus' trio of favorites—the "Three Caballeros," as Kent derisively called them—were grilled steadily for more than two hours. Little more was learned other than the fact that they had, indeed, been meeting with Jesus since the fourth day after Extraction, that he mostly told pithy agricultural fables which the Mexicans enjoyed but found puzzling, that he could quote lengthy passages from the old Castellano Bible without making a single mistake, and that he missed his old friends badly—and his mother. The men were sent out finally, exhausted, with vague threats of legal action ringing in their ears. Nichols and Donophan were then called for; they entered the conference room at a quarter past two in the morning.

"Caleb," cried Fuller, as the scientist appeared in the door. "Get in here, for God's sake. We need your input."

"It's worse than we thought, Donophan," said Kent unhappily. "He's been meeting with them practically every day. 'Making disciples.' He's got them eating out of his hand."

"Up to his old tricks, eh?"

"It's worse than that. They're reading the whole thing as a religious miracle! They're saying it's the Second Coming and God has picked them to carry the news to the world."

Caleb grinned sardonically, shaking his head at the unexpected quirk of fate. "That's a little ironic, isn't it?" he asked.

"It'll be ironic when the lynch mobs get here," said Fuller, his own face completely and totally straight.

"Look," said Caleb, "he's going back where he came from in just over 24 hours. And you were planning to publish the news in a few weeks anyway. Just hold these guys until then—after that they can sell their story to Oprah, the National Enquirer, whoever they want."

"But who's behind it all?" asked a panicky-looking Kent. "And how much do they know? We could be raided at any moment!"

"Are you sure we can't send him back until tomorrow night?" asked Breen.

"Send him back?" objected Flammerion. "He's talking now! This is a whole new start for the Experiment! Rather than sending him back we ought to be looking at extending for another three months."

"Impossible," cried Breen. "We've got to get him out of here before this leak draws down God knows what on our heads!"

Fuller was fuming. "Speaking of which, Mr. Nichols, you won't object if I ask what in God's name is going on here—security-wise? Haven't you got anything to report at all?"

"Yes, sir, I have," said Carter. "I'm reporting that this is the most sophisticated hack I've ever seen. Every last element of our security network is working flawlessly. Even a high-level inside job would leave some traces, but this thing is immaculate. It's mind-blowing, really."

"And yet somehow," said Fuller hotly, "I've got a bunch of born-again illegals on my hands, haven't I?"

3:12

"But it doesn't work that way!" said Rocklynne, on his feet now and pacing in the library. "The past can't be changed!"

"How would you know?" demanded Silverberg. "How would I? Because Fuller said so?" The point was taken; Rocklynne sat down again and wiped his hand across his face. "Listen, Gunny," the Rabbi continued, "what if Donophan and his experts are wrong? What if the past *can* be changed? Then a time machine—a real time machine—is the ultimate weapon. Nothing less. Poor Mintz saw it like the clear light of day. Want to stop radical Islam? Go back to the seventh century and murder Muhammad. Don't like Jews? Go back to 1939 and give Hitler the H-Bomb."

"That's crazy," said the Marine, eyes widening. "That's insane."

"Is it? You've got the machine to do it right here in this Compound!"

Rocklynne seemed at a loss, grappling with the implications. "They'd have been here by now," he said at last. "They'd have shut us down a long time ago."

"MacDonald's money might slow that process indefinitely—but only if they don't know Donophan's involved. He's the linchpin—'Mr. Time Travel'. If they can keep his name out of the equation, well…we could be making color TVs out here for all the government knows."

"I don't—I can't believe MacDonald would have gone ahead under conditions like that," said Rocklynne, shaking his head. "And I can't believe you're taking that chicken scratch seriously! What else is on that wall?"

"I don't understand it all—not yet," said Silverberg quietly. "The Rabbi had a powerful mind. Too powerful. Strong enough to hurt itself."

Rocklynne spoke dismissively. "Looked like a bunch of gibberish to me. Fuller said the same."

"It's not gibberish, believe me." It was Silverberg who rose to his feet now, looking pale and worried in the dim glow of the computer screen. "The geometry is based on the Shemhamphorasch, the 72 letter name of God from the book of Exodus. The mathematics is largely from Giordano Bruno, with some additional input from Kolmogorov."

"Oh, well, that explains it then," said Rocklynne, totally deadpan. "I thought it was something way out."

Silverberg ignored the sarcasm, still in deadly earnest. "Simply put, Mintz was trying to work out the relationship between prophecy, free will, and predestination in the light of a successful time travel event. For example, is it really true, Gunny, that everything you did while you were back there was pre-scripted in advance? That you couldn't have acted differently than you did, try as you might? And if the past can't be changed, what about the future? Does foreknowledge equal fate?" Rocklynne shifted in his seat uncomfortably, then reached across the desk and snapped on a small table lamp. "Basically," Silverberg continued, "the Rabbi was trying to convince himself that Donophan and his people are *right*—that the past really is fixed, solid, immutable by nature. Because if he could do that, he'd prove that his own fears of a Time Bomb were nothing but a bogey in the night."

"But he didn't succeed?"

"He tried desperately, I can tell you—read everything from Aristotle to Lewis Carroll. But no, God help us, he did not finally succeed."

"What about the obsession with Jonah?" Rocklynne continued. "What was that all about? He was going round and round with it by the end, like a dog chasing its tail."

"That's what puzzles me most!" said the old man, clenching his fist in front of him. "Mintz became certain that Jonah was the key to everything. Jonah convinced him that the past *can* be changed and thus, that Donophan's machine really is a doomsday device. But I can't follow his reasoning. There's not enough on the wall to piece it together."

Rocklynne went silent, knowing very well what was coming. "I need to see Mintz' project log," said Silverberg. "They've kept it, of course?"

"Don't know."

"You could find out, couldn't you?"

"I could," said Rocklynne finally, "if I weren't loyal to Mr. MacDonald. And to the project." He picked up one of the books absently and rose to his feet again. Leafing through the pages, not really reading but careful not to make eye contact, when he finally spoke it was with deep but carefully controlled emotion. "I may be a heathen and an atheist, Colonel, but they did teach me something about honor in the Marine Corps."

"I'm not asking you to betray anyone! I'm just trying to understand what we've got ourselves into the middle of out here."

"What you're asking me," Rocklynne insisted, "is to start sneaking around behind my employer's back *causing* security problems instead of preventing them. And that's not what I get paid for. Anyway, I don't even know what you're accusing them of!"

"I'm accusing them of being terrified—like me! They *did* go ahead under conditions like these. Whether deliberately or by accident, they've opened Pandora's Box out here and now they're trying to close it again. And keep a lid on it. You should have seen Breen's face when I asked him about the paint!"

"Well, if it's as dangerous as you say, that's the best thing to do, isn't it? Keep everything under wraps, dispense information on a 'need to know' basis, right? And neither one of us needs to know, as far as I can see."

"Hide it until this is over, yes!" the Rabbi agreed. "But what happens after that? What, ultimately, do you do with the damned thing? Dismantle it? Sell it to the highest bidder? MacDonald has proved it works now—in spades—so he could demand whatever price he likes!"

"Now you *are* talking crazy." The big Marine stood up again, as if he'd finally heard enough. "I know Mr. MacDonald—personally. I know what motivates him. He's had me up to his ranch house a dozen times. We go fishing together. We're both from the South and we have a lot in common, believe it or not. So you can trust me when I tell you, he's not in this for the money. He's got more than he can ever spend already."

"Are you sure of that?"

"Of course, I'm sure. And they wouldn't pay him, anyway. They'd just annex it all in the name of national security." Rocklynne shook his head. "No, no—you're way off base here, Colonel."

"Let me prove that to myself," said Silverberg passionately. "Get me those notes."

Rocklynne's eyes narrowed; his voice took on a tinge of exasperation. "Why?" he asked pointedly. "For what reason? What would you do if you did find out it was true? You gonna become a saboteur or something?"

Silverberg seemed caught off guard by this. His mind was racing; Rocklynne could see it in his eyes. When he finally answered, the answer itself was another question. "What would *you* do," he asked gently, "if you found out you'd been helping to enslave the whole world with this?"

The Rabbi had struck a nerve, just as he hoped. Rocklynne picked up the yellow pad again and thumbed through the pages some more. "I'm sorry, Colonel," he said at length. "I'm trying to take you seriously here, I really am—but it's just unthinkable." He tossed to tablet back onto the desk with a slap. "You can hardly get it into your head. No wonder Mintz lost his mind!"

"No wonder," repeated the Rabbi, his tone indicating neither agreement nor dissent. He said nothing else for several moments. Finally, he took Rocklynne by the arm. "Rabbi Mintz was a Shoah survivor," he said quietly. "Did you know that, Master Sergeant? I had an uncle in Brooklyn who sponsored our family's visa, otherwise I'd have joined him in the camps." The Security Chief did not respond. "So we know by experience, Mintz and I. Just because a thing is unthinkable doesn't mean it's undoable."

Rocklynne looked at his watch; it was 3:20 AM. "Come with me," he finally said.

"You'll do it, then? You'll get the notes?"

"I wouldn't count on it."

It was Rocklynne who took the Rabbi's arm now, shepherding him through the darkened atrium towards the exit.

"Then where are you taking me?"

"I'm going to drop you off at my apartment. That room of yours ain't fit to live in. How long since you slept in a bed?"

Silverberg pinched the bridge of his nose with one hand, rubbing his eyes heavily. "Some little while."

Both men stepped out into the desert chill. Rocklynne turned and used his key ring to secure the door behind them.

"Then get some rest, Colonel. Before you start writing on walls, too."

3:13

A young blonde, roughly Sylvie's age, was lying on the floor with her skirt hiked up around her waist. She was in the very act of giving birth. Sylvie could see the top of the baby's head through the girl's widely distended cervix.

Where was this taking place? It looked and sounded like the deepest pit in hell. Roaring columns of flame encompassed the laboring mother on all sides and the most godawful din filled the air, some kind of cacophonous pagan chant droning on and on at rock-concert levels; the woman's own screams were scarcely audible. Three other girls were cowering nearby, clutching their own small, hysterical children. All of them were watching the act of childbirth with wide, terror-stricken eyes, but offering no assistance. Finally, the baby spilled out onto the floor of its own accord, lying there wriggling and helpless in a lake of blood and fluid, the umbilical trailing back into the womb unsevered.

Suddenly, a running man appeared out of the billowing smoke, covering his nose and mouth with a wet towel. In his free hand he held a big, brutal-looking handgun. He stopped when he became aware of the women and children, paused briefly to check the ammunition remaining in the clip, and then, without any further hesitation at all, emptied the weapon on the cowering clutch of innocents. Heads popped back, limbs went rigid, more liquid emptied onto the floor. Even the newborn infant was quickly dispatched.

Sylvie turned her head away, squeezed her eyes tightly shut. When she opened them again she found that she could still see the horrific scene playing out as a series of distorted reflections on the surface of her chintzy little Bible Land snow-globe. She sat up in bed with a jolt.

Scanning the shadowy bedroom through bleary eyes, she saw that she was still at MacDonald's desert compound, still occupying the plush private apartment Caleb had assigned to her use the previous afternoon. She sunk back into her pillow, half dazed. Christ, what time was it? Rolling to one side, she picked out a set of glowing green numerals on the bedside table: 4:41 AM. A nasty lump of bile rose in her throat. She felt sick, very sick, she now realized. Nothing unusual, of course—just all of her regular complaints: nausea, headache, joints aching like a bad flu. More evidence for the power of prayer, she decided. Sylvie's Christus Experiment was a flop.

She didn't bother to dress. Still in her nightgown, she struggled into the borrowed wheelchair and draped herself in the Navajo blanket Jesus had given her a few hours before. Fifteen minutes later she was sitting in an empty hall in 'F' Building, repeatedly pushing the doorbell outside Fuller's office suite. The sleepy-looking tenant appeared at length, rubbing his eyes. "What do you know?" he said. "It's Miss Fortune knocking at my door."

"I know you're doing that on purpose," Sylvie growled, "so you can just quit, okay?"

"Sylvie, then," said Fuller. "What can I do you for, madam?"

Sylvie's eyes widened in disbelief. "You suck, you know that? You know perfectly well what I'm here for."

"No miracles yet, eh?"

"What's that supposed to mean?" said the girl, eyes narrowing again.

"Oh, I don't know. I thought maybe you-know-who had cut you some kind of a private deal out there on the terrace."

"You can go get bent, you pompous assbag. Are you gonna let me in or not?"

"How could I refuse, after a polite, affectionate request like that?"

Fuller opened the door wide, allowing Sylvie to enter his quarters. The first room was an elegant, stainless steel kitchenette; the second, a beautifully decorated living room with the remains of a fire smoldering quietly in a flagstone hearth. Beyond this, farther in, they came to an interior door with another keypad. When Fuller opened it and pushed Sylvie through, the atmosphere changed completely. This was some kind of medical lab, almost like being back in the hospital again. They'd told her Fuller was a doctor and here was the proof, but she hadn't expected him to keep his own private practice attached to the back end of his sleeping quarters. Yet here it was, cold and asleep, darkened for the night, the air sterile and smelling of cleaning fluids, the only sound the whir of the refrigerators keeping the doctor's stash fresh and potent. Sylvie disliked the feeling of this place right away. It made her think of a well-stocked morgue in a distinguished hospital known for its cleanliness. But at this point in her life she liked the thought of Dr. Fuller's stash very much indeed—and that was what kept her from getting too very finicky about the ambiance.

"Be just a moment," said Fuller as he opened one of the coolers.

"What do you do in here?" Sylvie asked in an unsteady voice.

"I've got my own private line of research. That's how I knew about you, actually. I've been following your exploits for some time."

Fuller took out a small glass bottle of completely clear fluid and took it over to one of the countertops. He switched on a fluorescent light above it which flickered, then buzzed to life. Sylvie watched hungrily as he produced a hypo out of the drawer beneath and began filling it.

"You see," Fuller continued, "we've got more in common than you realize. I've been interested in parapsychology for years—as a kind of an adjunct to my neurophysiologic work. So you're not the first psychic I've ever entertained." Sylvie wasn't focusing on any of this very well. She was feeling pretty bad by this stage and had started rocking back and forth in her chair like a little girl who needs to pee. "As a matter of fact, I was studying people like you long before this current experiment was ever conceived."

The hypo was ready now. Fuller left it lying on the counter and turned to prepare Sylvie herself. Dropping the blanket from off her bare shoulders, he began tying a black rubber tourniquet around her right arm just above the elbow. Sylvie winced. Fuller's hands were very cold. She closed her eyes, held her breath, and waited for some relief.

All at once, however, a strange new sound filled the room. Some kind of radio or intercom kicked in and an unnatural, ghostlike voice crackled out of it. Thin, eerie, bodiless, it seemed to come from a million miles away, like a distant AM station heard on a lonely highway at midnight. After a moment, words became discernable. *"Henry? Henry, is that you? Where am I? Where am I? Why don't you answer?"*

Sylvie's eyes flew open. The physical effect of hearing the sounds was exactly like the experience of being home alone at night and hearing an unexplained rap on one's bedroom window. Even through the pain of withdrawal, her mind was now fully alert. Scanning the room, she saw a loudspeaker mounted above another magnetically locked security door, a door which seemed to lead even deeper into Fuller's suite of rooms.

"What was that?" Sylvie gasped at last.

Alone and unanswered, the ghostly voice broke down into sobs, weeping. *"I'm still so cold…I can't think, it's so cold."*

"Oh, that," interrupted Fuller casually. "That's nothing. I'll switch that off." He stepped away from the wheelchair, moved to a PC nearby, and jiggled the mouse. It took a moment for the desktop to appear. During the interval the voice could be heard again: sad, female, with a slight Slavic accent of some kind.

"This cube is so narrow…and I've had too much sleep…The inductions have been closing in for some time now…too complex…maddening complexity…overcoming any instinct for self-preservation."

Sylvie blanched. She was enough of a psychic to know that a sound like that must come from a bad place. Fuller, meanwhile, clicked an onscreen button and the speaker went dead. "There," he said, "that's enough of that for a while."

"Is there someone behind that door?" asked Sylvie, voice wavering.

"Not really. Not in the usual sense."

"What's behind there?"

"More of my work. Psychic work. I'd take you in if you were feeling better. You'd understand, I think."

Fuller tapped the vein on Sylvie's arm and then paused before shooting her up. "Ready to go?" he asked. "This will make it all better, I promise."

Sylvie was very frightened, but sick as a goat and in a lot of pain. The final dark door to Fuller's inner chamber seemed to quiver just a bit—surely an illusion. She looked up into Fuller's face. His expression was kind, full of understanding. She closed her eyes again and nodded "yes." Fuller injected the chemical.

As soon as the needle penetrated, the girl sucked in a deep breath through clenched teeth. Her eyes opened, then rolled immediately back into her head. The relief was instantaneous. She smiled broadly and raw, shivering pleasure coursed through her body like a powerful orgasm. "Holy shit, that's good!" she managed. "Wow." Her head lolled happily backward and she slipped off into semi-conscious ecstasy. Fuller removed the needle, and began stroking her hair sympathetically. "Sweet dreams, butterfly. You deserve them."

A soft bell rang after a moment. Fuller looked up and a red light was flashing above the mysterious door. He silenced the ringer right away, opened the door with another key code, and passed through it into darkness, leaving Sylvie contentedly on cloud nine.

E X O D U S

What meditates thy thoughtful gaze, my father?
To tell me some new truth? Thou canst not so!
For all that mortal hands are weak to gather,
Thy blessed books unfolded long ago.

Elizabeth Barrett Browning
Ode to an Ikon of St. Gregory Nazianzus

4:1

The sun rose on the third day, a morning bright and clear, and its rose-colored rays fell upon the MacDonald Compound like the benediction of Heaven. The encircling containment ring was a tiara of light, the water tower a lofty guardian angel just completing the night watch. Welcoming this new day, standing at one of the tees of a spectacular driving range located inside the complex, was administrator Lance Fuller. This fantastic recreational perquisite, situated on a substantial rise along the eastern edge, commanded an impressive view of the entire circle. Also in shirtsleeves, Doctors Kent and Breen were enjoying the sight from other tees nearby, where they too were taking mighty whacks with expensive clubs. Though not yet seven AM, the desert floor below was thoroughly salted with the fruits of their combined efforts. In fact, they hardly noticed when Carter Nichols approached from behind, expecting another royal reaming-out from his client. Fuller, however, noticing his approach with an almost imperceptible sideward glance, remained calmly focused on lining up his drive and did not turn around.

"Good morning, Mr. Nichols," he finally said, with a rather artificial cheerfulness. "You're right on time." Breen and Kent offered a grunt or two as well, which Carter politely acknowledged.

"Did you sleep well?"

"I haven't actually been to bed, no," said Carter, and his appearance proved it.

"Working our problem, I would guess."

"That's right."

"I appreciate that, Mr. Nichols, I really do. I'm looking forward to your report."

However much that might be true, Fuller had, apparently, no intention at all of breaking off his golf practice. He positioned another ball, reared back, and sent it flying through space, nearly 400 yards, and watched it fall with silent pleasure.

"But, uh, before we get started, Carter—you don't mind me calling you by your first name, do you?"

Carter was somewhat taken aback (in his experience Fuller had always been the most formal of modern employers) but nodded his agreement right away.

"First, Carter, I wonder if I can be completely frank with you?"

"By all means."

"I think you ought to know that Master Sergeant Rocklynne has come to suspect that you, yourself, are the cause of our security problems."

"Is that a fact?"

"It is a fact. And, you know, to be honest, I'm not certain that he doesn't have a point."

"Go on."

"You wrote the surveillance software we're using, did you not?"

"I did."

"No one else had any serious input."

"No, it was me all right."

"So you could easily have manipulated the system in the way we've seen."

"That's true. I could have."

"And—well, Rocklynne has also looked a bit deeper into your background over the last couple of days."

"Has he now?"

"Yes, he has. And there's a surprise or two." Pausing, Fuller lifted his club again and completed another excellent drive. "You considered becoming a minister once upon a time," he presently continued. "You applied to an Episcopalian seminary at one point, am I right?"

Carter's features betrayed a mild irritation for the first time. "That was a long time ago," he said, shifting uncomfortably. "A man's opinions change."

"Indeed. Indeed, they do. But why did you feel it necessary to hide that fact from us? You never mentioned it."

"I wasn't sure it was any of your business."

"Maybe not," Fuller smiled, fixing him with a sharp, pitiless gaze. "But we did ask. And you didn't come clean. So now we're suspicious. That's logical, isn't it?"

Carter did not reply. His eyes dropped to the ground. There was a lengthy and uncomfortable silence. When he looked up and opened his mouth to speak, he found he was, once again, about to address the back of Fuller's head.

"One more thing," said the Boss at last. "We monitored your communications last night. You bypassed our rather draconian firewall and made an outside call, I think. After all, you're the only person in here who'd be capable of such a feat, are you not?" Still Carter said nothing.

"At 0423 this morning you tapped into an internet phone circuit and placed a call to a Holiday Inn hotel down in Reno. Looks as if you were talking to one of your employees, Mr. Will Jenkins, who, if I'm not mistaken, just went out of here on the bus yesterday morning. You asked him to run illegal background checks, I believe, on three persons currently residing within this Compound; myself, Dr. Caleb Donophan, and Miss Sylvia Fortune. Which three happen to be the only persons in the place you haven't investigated already. This, too, seems rather suspicious."

"I can see your point."

"Oh, before we go on," said Fuller, calmly teeing up a third ball. "I'll save you a few steps on those background checks. Dr. Donophan had a little too much to drink one night back in 1969 and killed his bride of three weeks in a drunk driving accident. Being of a scientific bent, he's been obsessed with time travel ever since. Made quite a name for himself in that field—but wouldn't have gotten anywhere, of course, if anyone had realized his ambitions were anything more than theoretical. The only thing his colleagues knew was that his drinking got worse and worse—thirty years of dead-ends will do that—and that he was thrashing around depressed and suicidal and finally had to be given a leave of absence. Happily, Mr.

MacDonald and I were there to catch him on the way down."

"That was fortunate."

"Providential even, as a more religious man might say. Me, myself, well…let's just say that his needs and ours were an exceptionally good fit."

The third ball went sailing *at least* 400 yards.

"Sylvie's story is even better—you'll like this. Back in June of 2000 she had a dream that she was competing in a diving meet. Still dead asleep, she jumped off the end of her bed onto the floor and shattered every bone in her pretty little neck. Her life's been pretty much of a freak show ever since."

Carter winced and then his features softened. No longer boiling up at Fuller's accusations, he was both fascinated and horrified to learn the truth about Sylvie's accident, having guessed up to now that she'd likely been in a car crash like himself. He also became aware for the first time of a genuine and growing dislike for Lance Fuller. The man's agitation over the security situation was understandable and Carter couldn't blame him, really, for his suspicions. But his tone here, the complete lack of pity for the most hideous of human misfortunes, made him seem bloodless, alien, like the Martians in *War of the Worlds*—an intellect "vast, cool, and unsympathetic."

"As for me," the Administrator resumed, "well, I'm the boy who opened Pandora's box, I guess. Most promising med student to come out of Harvard in years—threw it all away to follow some mad, impetuous dream. But hey, I gotta be me, right? What else can I be?" He stepped away from the tee and began putting his ebony driver back into his bag. "Now, what have you got to say for yourself, Carter?

"I think I'd like to be completely frank as well."

"Excellent! Progress being made."

"First of all," Carter began, "nobody could know about that outside call of mine unless they understood that firewall just as well as I do. But since you do know about it, that means you've got someone here with all the same skills I have, who is, therefore, just as likely to be responsible for those camera loops as I am. That's more logic, by the way."

It was Fuller's turn to go silent. Carter pressed ahead.

"Secondly, I've been down to the village this morning and had a very nice visit with little Maria Rosa, so called, and her family."

"The little girl with one hand?"

"The little girl who most definitely did have only one hand when I first interviewed her, along with her family, back in October. Now, she has two hands—as billed."

"A miracle, then. Cut and dried. Is that it?"

"Maybe."

Fuller smiled. "Maybe you guys could round up some rattlers tonight and have a good old-fashioned snake handling."

"Maybe. Or maybe Maria Rosa has a twin sister back in Guadalajara someplace. And maybe this twin sister—just guessing, mind you—is still getting along with just one hand."

Fuller looked at the security tech in an entirely new light. "What are you driving at, Mr. Nichols?"

"Just this. Did you ever see one of those old movies where Vincent Price dares a bunch of people to spend the night in a haunted house? And at the end it turns out that it was all done with smoke and mirrors? Well, I'm starting to wonder if maybe this isn't the same kind of set-up. With Mr. Anson MacDonald standing in for Vincent Price."

Suddenly, the howl of an approaching plane came into hearing. Both men paused to watch as the Gulfstream jet became visible in the east, clearly aimed at the airstrip nearby.

"Speak of the devil," said Fuller simply.

"I mean, he does have a long history of involvement with anti-God causes, does he not? 'Religion is for morons' and all that?"

The gleaming white jet swooped out of the sky and its engine noise forced the two men to raise their voices.

"So what about it, doc?" yelled Carter. "Am I on the right track?"

"It's an interesting theory."

"I mean, come on. Time Travel? Some guy in blue jeans who's supposed to be God? Chopped off hands that grow back? I'm thinking there's a simpler explanation."

"I don't suppose you'd be interested in seeing some proofs?" Fuller asked. "Video from the Extraction, maybe? Perhaps you could watch us fire up the machine tonight and send him back."

Carter shook his head. "I'm not sure that would help, to be honest. Sixty-eight billion dollars buys a lot of special effects."

The plane touched ground and slipped swiftly to the end of the runway where it came to rest. A moment later the pilot cut the engines and all was quiet again.

"You're a clever fellow, Carter. More clever than I've been giving you credit for. Tell you what. I've got to go down and meet Mr. MacDonald right now. But why don't you come to my office about, oh, six o'clock this afternoon, and I'll lay all my cards on the table. Sound right?"

"I'll be there."

Carter offered his free left hand again. Fuller grinned and shook it warmly.

4:2

As might be expected, Sylvie slept late on the third day and as she did, she dreamed again. This one, however, was no vision of Christmas past, nor even a glimpse of Christmases yet to come. It was the Spirit of the Present that came upon Sylvie now, of things that were happening today, or at least recently—certainly since she herself had been at the Compound. Caleb Donophan was drinking heavily. His apartment, the one next door to Sylvie's, was dark, though the windows were open and the desert air flowed in freely, mitigating the sickly sweet fumes of spilled Scotch whisky. The chief technician was alone, sprawled across his couch and nearly nude, listening to music; a sad, intense and ravishing bit of classical Sylvie would not have known in her normal state of mind, but which she recognized here somehow as Mahler's Symphony #9. But no—another moment and Sylvie knew that Caleb wasn't listening alone. He and his wife were listening together. The symphony was the recording of a recording, the mere background score of a closer, more immediate layer of sound.

Sylvie's psychic gaze grew sharper; more visual details began emerge. Situated in the midst of a wall-sized entertainment center heavily laden with several decades worth of framed academic awards, a big outmoded reel-to-reel tape deck was slowly unspooling its load from right to left. On top of a loudspeaker nearby was the empty cardboard sleeve in which the ribbon had been stored for over four decades; without even looking Sylvie knew that the title penciled onto the surface read *"Charley's Acid; Cape Cod; Sep '69."* And on this cherished old tape, she knew, was the record of a journey in space, in time, a pharmacologically-fueled adventure in the Fifth Dimension straight out of the Age of Aquarius: Caleb and Marie, both 22 and just married, listening to Mahler and tripping out of their skulls. The girl's voice was gentle, touched with the barest trace of her mother's Scottish lilt; and she had a tiny tinkling laugh (heard quite a lot near the start of the tape) which sounded like wind chimes on the portico of a beach house. Sylvie liked her intensely the minute she heard the voice. Caleb's was, of course, a younger, purer edition of his current speech; an aural reflection of his then-unlined face, his then-unmarked wrists. His voice was heard less often on the tape than hers. Marie expressed, after the usual cosmic laughter died down, a strong desire to talk—and immediately backed it up. She talked about eternity, about destiny, about music, and about love. She asked the big questions and grappled excitedly with new and revelatory trains of thought. Caleb's focus stayed mainly on Marie.

Presently, the girl announced with great solemnity an unshakable resolve to find her paperback copy of Elizabeth Barrett Browning and make Caleb understand just how much it meant to her, no matter how long it took. After a few minutes of audible scrambling, she did find it and, after one or two false starts with which she was loudly dissatisfied, delivered at last a passionate and moving performance of Mrs. Browning's exquisite translation of the *Fifth Anacreontic Hymn* by Maximus Margunius:

Take me as a hermit lone
With a desert life and moan;
Only Thou anear to mete
Slow or quick my pulse's beat;
Only Thou, the night to chase
With the sunlight in Thy face!
Pleasure to the eyes may come
From a glory seen afar,
But if life concentre gloom
Scattered by no little star,
Then, how feeble, God, we are!
Nay, whatever bird there be,
(Aether by his flying stirred),
He, in this thing, must be free --
And I, Saviour, am Thy bird,
Pricking with an open beak
At the words that Thou dost speak!
Leave a breath upon my wings,
That above these nether things

I may rise to where Thou art,
I may flutter next Thine heart!
For if a light within me burn,
It must be darkness in an urn,
Unless, within its crystalline,
That unbeginning light of Thine
Shine! oh Saviour, -- let it shine!

Sylvie understood little of this; it seemed to be directed at God or Christ or somebody—a personage whose attributes had only grown more obscure in her mind since meeting the Palestinian in blue jeans. Yet she was *unstrung* by the reading; shaken and appalled by the beauty of it, as if she herself were on Charley's acid, tapped into its power vicariously. Mahler's music continued behind, underscoring every phrase with uncanny perfection. And Marie—oh, the lost Marie! At this moment, Caleb himself could hardly have loved her more. The new bride had struggled with the piece toward the end, many of the words distorted by her efforts to clutch back a sob. She'd come apart completely before it was over and (though Sylvie could not actually see) had very obviously fallen into her bridegroom's arms, weeping.

"I've seen things, Caleb," Sylvie heard her say, in a taped voice which now sounded more like the voice of a child. *"I know too much."* There were whispers, more heavy sobs. "And...and I'm responsible for what I've seen!" Marie wailed suddenly. "I don't deserve what I've already been given!" Poor Caleb, on the tape, could hardly be blamed for the inadequacy of his response. Impaired as

he himself was, he managed only a few platitudes, a few promises that everything would be okay by daybreak, in a tone of voice which implied only a few worries about the quality of the acid. But when Marie spoke again, asking, or rather insisting, that the Caleb of 1969 rise and turn off the tape machine—that he stop, in other words, the recording which would one day be his only link to this precious, vital creature—Sylvie expected the worst from the Caleb on the couch. What would happen when the voice on the tape went silent? Would he fling his whiskey bottle at the machine? Would he make another suicide attempt? After all, Donophan had actually accomplished the thing! The impossible dream of so many bereft lovers through the ages, the gnawing, hopeless fantasy of so many sleepless nights, this the man had already done. He'd built a *time machine,* for God's sake; a real, working time machine capable, it would seem, of miracles. And yet there he still sat, naked and drunk, the gulf between himself and Marie as wide as on the night she died. They had told him it wouldn't work—Aristotle, Aquinas, and the rest. The past can't be changed. And Caleb had told Sylvie he believed them. And yet he built the damn thing anyway. Then he must have built it *knowing* it wouldn't work, knowing that fate would have the last laugh after all, just as everyone predicted. It couldn't be used for the only purpose that mattered to Caleb, for the one project that had secretly motivated his entire, brilliant scientific career. Now, why the hell would a person do that? How the hell? Could you really waste a whole lifetime circling in that kind of tiny mental loop? And yet Sylvie knew the answer to these questions the instant they occurred to her. He did it for the same reason she filled her own veins with poison every day. Because...well, what else was there to do?

Caleb surprised her, though. When the voices from 1969 went silent, when the free end of the tape came off the empty right-hand reel and went flapping around unattended, he neither raged nor wept. All of those violent emotions had, of course, been spent long ago, Sylvie realized; sometime during the Ford or Carter administrations, most likely. What feeling remained was not violent but deadening, nothing but a pure, mechanical obsession. Caleb got up from his sofa quietly, shuffled drunkenly to a full-length mirror and began to speak.

"I have something to tell you that will be hard to believe. You always had an open mind, Marie, so I know you will listen first before calling me crazy."

The words had a rote quality, as if they'd been spoken many times before.

"You're in danger. You mustn't go to the party tonight, the one at Sheffield's. No matter what your husband says, no matter how he begs—just refuse. It's a matter of life and death."

It was a prepared speech, Sylvie realized, and one that Caleb had rehearsed to perfection.

"How do I know? Because I know the future. I've come here *from* the future to warn you, in a time machine I built myself. I am your husband, Caleb Donophan. And I love you, Marie. I love you so much I could die."

Sylvie did not want to see the rest. She had no business in such a private fantasy, or in such a terrible, godforsaken place. She willed the vision to stop, but like all of her visions, it wouldn't stop. It played out, straight through to the bitter end.

4:3

Silverberg hadn't slept long—perhaps 45 minutes on the sofa in Rocklynne's apartment—but when he woke he found the big Marine gone and Mintz' project notes stacked neatly on the coffee table before him. It didn't take him long to realize why (or one of the reasons why) Fuller had them suppressed. Yes, they contained the Rabbi's reflections on Jonah, on time travel, on the case for and against the changing of the past. But they also contained Mintz' own personal diary for most of the previous three months...and it was a horror story, nothing less. Silverberg, having read it to the end, was still trembling like a soldier in a Higgins boat on D-Day. Things had begun well enough; despite prejudices similar to those of his colleague, Mintz had found the Palestinian prophet a pious and likable young man who seemed to like him in return. In fact, Jesus had shown him great deference as "a teacher of the Law" and had demonstrated a desire (which Mintz found difficult to reciprocate) to pray with him and study Torah together. But when, after a few weeks, the Rabbi's meditations led him to his sinister Time Bomb conjectures his attitude began to change. The sheer power of the Nazarene's effect on history, the enormity of his place in the world's consciousness, began to affect Mintz's imagination like a talisman of doom. He got to the point where he wouldn't touch him, wouldn't even speak to him for fear of creating incalculable consequences in the ripples of time. The Rabbi grew terrified of Jesus, developed what

Silverberg could only call a superstitious fear of the man as the world's great nexus for infamy and ill fortune. He begged Fuller at last to relieve him of his rabbinical duties. Yet when Fuller agreed and offered to send him out and bring in a replacement, Mintz changed his mind and backtracked, feeling, as Silverberg learned in the diary, a huge, smothering weight of responsibility, an obligation to keep an eye on the time machine and to ensure that its existence remained a secret. This was when Mintz began his calculations in earnest, his increasingly panicked effort to calm his own fears about the wanton changing of history. And this was also when the diabolical manifestations began, whether in reality or just within the Rabbi's own tortured mind. Ugly voices in the night, bad smells in the room, the mocking caresses of a woman's hand when no woman was to be seen. Blasphemies, obscene words, encouragements to suicide. One particular sleepless night Mintz heard a swarm of rats devouring the curtains, yet when the sun finally reappeared the curtains were undamaged. He concluded finally that someone in the unseen realm was sending him a message: keep your nose out of any potential Time Bomb applications. This—rather heroically in Silverberg's eyes—the Rabbi refused to do.

Instead, Mintz began to pray; something which, like many Reform-minded Jews, he hadn't done seriously since childhood. Like Silverberg, Mintz' Judaism had consisted heretofore of a mixture of tolerance, political liberalism, and vague munificence toward mankind; theologically speaking, he was practically an atheist. The demonic activity, in other words, succeeded in accomplishing just the opposite of its supposed purpose. If devils and ghosts and satanic plots can be real, Mintz seemed to conclude, then perhaps the angels and patriarchs and the Lord of Hosts Himself are real, too, and might also be prevailed upon to make themselves known in such a situation. As he read, Silverberg's interest in this same subject had also grown increasingly acute, any inordinate skepticism having been softened during the brief time he himself had occupied the Chaplain's Quarters. Sadly, his predecessor did not appear ever to have received the help he called for; not, at least, while here in the desert. The diary entries grew less and less coherent, more and more feverish and fantastic as they continued, degenerating finally into a long stream-of-consciousness tirade about destiny, doom, and human damnation. When Rocklynne finally returned to the apartment about 9 AM, Silverberg learned that lack of sleep, mental exhaustion, and constant fear finally put Mintz into the cafeteria one night, waving a straight razor at the Theos and raving in the patented "End is Nigh" style. Fuller shipped him out the next day and turned his notes over to the Master Sergeant for safekeeping.

Despite the early hour, Rocklynne went to his wet bar and poured Silverberg a small shot of cognac, which the Rabbi gratefully accepted into trembling hands and brooded over for the next hour as the two of them talked. Rocklynne thought he saw a new look on the old gentleman's ashen face; emotions deep, disturbing, but not entirely negative. "I had that kind of faith once," said Silverberg, almost to himself. "I had those feelings, that idea—that God really might tug on the other end of the rope someday. It seems like a million years ago."

"I don't think it did Mintz much good," observed Rocklynne caustically. "He's still in the hospital."

The Rabbi looked up from his drink, eyes sparkling. "Maybe not. Maybe all of this is driving me insane, too, just as you feared. But Donophan's time machine is no hallucination, is it? And if not, I'm more convinced than ever that it's the most dangerous discovery ever made." He lifted the stack of papers off the table. "Have you read this yourself? All of it?"

"I'm a busy man, Colonel. I read enough to know."

"Jonah *was* the key. Mintz was right."

"I know he believed that—but none of us here could make heads or tails of it. And we got some pretty heavy theological hitters around this place, don't you think? I mean, okay, God sent Jonah to Nineveh. 'Tell 'em to turn or burn,' he says—all the standard stuff. Kind of a cut rate 'Sodom and Gomorrah.' Only this time, the pagans do turn...and so the city doesn't burn. I guess that does show that the *future* can be changed—that the Ninevites weren't predestined to be destroyed after all—but surely that wasn't the big revelation? What's it got to do with time machines?"

"But you've missed the most important point! You've quoted the story incorrectly. God didn't say turn or burn—He just said burn!"

"What do you mean?"

"There's no *if* in the prophecy! *'Yet forty days, and Nineveh shall be overthrown.'* And yet it wasn't overthrown. The people repented, the city was saved, even though God had made no such promise!"

It was Rocklynne's gaze that turned inward now, as if he also were tapping into some long lost part of himself—ransacking dusty cupboards, unsealing locked off rooms— looking for the young man who had thought about such things once, who had himself once read the Bible expecting the tug on the other end of the rope. It lasted only a moment.

"I still don't get it."

Huffing slightly in frustration, Silverberg backed up a few conceptual steps. "Fuller and Donophan say the past can't be changed, that the only version of time travel which makes any sense is the one where every action taken by our travelers has already been factored in, on the one single timeline that exists. That seems to them the only way to avoid the paradoxes and contradictions which every trip into the past would otherwise create. And they'd be right, of course—if we knew for a fact that there *is* only one timeline. But do we really know that?"

Rocklynne was listening again, but still affecting a pose of impatience.

"What if every trip to the past," the Rabbi continued, "actually creates a *branch point* in the universe? A place where the river of time, so to speak, splits into separate streams, just as the one mighty Nile River splits into the Blue and White Niles at Khartoum? If that were true, then the past could be changed—not our original past, mind you—but the as-yet-unseen past of an alternate reality!"

"You're losing me, Colonel..."

"No, think of it! The past which the time traveler enters becomes a *different* past right away—the past of a parallel world. It would have to, since he wasn't there originally! And because of that, it would begin to diverge from the past he knew, more and more, starting at that point."

"Let me get this straight. You're saying that whenever somebody travels into the past it isn't really their own past that changes—but somebody else's?"

"There's a better way of putting it: every reverse time travel machine is really *a machine for creating alternate universes*—not so much a 'time machine' as a 'multiverse machine'."

"Now you really have gone 'round the bend."

It was Silverberg who lost his patience now and it was no act. His face clouded over and he became, for the first time in Rocklynne's acquaintance, something less than the perfectly well-mannered clergyman. "Look, you drugged Jesus Christ and kidnapped him, you jackass! Can anything be more incredible than that? I mean, haven't we already established that there are some pretty radical possibilities in this universe of ours?" The Rabbi was years younger all of a sudden, the Army colonel again speaking to an enlisted man. "I don't know who you are, Marine, or what's happened in your life to put you here, but you've got to get your head back into the game, son! There's no time for this!"

For a moment, it seemed as if a dam would break in response to Silverberg's outburst; Rocklynne had, of course, plenty of anger of his own bottled up in a private Lake Mead someplace. But his many years as a man under authority, his long training in self-discipline and his instinctive, practically hard-wired response to this tone of voice prevented the disaster from happening. His face grew stonier, his jaw clenched tighter, but when he finally spoke he just said, "So getting back to Jonah…"

"Jonah ran away at first, remember? He didn't want to go! Why not? The Bible doesn't say."

"I always heard he was afraid. Or that he despised the Ninevites and wanted them destroyed."

"Those are two of the common theories, yes. But Mintz discovered something more obscure—something phenomenal." Here Silverberg took up his colleague's notes again and located a page he'd carefully dog-eared a few hours before. "Here it is," he said, rising to his feet and moving to the center of the room. "Mintz finally narrowed his focus to this one bizarre little passage. It's in Greek—a selection from Gregory Nazianzus, one of the Byzantine church fathers from the 4th century. It's part of his commentary on the Twelve Prophets, including the Book of Jonah." The Rabbi held the page at eye level and began to read aloud, translating on the fly. "Listen to what St. Gregory says: '*He fled from having to announce the awful message to the Ninevites, and—if the city should happen to repent and be saved—from being called a false prophet. It was not that he would have been displeased at the salvation of the wicked, but that he was ashamed at the possibility of being made the instrument of a falsehood. For Jonah was exceedingly zealous for the reputation of prophecy, and feared that he himself would be thought to have discredited it, since most men are not able to penetrate the depths of the Divine plan in such cases.*'"

Silverberg dropped the page; Rocklynne stood pondering a long time, lost in thought. "Jonah was worried about being killed, wasn't he?" said the Marine at last. "The Hebrews stoned false prophets to death." Silverberg smiled; Rocklynne saw the point. "God said Nineveh would be overthrown," Rocklynne went on. "Not that it *could* be overthrown, or *might* be overthrown if you're not careful, but that it *would* be overthrown: '*Thus saith the Lord.*' But it wasn't overthrown! And God can't lie—not if you believe your Sunday School lessons, anyway."

"Exactly!" cried Silverberg. "And Mintz *was* starting to believe them again! And if you do believe in prophecy—or foreknowledge, as it's sometimes called—then the foreknowledge has to have an *object*. Must necessarily have one. Because foreseeing something that *might* happen isn't foreknowledge at all, it's just guesswork. Which means that somehow, somewhere, God did see Nineveh destroyed—or else God is a liar. But He isn't a liar. God is merciful. And a time-traveling bit of information can change the past, too! After all, that's what a prophecy *is*—a bit of future history travelling backward in time. So in His mercy God, by sending the prophet, has created the opportunity for..."

"...for a branch point," finished Rocklynne quietly. "An escape hatch, to a universe where Nineveh does repent and stands another 400 years. *Our* universe, in other words."

"That's it exactly."

Rocklynne was pacing now, his mind racing in ways long unaccustomed. He stopped at the bar and took a shot of the cognac himself before pausing suddenly, turning back to face Silverberg, and speaking again. "That's great, Rabbi. Truly great. First class deductions.

But you're forgetting one thing. You forgot the reality check."

"What reality check?"

"I told you before—I know Mr. MacDonald. I know what makes him tick. And if this machine could do what you say it can...well, he wouldn't have bothered with Jesus at all. I know something about his *life,* Colonel—something in it he would already have changed, right away if he had the power."

"And what would that be?"

Rocklynne frowned. "I...can't say. You'll just have to trust me. But you can bank on this, Colonel: if there was even the ghost of a chance of really changing the past with this thing—his own past—he'd have done it long ago. And you and I wouldn't even be having this conversation."

Silverberg stood very still a moment, almost like a waxworks, looking directly into Rocklynne's eyes. Then he said, "I want to talk to him myself. And to Fuller. I have questions, Gunny."

Rocklynne grinned broadly. He seemed relieved, as if released from some heavy responsibility. "That's okay, Colonel! That's fine. I was just about to tell you—I've been to see Fuller this morning. I briefed him on our talk. And he's already suggested a meeting. Sent me here to get you and set it up."

"He did?"

"Yeah. But...well, he's got a busy day today, so it won't be right away—we got the Reinsertion coming up tonight, as I think you know. He'd like you to wait for him. In the village."

"The village?"

"Yeah, in the synagogue. Have you seen it yet?"

Silverberg shook his head.

"It's a reproduction of the 1st century synagogue found at Capernaum. Very detailed, replicas of the scrolls and everything. Cost a fortune. Should be plenty there to keep you interested for a few hours."

The Rabbi hesitated, looking very tired and still quite troubled. He finally gave a nod of silent agreement however, and started gathering his things.

4:4

"Fuller ordered all the gates opened?"

"Not Fuller," replied Kent from behind the wheel of a company SUV. "MacDonald."

"Incredible," said Dr. Flammerion, shaking her head. "Simply incredible."

Kent's other passenger, Joe Breen, wore a look of disgusted resignation. "What difference does it make now?"

Flammerion ignored the question. "And the man is talking? At length?"

"About an hour, so far. Off and on."

"On the last day. The last day of the Experiment!"

The SUV passed through the Palestinian Village and emerged at the other end, where the cobbled street petered out onto a rocky beach. The gigantic cobalt dome of the Nevada sky hung overhead with an almost sensible weight and the sun in the center of it was just past its zenith. The strange rock formation which gives Pyramid Lake its name jutted up from out of the waters to meet the sky like a monument. About fifty yards out from the shore the brilliantly white structure of the dampening ring crossed over the water like the monorail track at Disney's EPCOT, shaving off one corner of the shimmering lake and enclosing it within the MacDonald compound. Practically the entire support staff could be seen a few yards up the beach, assembled at the water's edge and watching as Dominguez, Bautista, and Ramirez stood hip-deep, baptizing a small group of other Mexicans. Jesus himself, still in blue jeans, sat on a rustic bench halfway up the beach, whittling on a piece of wood. He was surrounded by a happy brood of small, babbling children.

The wheels of the big vehicle ground noisily to a halt on the pebbled surface. Flammerion rolled down her window to better observe the striking scene, taken aback suddenly by its beauty and simplicity. Though she had spent many hours with Jesus, in cramped recording booths and harshly lit interrogation rooms, this was the first time she had seen him smile.

"*Suffer the little children to come unto me,*" she quoted, with a touch of awe in her voice and to no one in particular, "*for of such is the kingdom of God.*"

4:5

Caleb stood in the hall outside Sylvie's room, pounding on the door with little to no visible effect. It was nearly two o'clock in the afternoon.

"Sylvie. Are you in there? Open up."

The room was silent as a tomb. Finally, the scientist simply opened the lock with his own key ring and entered. Inside, he found the girl in a dreadful state. Wearing only a diaper and the short, teddy-style nightgown, she was sprawled awkwardly across the bed with her ugly, atrophied legs fully exposed to view. A narrow tube could be seen piercing her abdomen and entering her left kidney for purposes of urine collection. Her colostomy bag had ruptured during the night, leaving the bedclothes smeared with diarrhea (which, of course, also fouled the air in the room). She was a pitiful sight to say the least and Caleb winced at the spectacle in spite of himself.

"My God."

He stepped into the bathroom and emerged with a stack of clean towels, then set to work cleaning Sylvie up. With his first touch she began to stir.

"Wonderful," she managed after a moment, looking down at her self through bleary, bloodshot eyes. "Just bloody wonderful." And at just that instant Carter Nichols bounded through the door, an oblivious bull in Sylvie's very fragile china cabinet. He saw only Donophan at first.

"Is she ready to go? MacDonald is waiting. I've got…"

The actual scene registering at last, Carter looked at Sylvie on the bed and focused almost immediately on the awful heroin tracks pockmarking her arms—something he hadn't been aware of to this point. His voice trailed off, but he did succeed in completing his opening sentence.

"…the van parked outside."

Sylvie looked up, meeting his gaze, about as miserable and hung out to dry as any human female could be in this vale of tears. Carter couldn't help it; the look on his face communicated deep shock and an unmistakable measure of revulsion. Caleb rounded on him angrily.

"God dammit, man! Don't they teach people to knock where you come from?"

"The door was standing open."

"Get the hell out."

Carter backed away, then turned and disappeared.

Sylvie started to cry. Caleb pulled the coverlet up over her legs and most of the mess. She tried to speak but he couldn't understand. He bent over to hear better; when he did, Sylvie clutched at his shirt and pulled him down close.

"I've got to get off of this junk, Caleb. I've got to. I can't—I can't get my head clear enough to figure this out. Help me."

Caleb allowed her to hug his neck like a little girl after a bad dream. He had, of course, never fathered a child of his own.

4:6

Most of the baptisms had finished and the people—even the Theos—had started gravitating around Jesus himself, still sitting at his bench whittling. Though intensely curious, doctors Flammerion and Breen hung back toward the rear of the crowd; their attire contrasted strongly with the plainer dress of the peasants and several of the ladies had taken up their scandalous habit of feeding the baby again. As the group watched, the Nazarene put the last touches to a little toy lamb he'd been making and he presented it as a gift to one especially bright-eyed five year old. The quality of the carving really was very good; the man had obviously worked with wood before. The Mexicans fell silent, anticipating another word or two from

"Josue." Jesus put his hand on top of the child's head and began to oblige.

"You must all come to me as this child has come, and I will give gifts to you as well."

"What kind of gifts, Señor?" asked Ramirez, also in Spanish.

"Gifts of the Spirit," said the Israelite, rising to his feet and scanning the faces of his hearers with an expression of youthful enthusiasm. "I'm telling the truth, I am not lying: whoever believes in me will do the same works that I do; yes, and even greater works. But unless you come as a little child I can give you nothing." Here, the Preacher's eyes fell upon the Theos and upon Kent personally, standing back with his arms crossed in wordless skepticism. "To what shall I compare the rulers of this city?" Jesus asked when he spoke again. "They are like the servants of a great landlord whose Master planted a vineyard and then went away on a journey to a far country. While he was gone the servants grew lazy and began to think of themselves as the true owners of the vineyard. Their Master's return became, at last, nothing but a rumor. Finally, they convinced themselves that there never had been any Master to begin with." Jesus sighed, but his expression brightened when he looked back on his peasant friends, all of whom over the past three months, he had come to know on a first name basis. Their open, agricultural faces—many of which were so purely Mexican that they might have come straight off an ancient Olmec sculpture—shone with pleasure at his mere presence among them. Jesus broke suddenly into a tremendous smile and, with sparkling, misty eyes, lifted his gaze up to heaven and called out to the Sky. "Father, I thank you because you have hid these things from the wise and the learned and have revealed them to children. So be it, for this has seemed good in your sight." He lowered his face and addressed the disciples again. "Privileged indeed, and happy, are eyes which have seen what your eyes have seen. I tell you that many prophets and kings have longed to see what you have seen here and have not seen it; and to hear the things you have heard, and have not heard them."

At this, one of the women called out: "We love you, Señor! Pray to the Father for us."

"The Father himself loves you," Jesus replied, "because you have loved me."

Dr. Kent, who had picked up a word or two of all this with his high school Spanish, stepped over to Ramirez and whispered something in his ear. Ramirez nodded, agreeing to translate for him.

"Lord," began Kent in an impressive voice, "we have asked you a great many very sincere questions since you came here. Why have you not answered?"

Jesus waited patiently for Ramirez' translation, then responded, to the astonishment of all, in his own gently accented English. "Why do you call me Lord when you will not do as I tell you?"

The knowledge that Jesus possessed such a complete command of their language sent a wave of visible consternation over the Theos. "But you haven't spoken to us at all until now!" sputtered Kent at last.

"I've been speaking to you since you were children."

The Theos fell silent again.

"The prophet Isaiah was right when he prophesied of you: *'This people's heart has grown callous and their ears have grown dull from too much hearing. Their eyes they have closed for fear of seeing. Otherwise, they would see, and having seen, be compelled by their hearts to turn and find healing.'* "

Kent was unimpressed. "That's very clever. St. Paul used that line on the Pharisees in Acts 28. You *have* been reading that Bible we found, haven't you?"

Jesus ignored this. "I ask you all plainly: do you believe in the Son of Man?"

"What do you mean?" asked Breen plaintively. "Of course we believe. We've spent our entire lives in theological study, all of us!"

Flammerion picked up this thread. "But here in the 21st century," she said, "we believe each person has to understand those words in his or her own way."

"My words were given to me by my Father," said the Nazarene. "Not even I can cut them to suit myself. His word is Truth. So I ask you again, do you believe that the Father is in me and I am in the Father?"

Ramirez, the only English speaker among the help, was also the only person to respond. "I believe, Señor! Ask me!" The Theos only gawked.

"Because I warn you, the time has grown short. And whatever state I find you in at the end, that is the state in which I will take you."

4:7

The van with the wheelchair lift pulled up in front of "A" Building, a bare, sunblasted shoebox of a place standing apart from the rest, completely nondescript.

Neither Carter on the passenger side nor Sylvie, seated in her chair and strapped in the back, had seen this particular structure yet; it presented quite a contrast to the lavish styling elsewhere and might almost have been a storage facility for aluminum siding or a building supply warehouse. When Caleb had parked the vehicle and engaged the handbrake he and Carter clambered into the rear and teamed up releasing the wheelchair; this was a five to ten minute process even for experienced caregivers. As they worked, Sylvie—considerably cleaned up since Carter saw her last but still looking a bit delicate—had questions to ask.

"MacDonald's in here?"

"Not yet. But he'll be here. I've never known him to be a minute late for anything."

"What is this place?"

Caleb shrugged as he worked. "Dunno. None of us have ever been inside."

"You're kidding."

"No, it's some kind of private sanctum, I guess. I know MacDonald spends a lot of his time here whenever he's onsite."

Once the chair was freed Carter climbed out the back and took hold of a big square remote wired to the chair lift. Caleb rolled Sylvie out onto the metal platform. She sat quietly as it was lowered to the ground with a soft pneumatic whine. All this time Sylvie thought Carter seemed reluctant to look her in the face, which was okay with her since she still had a vivid mental image in her mind of what he must have seen from the doorway an hour or two ago; a pathetic little junkie, a greasy drowned rat wallowing around in her own waste. It still made her throat burn to think about it, so she tried not to. Alas, Caleb left the two of them alone for a moment, stepping away with his keys to unlock the gray metal and wholly unmarked door to the building. But instead of the awkward silence Sylvie feared, Carter turned his back to Caleb and to the door and used the brief moment of privacy to speak.

"What are you doing for dinner tonight?"

"I beg your pardon?" said Sylvie, looking up at him in blank incomprehension.

"I want to have dinner with you. In the cafeteria."

"Why?"

"Why? Because I like you. I think you're pretty. And very sweet."

"You're joking, right?"

"Nope. Serious as a Russian play. So how 'bout it?"

Caleb interrupted by calling out—the door was open. Behind him, Sylvie and Carter could see the yawning black entrance beckoning.

"I don't think we better, Carter. But thank you for asking."

"Why not?"

"I'm not…myself right now." For a moment, Carter thought she might cry again, but she'd didn't. Instead, she just put her right hand to her temple and rubbed it worriedly. "And besides, I got a real bad habit of making unhappy endings for people."

Carter screwed up his face in a gentle spoof of her serious tone, like Snow White mocking Grumpy. "Well, you don't scare me none, Miss Fortune. Not a bit. I don't scare easy."

With her weepy eyes blood red and the rings under them making her look like a sick raccoon, Sylvie looked up. "Don't you, Carter?" she asked, smiling another of her crooked, endearing smiles. "I'm glad."

Caleb interrupted again with a distinct time's-a-wastin' tone in his voice, so Nichols finished his overture with a simple, casual grace. "Anyways, let me know if you change your mind." He took control of the chair and piloted it firmly toward the mysterious door.

The darkness was palpable inside, the atmosphere heavy with an artificially air-conditioned chill and a powerful antique smell that none of them could quite place at first. Caleb fumbled for a light switch. When he did the whole trio stood astonished at what the lights revealed.

They had entered the lobby of the Bible Land Wax Museum. Any doubt about that was eliminated right away by a lighted marquee to that effect hanging above an old-fashioned ticket counter. This was nothing more or less than a roadside American tourist attraction straight out of the early 1960's, transported to the Nevada desert as if by magic. The centerpiece of the lobby was a wax figure of the traditional blonde-haired, blue-eyed Jesus standing behind velvet ropes, his arms wide in a gesture of welcome. A rack of travel brochures stood nearby, encouraging visits to similar places from Rock City in Tennessee to Wall Drug in South Dakota. Somewhere, a hidden tape player started up with the dated sounds of a hushed choir in full George Beverly Shea mode. Simultaneously, a sunny picture window blinked to life, rigged with a color transparency of what must have been the original view into the parking lot, full of cars with tail fins. Every detail was perfect, from the art-moderne water fountain to the classic Perey turnstiles, and the total effect was downright surreal.

"I'll be damned," said Carter bluntly.

Sylvie took control of her own chair again and wheeled it over to a souvenir stand, crowded with big pencils and Viewmaster reels. One item in particular arrested all of her attention: the exact same snowglobe she'd been seeing in all of her visions. She was reluctant to touch it at first, associated as it was in her mind with so much anguish and terror. She did finally steel herself to the task, however, and when she did...she felt nothing. Nothing at all. Caleb, meanwhile, was having a closer look at the wax Savior.

"Not much of a likeness, is it?"

"What's that?" asked Sylvie, stirred out of her reverie.

"I said it's not much of a likeness. This guy looks more like me about 1968."

Sylvie shook up the snow globe, watching the tiny blizzard swirl around the baby Jesus inside.

"It even smells like the Sixties in here," Caleb concluded.

"Do you ever talk to him, Caleb?" Sylvie asked suddenly.

"Not since I was an altar boy."

"No, I mean here. While he's been here."

"I try to stick to the technical end, Sylvie."

Nearby, Carter looked up from a stack of picture postcards. "What's this all about anyway?"

A new voice responded from the entrance door—with a distinct Southern accent. "Just an old man's hobby, Mr. Nichols. I hope you can find it in your hearts to humor me a little."

"Mr. MacDonald," said Caleb in reply.

Anson MacDonald entered the lobby; a tall, well-groomed gentleman in his mid-seventies; tanned, good-looking, probably quite a rake in his day, with a white cowboy hat in one hand.

"Some fellas spend a fortune gathering up baseball cards," he said. "The ones they owned as a kid. I guess my paradise lost was even more expensive to regain...but it's the same principle." He closed the door behind him and moved to stand near Sylvie. "They were gonna tear the place down back in '92. I couldn't let that happen so I bought it instead. Had it put into storage until I could find a place for it." He extended his hand to Sylvie. "I'm Anson MacDonald, Sylvie. You can call me Andy." Sylvie shook the hand sheepishly. "Dr. Donophan's been taking good care of you, I trust? Hello, Caleb."

Donophan nodded in response. Carter's worst habit, a superstitious worship of mere wealth, left him looking a little awestruck and silent.

"It's just that I had my first religious experiences in here, I guess you'd say" MacDonald continued. "As a boy of 13. Really shook me up. Wrote a letter to Billy Graham the next day, asking to go on staff with his crusades. He told me to finish school, of course. Quite right, too. I'd like to give you the tour, Sylvie, if your friends don't mind. I won't even charge you the 75 cents admission."

Sylvie looked at Caleb as if to get his permission. He took hold of the wheelchair in response and delivered it to MacDonald. The billionaire, meanwhile, lifted the arm on the gate which led into the exhibit itself. Caleb and Carter were left unceremoniously behind.

The first wax tableau was a lush Garden of Eden, complete with taxidermied wildlife, a real running waterfall, and a rather demure Adam and Eve. The scene was cordoned off from the public with an incongruous split-rail fence which would've been more appropriate, Sylvie thought, for a scene of the Beverly Hillbillies.

"We've got a lot to talk about, you and I," said her host, pushing Sylvie right up to the fence for a good view. "Or so I've been told. And, well, this just seemed the appropriate surroundings. It's a little creepy, I guess. I'm reminded of what Flannery O'Connor used to say about us Southerners."

"What was that?" asked Sylvie, finding her voice at last.

"She said that the South isn't so much Christian as it is 'Christ-haunted.' And I guess I'm 'Exhibit A'. But like I said, maybe you'll humor an old Southern gentleman?"

4:8

The black starless void was terrifying in its awful, airless emptiness. Sound was impossible, heat non-existent. It was a vision combining all the terrors of height, all the panic of falling, with the closed-up claustrophobia of a vacuum-tight room where no atom of air was nor ever would be available again. And tumbling silently through this appalling void, closer and closer, was the tiniest blue speck—indiscernible as yet, but undoubtedly a portent of things gone horribly wrong.

Then the voices began—an unintentional eavesdropping on a dialogue happening somewhere else entirely. The conversation seemed to happen in the mind, however—the deadly, stifling void remained as silent as the grave. There were two voices: the first recognizably that of Dr. Lance Fuller, speaking in low, conspiratorial tones; the second was strange and new, a commanding, imperious voice using female vocal chords, it's true, but with no hint of the warmth or humanity of a woman.

"I'm concerned," admitted Fuller. "Concerned about interruption."

"Have no fear, Lance. No fear. Everything will come right at last. At long, long last..."

"What about these Mexicans?"

"The new apostles you mean?" The second voice was amused. *"Ignorant rabble—just like the last time."*

The tiny blue speck had come much closer. It was discernable now as a human figure spinning weightlessly forward, like the dead and drifting astronaut in *2001*.

"They will try to free him, won't they?"

"I expect they will. You mustn't allow it, of course. Nothing must prevent us from sending Him through."

"You mean sending him back."

"Yes. Yes, of course. Sending Him back."

The tumbling figure rolled closer and closer, until it was all too recognizable—the body of Jesus, frozen stiff, covered in frost, his throat cut from ear to ear.

"What about the old Jew?"

"Keep him away from Donophan if you can."

The Rabbi's eyes flew open. He yanked himself erect from the bench upon which he had been praying. He'd fallen asleep in the synagogue, with a beautiful illuminated scroll of the prophecy of Jeremiah as his pillow. A long shaft of afternoon sun fell golden through the window but the ghostly voices of the plotters were still ringing in his ears.

Silverberg staggered to his feet, rushed to the door at the rear and passed through it without any trouble at all, before hastily departing onto the streets of the Palestinian Village. He must find Donophan as quickly as possible, with what waning mental health he still had left at his disposal.

4:9

Sylvie and MacDonald entered another musty, theatrically lit diorama, this one depicting the patriarch Abraham preparing to sacrifice his son Isaac to God on a crude stone altar. Sylvie remembered the story pretty well, but if there had been any lingering doubt the whole tale was reiterated succinctly on a very sincere and nicely lettered signboard to the right. The wax Abraham had been caught by the sculptor at precisely the penultimate moment, with an anguished but impassioned gleam in his glass eyes and a real brass knife flashing high over his head, ready to strike the fatal blow. MacDonald, who knew every detail of the museum by heart, kept his eye fixed on Sylvie as they toured.

"I don't mind telling you, young lady, I'm pretty fascinated with you."

"Well, one tries," the girl said archly. "You should have seen me in my heyday: pretty as a peacock and about as smart. The perfect woman, in other words."

MacDonald ignored her. "I've never gone in for ESP, stuff like that, until just here lately. Bunch of baloney, I always figured. But Fuller's been right about everything else he's proposed to me so I gave it a shot. I've gotta tell you, though, that nail was a budget buster even for me."

Sylvie's expression darkened at the thought of the nail. She glanced up at the long, scary-looking knife in Abraham's fist and (though she did it instinctively rather than with any theological motive) linked the two in her mind.

"And then he spoke to you on the terrace," MacDonald continued, in a tone of amazement and reverence. "Do you know I've dreamed about an interview like that my whole life long—ever since I first came out of this place. No bowed head, no memorized words or any of that rigmarole. Just him and me, face to face. God, what was that like?"

"I upchucked all over the floor. He had to clean it up."

MacDonald didn't look shocked. "Well, you would, wouldn't you? I mean—that seems natural to me. What did he say?"

"He told me things that only he would know."

"What kind of things?"

"About me. And my life."

MacDonald's eyes held a new excitement. He seemed to look past Sylvie or through her, his thoughts racing far ahead of their current conversation. "Do you think he would talk to me now?" he asked presently. "He never would before, you know."

"I don't know what to think anymore."

4:10

Caleb emerged from the wax museum, leaving Carter puttering around in the gift shop inside. How long Sylvie's tour would continue he had no way of knowing so he leaned against the van, lit a cigarette, and stood quietly in his thoughts, watching the sun sink over Pyramid Lake. It was less than five minutes, however, before Rabbi Silverberg appeared on foot, winded and agitated. "There you are..." said the Rabbi in greeting. "...Dr. Oppenheimer."

There was a long, significant pause before the Chief Technician finally responded. When he did he simply said, "It's Donophan, actually."

"I spoke figuratively, of course."

"What's on your mind, Rabbi?"

"How long till your infernal machine is ready again?"

"Should be right on schedule—couple of minutes past midnight tonight. Worried you won't get to say goodbye?"

Silverberg dismissed the flippant remark. "Is there anyplace in this damned circle where two gentlemen can talk frankly?"

"My office?"

"Someplace without bugs. Or cameras."

Caleb paused again. Plainly, the Rabbi was frightened and completely in earnest. In fact, he could see the old man's hands shaking.

"Get in the van."

4:11

Gradually, Sylvie realized that she ought to be frightened of MacDonald. The immaculately preserved waxworks, the billionaire recluse obsessed with his lost innocence—these certainly invited easy comparison to Howard Hughes' Spruce Goose and Michael Jackson's oxygen chambers. Her mother—indeed, any outside observer—might very well be screaming at her to get out by now. But Sylvie didn't feel that way. She wasn't sure why, but MacDonald saddened rather than frightened her. He was loved by many once, she felt, and had loved many in return. But now there was a kind of dark light inside of him, a widening purple blaze which was slowly consuming him from within. She found herself wishing—or tempted to wish, perhaps—that it had killed him already and spared him the trouble of suicide.

The next display was an elaborate Nativity scene bathed in artificial moonlight. MacDonald shoved her right up to the barrier for a front row seat. The shepherds and wise men were all in place. There was frankincense and myrrh, a lowing ox and ass, a wax baby, the whole nine yards. Sylvie couldn't help it; she was submerged right away in a sea of pleasant, involuntary of recollections of Christmases long, long ago. MacDonald, smiling broadly, stepped over to the rail where a big red button was marked *"Push Me."*

"Oh, this is great," he said with childlike enthusiasm. "Watch this." He depressed the switch and a sumptuous choral arrangement of "Silent Night" poured out of a hidden loudspeaker, accompanied by the stentorian tones of a very square period narrator: *"No matter at what season of the year we gaze at a representation of the humble manger scene, our hearts are touched with deep seated admiration and humility as we recall the biblical passages telling of this world changing event. 'Now when Jesus was born in Bethlehem in the days of Herod the King, behold there came wise men from the East to Jerusalem, saying, 'Where is he that is born king of the Jews?..."*

As the narration continued, MacDonald raised his voice and spoke over it. "I had the old tapes digitally remastered," he said with obvious pride. "Sounds great, doesn't it?"

Sylvie didn't quite know what to say, but nodded in agreement anyway. As she did, a smile broke out on her face—the first in a couple of days. And this made her angry for some reason. It was like she was Pavlov's dog or something. *"Silent night, holy night; Son of God, love's pure light..."* She was ready to join in, for God sakes, with a complete set of lyrics on hand, already pulled up from her internal hard drive. They'd schooled them into her as a little girl, of course. It was what they taught people instead of more useful things: such as how to keep on getting up in the morning when half your body is a useless lump of tissue. And why did she have to keep having her nose rubbed in all this, anyway? She hadn't asked to get involved. If they'd told her what it was ahead of time she'd have told them to take a freakin' hike. And it wasn't her job to figure out who the man on the terrace was—what he was and what it all meant. That was for the Theos, who got paid—pretty *well* paid, she imagined—for deducing how many angels fit onto a pinhead. She didn't know and she didn't care. She was tired of wondering. But, no. No. She was tired, but not of wondering. She still wondered, dammit. She wondered intensely. But the wax baby was no help. He simply sat there smiling, happy as a clam, while the narration continued:

" *'And there were in the same country, shepherds abiding in the field keeping watch over their flock by night,' when suddenly the angel of the Lord brought to them the tidings of great joy, 'for unto you is born this day in the city of David, a savior which is Christ the Lord.'* "

"Silent Night" faded gently away. Automatically, a little brass sign lit up above the next doorway with the polite phrase "This Way Please."

MacDonald's mood seemed to change suddenly. When he spoke again he was brooding, troubled.

"Too bad it's all bullshit, huh? You're lucky, Sylvie. You found out while you're still young. I only wish my own..." The publishing magnate cut himself off in mid-sentence—but Sylvie decided to press.

"Your own what?"

"Nothing. I...had a daughter your age. And a grandson, too, they tell me."

"What happened?"

"There was a fire. In Texas."

The lights over the Nativity faded to black, encouraging visitors to move on to the next scene.

4:12

Caleb took Silverberg to the beach—the same beach where Jesus and his disciples were still congregating, but several hundred yards upshore from the crowded baptism site. The doors of his van flew open and the two men stepped out onto the sand.

"You can say what you like out here," said Donophan.

"Have you seen Rocklynne?"

"No, I can't say I have. Fuller's had him on some kind of extra security detail all afternoon."

Silverberg was almost literally wringing his hands in anxiety. "I'm taking a terrible risk coming to you, Donophan," he said. "It makes me sick to think of it, but I don't know what else to do."

"Oh, I know what you're here for," said the scientist quietly. "You know, I actually met Oppenheimer once. I almost asked him—didn't he give some thought to hanging himself first, rather than accept the responsibility?"

Silverberg stared at him, his elderly eyes darting over the younger man's features, searching for any sign of deception or duplicity.

"But it's all nonsense, Rabbi! The past can't be changed. It's the only way to save any rational concept of the universe!"

"You're not sure of that! I've been reading excerpts from your work. What about Everett, Hugh Everett?"

"Everett? Is that what you're losing sleep over? Everett's is a minority opinion. A fringe theory."

"You said yourself that it's never been disproved! The 'many-worlds interpretation of quantum physics,' the theory of alternate realities, with parallel time tracks. You may have split the universe into two separate branches the moment your time travelers entered the past!"

Looking down the beach, Caleb could see the figure of Jesus in the distance, still standing at the water's edge, preaching to the Mexicans.

"Look, Rabbi," he said after a moment. "You've got to trust me on this. You're letting your imagination run away with you. The Government knows nothing. The men in black are not coming."

"I'm not worried about the Government anymore!"

Caleb was puzzled. "You're not worried somebody's going to come and take all this away from us? Use it to reshape reality in some horrible way?"

"No!" the Rabbi cried. "Someone *is* using it already—right now! Tonight!"

4:13

MacDonald pushed Sylvie up to another red button, this time in front of an impressive crowd scene: a dozen or so New Testament peasants in authentic costume, listening to a wax Jesus with rapt attention.

"I'll let you do it this time."

The girl leaned forward and depressed the fat button with two of her frail white fingers.

"Down through the ages, above the din of discordant earthlings absorbed with their greed for gain and envy of their

fellows engaged in the same pursuit, echo the calm, clear words of the great Teacher in His Sermon on the Mount: 'Blessed are the poor in spirit, for theirs is the kingdom of heaven. Blessed are they that mourn, for they shall be comforted. Blessed are the meek, for they shall inherit the earth. Blessed are the peacemakers: for they shall be called the children of God. Blessed are they which are persecuted for righteousness' sake: for theirs is the kingdom of heaven...' "

MacDonald turned away from the scene with an unpleasant smirk on his face. "You know those Mexicans want us to set him loose on the world again," he said. "They've actually got the idea that this is the Second Coming or something!"

At these words, a new realization came over Sylvie's face. "Isn't that just what it would be?" she said, at last. "I mean, what it *is*? Literally?"

It was plain that MacDonald hadn't thought of this. "I didn't...I mean, I don't know whether..." He went completely silent for a full minute at least, his eyes gazing vacantly at the pious dummies in the display, lost in his own thoughts. Finally, he crouched suddenly next to Sylvie's chair and addressed her in a very grave tone.

"Listen, young lady. You don't really think this man is—well, you know what they say. I heard you were a solid atheist."

Was she an atheist? Was she anything? By this point, Sylvie's thoughts revolted against labels of any kind. After all even an atheist claims to know *something* about the ultimate nature of things, even if that something is a mere denial. And Sylvie didn't even have that much faith right now—in her own intellectual powers or in the validity of human reason itself. So did that mean she was a Christian again, like that silly, childish thing in the mirror? Was her response to the man on the terrace a true insight—or just the inevitable psychological leftovers from years of conditioning? These questions raced around in her head like a gerbil in its exercise wheel. But she was too sick to work these damned puzzles! Couldn't they all see that? Why did she have to *be* anything? Why couldn't they just leave her alone to crawl under a rock like she wanted to and shrivel up in peace?

"I don't know what they told you, Mr. MacDonald, but I'm just a junkie. I don't know my ass from a hole in the ground."

MacDonald's voice sparked with anger now, but not at Sylvie. "But—oh, c'mon, if Jesus is God then I'm greater than God, 'cause I snatched him out of his own life!" Sylvie said nothing, but simply began nervously fingering the silver cross around her neck, head throbbing. "And the real God would never have allowed such a thing, would he? Not if our Jesus is who he's supposed to be. God wouldn't allow his own Son to be just thwarted and kidnapped and humiliated like that..." Whether or not Sylvie noticed the theological mistake in this—that the capture and humiliation of his Son is just exactly what God, in the Christian scheme, *is* supposed to have allowed even the first time around—she certainly did permit a new pensiveness into her features at the thought, a new willingness to follow religious arguments in ways that would have been emotionally impossible even twenty-four hours earlier. MacDonald, not having known her earlier, noticed nothing of this. "Anyway, I did it to free people,

Sylvie! To save them! There's millions of folks around the world throwing their lives away on what I have now *proved* is a superstition! Don't you think at least a few of them would like to know about it?"

The room fell silent again, except for the sonorous voice of the old Sixties narrator: "*Here it was, too, that the Master gave to us the prayer of prayers, which the voices of the Bible Land choir now bring us in reverent praise and supplication...*"

Another song began, Malotte's familiar arrangement of "The Lord's Prayer." "*Our Father, which art in heaven, hallowed be thy name. Thy kingdom come, Thy will be done on earth as it is in heaven...*"

Sylvie had always been moved by this song. It surged in the middle, she felt, to a near-panic of desperate entreaty, then faded away at the end to an afterglow of ecstatic resignation. Thy will be done, it said. Not my will, but thy will. Was it God's will that she was here now, experiencing all this? A lump of angry bile rose in her throat at the thought, and she made a face thoroughly appropriate to its awful taste. Sylvie had heard enough about the will of God to last her three lifetimes. Half the damned fools who'd ever tried to be nice to her since the accident had thought she might enjoying hearing their particular theory of God's will; of hearing, that is, about how her supposed calamity had actually been the best thing for all involved if only she had the faith to see it. So Sylvie had, of course, promised herself long ago never to waste another thought on the damnfool subject. But that was just the trouble! She couldn't *stop* thinking, no matter how hard she tried. She'd protected herself for a long time, she realized, by never succumbing to the temptation to think; the temptation, that is, *to stick her neck out,* as Carter had put it. To imagine, hope against hope, a world where her accident wasn't just a chance event, with no more real significance than the death of one given tuna out of a trillion in one given patch of the Atlantic eaten by a given shark on a given day. Because if she did stick her neck out, she reflected bitterly, the headsman might just be there with his axe, waiting. Her heart leapt queasily at the thought. But then…what more could this headsman do, really, than what she had already done to herself?—and not least by her resolute refusal to hope! Would he threaten her with a horrible death? A loss of faith and happiness? Would he wag his finger in her face and say "Toldja so"? Was that the specter that had made her surrender as she had? And wasn't this, after all, a bit like the man in the proverb who committed suicide from fear of death?

Suddenly, MacDonald rose to his feet, looking just as conflicted as Sylvie. She watched him as he scanned the reverent faces of the artificial crowd, his eyes beginning to water. He started pacing, back and forth in the semi-darkness. "Was it all a mistake?" he asked, not necessarily of Sylvie. "Have I been doing wrong?"

"Maybe it was meant to happen this way," Sylvie offered, with a dreamy look on her face. "I mean, maybe this is how the Second Coming *happens*."

"With a time machine?" replied MacDonald, incredulous.

"They always said he uses our evils to bring about good…"

"That's right!" the billionaire said, in a distinctly altered tone of voice. "That was the way with the cross, too." MacDonald rose to his feet, his face shining with a new light. "Maybe it's all part of the Divine plan. Maybe I'm meant to *help* him now, rather than…"

"And lead us not into temptation," the Choir continued, *"but deliver us from evil…"*

"I need time to think this over," the billionaire finished. His expression became trance-like as he followed this new train of thought wherever it might happen to lead. At any rate, he quickly lost all interest in Sylvie or the wax museum. Taking hold of the handgrips perfunctorily he piloted the chair directly to the exit, skipping entirely what had been the highlight of the whole tour back in the day: a faithful recreation of Leonardo's Last Supper, with all twelve apostles, an authentic painted backdrop, and a table full of fruit made from the very same wax as the blonde Messiah Himself.

4:14

"They mean to keep him, Donophan! They mean to destroy him, to wipe him from the pages of history."

Caleb was getting angry. "Who's they? MacDonald? He's not even convinced it *is* Jesus. Doesn't look enough like the guy in the wax museum."

Silverberg didn't understand this comment, but he let it pass.

"And Fuller…" the scientist continued. "Hell, Fuller can't wait to get him out of here. This hacker's got him scared to pieces."

"I know it sounds crazy," said Silverberg, "but…"

He was interrupted by a huge, resonating *clang*; and then by a powerful hum that seemed to throb in the bedrock under the pebbled beach. Both men winced, as if hit by a wave of dizziness.

"What was that?"

Caleb looked at his wristwatch. "They're bringing the field coil up to speed. For tonight." Sure enough, ripples generated by the containment wall offshore came rolling onto the beach at their feet. "That means he's leaving in six hours, Rabbi. Six hours from right now. So relax, okay? Anyway, I'm needed at the Cave."

The Chief Technician turned toward the van but Silverberg arrested him with a hand placed firmly on his shoulder. "I'm telling you," the Rabbi said, "someone will try to stop you before then. Don't ask me how I know..." Caleb was shocked to see a small tear break out of one of the older man's eyes, to be swallowed in one of the many wrinkles on his face below. "I should never have come," said the learned Jew in a faltering voice. "It's not my religion. He wasn't my holy man. So I decided he was fair game. We could dig him up, put him under a microscope—like digging up an Indian burial mound, putting the bones under glass for the white man to gawk at."

Caleb looked very uncomfortable here. Noticing this, the Rabbi chose to confront him directly. "What happened to your conscience, doctor? What's driving you in all this? You've been happy enough to let MacDonald finance your research, I suppose. Has he given you first dibs on the second trip?"

Caleb turned decisively away. "I've got to go."

"I don't know why, Donophan," Silverberg called out, though the scientist had shown him his back. "But I believe you're a good man at heart." Caleb paused, not really turning around but glancing back over his shoulder. "You've got to get him safely back where he belongs!" the Rabbi implored. "Whatever they say to you, whatever they do. You've got to get him back tonight."

"Is that why you came to me? To give me a pep talk?"

"No. I came to ask you for something."

"And what was that?"

"An outside line."

Caleb raised an eyebrow in disbelief. "You want to call the authorities? Is that how you plan to make the world safe from all this?"

"If you're not willing to help."

"Who's playing Oppenheimer now?"

"You don't understand!" Silverberg exclaimed, out of an agony of anxiety. "Something *dark* is behind this, Donophan. Something that hates humanity. Haven't you ever felt it out here? At night, when the stars shine so cold on the desert?"

Caleb hesitated, almost as if he did recognize the emotions the Rabbi was expressing. But no, this was just the sort of thing that Mintz had raved about—before they put him in an institution. "I couldn't help you if I wanted to," the scientist said, finally. "The only phone is in Fuller's private lab and I don't have the access code. We'd have to get Nichols involved." He broke free completely, walked to the van, got in and drove away.

Silverberg sagged and hung his head in hopeless frustration. One of the rustic benches was a few steps away—he stumbled over and lowered himself onto it in defeat. Just faintly, however, he could hear the voice of Jesus in the distance. Looking up, he saw him at the water's edge, bathed in the golden light of the dying western sun, still preaching to his little band of followers. The Rabbi tried to make out the words for a while but could not. Finally, he rose to his feet again and began walking in that direction.

When Silverberg had covered about half the distance, the words did become clear and he recognized them immediately; Jesus was reciting—or perhaps translating himself as he went, since the Rabbi was not familiar with the precise English phraseology—the 62nd Psalm: *"Shall my soul not sit in silence before God?—my salvation comes from Him! He alone is my Rock, my savior, my fortress. I will not be moved much."* Yes, he was reciting, Silverberg reaffirmed, but the words did not seem "canned"; there was no hint of time-honored ritual, no tone of religiosity however sincere. The phrases seemed to be coming from the man himself somehow, from the very heart of him, as if he were making them up on the spot—though the words, as the Rabbi very well knew, were already at least 400 years old in Jesus' day. The Psalm continued now, Jesus turning his gaze away from the Mexicans and onto the remaining Theos—Kent, Breen, and Flammerion. *"How long will you work to shatter a man, as if you were tearing down a leaning wall or a tottering fence? They only work to cast him down from his heights; they take pleasure in a lie, they bless with their mouths but inwardly they curse.*

Selah!" The Mexicans repeated this obscure Hebrew word—though they had no very clear idea of what it meant—like a backwoods congregation shouting "Amen!" Casting his eyes back on them with pleasure, Jesus continued: *"My soul, wait in silence—for my only hope is from Him! For He alone is my Rock, my savior, my fortress. My safety and my honor rest on God alone; my mighty Rock, the God of my help, my only hope. Trust in Him, my people, at all times. Pour out your hearts to Him! God is a refuge to us."*

Silverberg reached the main group just as Jesus finished the recitation—and just in time to see Kent and Breen (who perceived that Jesus had been speaking of them) drift away, deeply offended. Flammerion lingered a moment, indecisive, but then joined her colleagues at last in walking away. Meantime, Jesus continued his address, in words that Silverberg had *not* yet heard.

"Do not be afraid, little flock; for it is your Father's will to give you a vast and wonderful kingdom. Even now He is working to that end with all His might. And in that kingdom all things will be made new." The faces of the disciples shone now, soaking up every delicious and unexpected word. He bent over and picked up one of the tiny beach pebbles and held it up for their inspection. "As it was with the Son of Man, so will it be with you. Even if your faith is no bigger than this stone, the wind and the waves will obey you."

Silverberg did not see, but Ross Rocklynne had now appeared and was lingering at the rear of the crowd. His face was hard and emotionless. As he waited for the sermon to end he gave the impression of a very illiberal chaperone at the high school dance, looking for an excuse to send everyone home early. The Rabbi did not notice—but Jesus did. He paused briefly and acknowledged the Master Sergeant's arrival with a wordless glance which might almost have been interpreted as a welcome. Rocklynne, who had never been comfortable in the presence of the man himself, did not respond, wordlessly or otherwise. Jesus turned his full attention back on the Mexicans, with a special focus when he spoke again, on his "Three Caballeros."

"I am leaving soon. And you must be ready to leave as well." An audible ripple of excitement ran through the group at this momentous if not entirely unexpected announcement. "Go back to your rooms, pack your things. Bring enough food and water for three days journey across the desert. Then wait for the outpouring of the Holy Spirit." The help staff stood stunned for a moment, not knowing how to interpret this final phrase, but when it became clear that the Israelite had finished his discourse their leaders finally began shepherding them away obediently. Only Silverberg stayed close to Jesus—joined by Rocklynne, who now stepped forward as well.

"What of me, Yeshua bar Yosef?" asked the Rabbi. "What shall I do tonight?"

"Why do you ask me?"

"I don't know. I don't know anything anymore. Perhaps I should do nothing. Perhaps they're right and the world *would* be better off without you."

"Is that a warning?" Jesus asked.

"Yes," said the tired old cleric. "I will do that, at least. You're in danger here. Terrible danger. I had…a vision."

At these words, Rocklynne moved between them. "That's enough, Colonel. How'd you get out of the synagogue anyway?"

"How did I...do you mean you had me locked in?"

"For your own good. To prevent an embarrassing episode like this. How'd you manage it, Houdini?"

Silverberg hadn't managed anything. The door had simply come open at his touch, entirely without incident. His eyes darted back to the face of the Nazarene; it was open, unperturbed, innocent as that of a child. Rocklynne took Silverberg's silence as a refusal to answer.

"Either way," said the Marine, "it's all over now."

"What do you mean?"

"Time's up for this trip, Rabbi. We gotta put him back in the storybooks."

Rocklynne took Jesus firmly by the arm. The Nazarene responded by looking him directly in the eyes; an appeal, as Silverberg thought, to the big man's better nature. In response, Rocklynne simply lifted his jacket and displayed a set of handcuffs hanging from his belt.

"Where are you taking him?" asked the Rabbi, half-panicked.

"Someplace safe, behind locked doors. Close to the time machine."

"Fuller's not to be trusted, Gunny! You've got to see that..."

"I said that's enough, Rabbi!" Rocklynne truly was angry now, with a bitterness in his voice even he must have known had little to do with the harmless Jewish grandpa. "You don't seem to get it. I believe in this

Experiment!—maybe the only one who still does. If you don't—well, the code for the outer doors is 911."

Silverberg backed up a half-step. Anguished, he spoke to Jesus again.

"If I try to interfere, they will kill me."

"You and I must be gathered to our fathers soon in any event, Yakob. Go to them as a righteous man."

Jesus smiled and extended a hand in friendship. Silverberg took it willingly, using both of his. The hand was soft and warm, full of life—and the young man still made him think of his nephew Haim. After a moment Rocklynne pulled the visitor away; he manhandled him into the back of his Jeep and drove off in the direction of the Time Cave, leaving Silverberg standing on the beach alone.

4:15

Carter looked up from his reading—a four-color flyer for Santa Claus Land that smelled like his grandma's basement—when Sylvie and MacDonald re-entered the lobby. He noticed right away that Sylvie had started looking unwell again. She was holding her arms close to her body as if chilled, and he saw tiny beads of sweat on her forehead.

"You feeling okay, Sylvie?"

"Prone to relapses, I'm afraid."

Carter spoke to MacDonald. "They've powered up the dampening field, sir. It won't be long now."

"The field?" MacDonald repeated. He did not seem happy to hear this. "I've got to go."

The snow globe caught Sylvie's eye again. She reached forward to pick it up.

"Mister....um, Andy?" she asked.

"Yes?"

"Would you allow me to take home a souvenir?"

MacDonald saw the globe in her hands and brightened immediately. "Good choice!" he said. "I brought that very toy home from my first visit. Used to keep it under my pillow at night—in case of bad dreams."

Sylvie looked disappointed. "Then you won't want to part with it..."

MacDonald surprised her. "No, take it. You should take it. I think I'd like that, in fact."

Sylvie did take it and dropped it right away into the pocket of her oversized black sweater. MacDonald smiled at her, then turned her chair over to Carter and drifted out the door, his mind someplace else completely. Sylvie watched him go. The lobby grew quiet again, except for a canned track of the Bible Land Choir performing a gushy rendition of "Go to Dark Gethsemane" accompanied by the Hammond organ.

"Carter," asked Sylvie at last, "why don't we have anyone here who actually believes in Jesus? I mean, look at us. We're a whole village of village atheists."

"Well, let's face it," Nichols replied. "Nobody with anything like a traditional Christian faith would have come within a mile of this Experiment. Just the very nature of the thing forced us to choose skeptics."

"And cripples, right? People with an axe to grind against God."

Carter looked distressed at this. "We needed people who could keep an open mind!"

"Then you screwed up big time, 'cause it ought to be obvious by now that none of us in here has got one! Not when it comes to the most radical possibility of all…"

"What's that?"

"The possibility that *it's all true*."

If Carter was caught off guard by this idea he didn't show it. "There you go again," he said in a concerned voice. "Going way out on that limb. I'd be careful if I were you, Sylvie."

"God, Carter," said the girl, thoroughly exasperated. "What would it take with you? I mean, hell, if you *died* and were standing at the effing Pearly Gates talking to St. Peter you'd find some other explanation!"

"Well, you do raise an interesting point there. I mean, how could you know for sure that you were really dead?—that it wasn't just hypnosis, or drugs, or something? Hell, we already know they've got this Vitamin 'X' or whatever. Maybe Fuller's spiking the water supply."

"You really are a retard, you know that?"

Carter just laughed. "Maybe so. But didn't you ever learn about David Hume in school?"

"Who?"

"Hume—Scottish thinker of the 19th century. They teach him in first year philosophy."

"Guess I missed that," said Sylvie coldly. "Did a whole year of surgery instead—as the patient."

Now Carter did look a little embarrassed, but decided the best comeback was to simply soldier on.

"Well, anyway, Hume proposed a formula for such things—and it really is awfully hard to get around. If anyone came to me, he said, claiming that he'd seen a dead man restored to life, I'd ask myself which was the more probable: that this person, no matter how smart or how previously reliable, might have been deceived about what he'd seen or else be deceiving *me*—or that a dead man really did come back to life. And then I'd weigh the one improbability against the other and always reject the greater improbability. So any claim of the supernatural, according to Hume, is always more likely to be the result of trickery or misinterpretation than an actual miracle."

Sylvie looked sicker than ever. "Christ, that's a jaundiced view of things, Carter. I don't know that I've ever...*damn*."

"I'm not trying to be cynical, Sylvie. I'm known as a pretty cheerful guy, in fact. But I just don't like the idea of being led down the garden path, that's all."

"But...didn't you say you were a libertarian? I thought you had an open mind to all points of view."

"I do! And it has to *stay* open. That's precisely what's wrong with the idea of a miracle. It leaves no room for an open mind. Miracles are connected to this crude idea that there's some sort of truth that's just *out there*—a big brute fact like the Rock of Gibraltar. But everyone has to find their own truth! That's what's so great about liberty. Everyone gets to create their own universe and live in it."

Sylvie stared at him glumly; Carter couldn't tell whether she was disgusted at him personally or only ill from her "relapse." "So Jesus Christ has to find some way to gain admission into Mr. Nichols' universe, then?" she asked finally. "I'll make sure and tell him when I see him."

Suddenly, the girl drooped her head as if to gag again and put up her hand to silence the conversation. Carter hastily snatched up a nearby wastebasket and offered it to her. "Can I take you someplace?" he asked. "Fuller's office, maybe?"

Sylvie looked up sharply at these words, wavering, not answering.

"I'm due there myself in a few minutes," Carter continued, looking at his watch.

"No," said Sylvie at last. "I'm not going there. Not tonight."

"Kind of a lousy time to go cold turkey."

Unexpectedly, Sylvie reached up and took Carter by the hand. "Take me to Jesus' house, Carter."

"Why?"

"I've got to see him again. One more time before it's too late."

4:16

Caleb Donophan hadn't worn his white lab coat since the Extraction; in fact, he only wore it on days when the machine was actually being operated. He'd had it on about half an hour tonight, supervising the cooling of the central solenoid, when the call from MacDonald came asking for a meeting in his office. Caleb tried to beg off. No, he wouldn't be able to come out right now. No, it wasn't true that it wouldn't make any difference at this point. To his surprise and consternation, the big boss continued to insist, even though he had always, up to now, been quite deferential in technical matters. Most shocking of all, however—and the thing that finally moved Caleb to accept—was MacDonald's cryptic reference to a "change of plans." On that word (and with a sick feeling in the pit of his stomach) Caleb surrendered the con to Spaz immediately, with strict orders to keep the standing wave modulated and an iron-clad promise to be back in the Cave in not more than fifteen minutes.

He made the trip to the Administration Building on foot, at something between a fast walk and a run. He strode into MacDonald's office, slightly winded, to find the billionaire seated at his mahogany desk, an open Bible spread in front of him and his computer monitor alive with bizarre-looking woodcuts illustrating scenes from the Book of Revelation. There was a half-empty tumbler on the desk as well, a jug of bitter green tea, and half-a-dozen bottles of prescription drugs.

"You called for me."

MacDonald looked up from his reading, eyes sparkling with a life and an enthusiasm Caleb had seldom seen in the man. He had stripped to his A-shirt above the waist, displaying a tanned, well-toned physique that was quite impressive for a man his age.

"We're going to stand down tonight, Caleb. Fuller was here earlier, I notified him personally as well."

"Stand down?" The words did not register at first.

"Yes. I'm aborting tonight's return trip. I want you to go back to the Time Cave and start bleeding off the power."

"That's not possible!" Caleb balked.

"Sure it is. I've been on the phone with the power company. We can start selling the juice back to them any time after 10:30. They're happy to be getting it with summer coming on."

"We can't do that! What about this security breach?"

"Fuller assures me that he's got a handle on that. Anyway, it won't matter once things start to fall in place."

"What are you talking about? How can it not matter?"

MacDonald smiled and looked at his chief technician quizzically. "You surprise me, Caleb. Aren't you the teacher of us all? The past can't be changed, remember? Nothing that happens to him here can alter what we know about him *there*."

"You can count me out. This is totally irresponsible."

"Have it your own way. But I'm sure your staff can manage a simple bleed-off for us."

"You'll need me whenever you do decide to send him back."

Here, MacDonald hesitated, with a strange, exalted look on his face. "I'll cross that bridge when—if—we come to it. Till then, I don't like to be pressured. I'll thank you to remember that machine down there isn't yours, it's mine. I bought it, I paid for it."

Caleb's eyes flickered with panic, but these words quieted him effectively.

"I don't want you to go, Caleb," MacDonald said, reverting to an affectionate, conciliatory tone. "We've been through a lot together. And if I'm right about what's happening here tonight, they'll be a whole new order of things soon. This is a chance to get in on the ground floor. The seven cycles of Revelation are playing themselves out before our eyes."

Caleb watched him now as if observing a man coming mentally unglued. His mind raced ahead, frantically trying to puzzle out his next move.

"So go back to that Time Cave," his boss continued, "and start that sell-back procedure. Then just stand back and watch the fireworks. Do this for me, Caleb, and I won't forget you in the new Kingdom, I swear it."

4:17

"I'll reclaim that electric razor of mine, Kelvin," said Joe Breen, appearing in the open door between his room and Kent's.

"By all means, Joe," replied Kent, not looking up from the suitcase he was packing. "It's in the medicine cabinet over the sink."

Flammerion came through the door behind him, looking thoroughly nonplussed. "That's it then?" she asked in disbelief. "You two are just leaving?"

"That's right. First thing in the morning," said Kent.

"I can't believe you'd let it end like this! There's still so much we have to learn."

"It's no use, doctor!" her colleague snapped. "It's just as we feared. The whole thing has been corrupted."

"Why?"

Breen reemerged with his razor and broke in with the answer. "Well, it's all become a self-fulfilling prophecy, hasn't it?—what Donophan used to call a 'causal loop'."

"You heard his talk," added Kent. "Jesus has been studying that book! He's already aping some of its phraseology in his speeches."

"Now he'll go back to his own time," said Breen, "determined to *become* the man he read about!"

Flammerion sagged at these words, the wind sucked out of her sails. A very resigned looking Breen drew the obvious conclusions.

"Perhaps Fuller was right. Maybe it is all destiny. Maybe it was fated to happen this way. In order for Jesus to become who we know him to have been, it was necessary for him to come here and learn what he has learned."

"Who invented the myth of the Divine Christ?" asked Kent, with a sardonic smile. "Congratulations, doctors. It looks like we did it ourselves."

4:18

There was a jubilant mood of expectancy at Jesus' house. Ramirez, Reynoso, and Dominguez were filling boxes as quickly as the empties could be placed before them and the rest of their clan was equally busy, stuffing clothing into bundles, foodstuffs into bags, and giving the general impression of a big close-knit family preparing for a camp-out. Everyone was singing, too—in Spanish—and though the song was not actually religious in nature (none of them knew any religious songs) it was something bright, upbeat, and inexpressibly cheerful. The words were simple, primary, and wholly out of touch with modern life;

all about springtime and planting and the birthing of new babies into the world. All of these things then, made it seem quite incomparably bizarre—comic, in fact—when the pale glowering Goth chick juxtaposed herself into the scene, creaking suddenly through the front door like Winnie-the-Pooh's little black raincloud. Behind her, through the open front door, Ramirez saw Carter pulling away in the van, headed for his appointment with Fuller.

"Where is he?" demanded the little sunbeam, forgetting to use her Spanish.

"The Master?"

"Yes."

"We thought he was with you," Ramirez replied. "With the bosses, I mean."

"He's not here?"

"No, he never came back from the beach."

Sylvie was shivering badly now, her withdrawal symptoms beginning to return in earnest. There was a frantic note in her voice as she continued.

"I've got to find him!"

"Why don't you wait here with us, Miss Sylvie?" Ramirez gently asked.

"You don't understand! He's leaving in just a couple of hours. Forever!"

"I know. We're all leaving. But he told us to wait here until the appointed time."

Sylvie shook him off, turned, and rolled herself back out the front door. Ramirez called out as she went.

"He wouldn't leave you behind, Miss Sylvie. He loves you very much. He told us so."

4:19

Rocklynne and McCandliss, his second in command, stood near the Village gate, holding a heavy steel chain and padlock. It was almost completely dark now and the gas lamps flickering on the inside (centrally controlled by computer, of course) really did begin to give the unmistakable feel of Disneyland after dark. The rapid cooling of the desert had begun, as well, when Rocklynne's walkie-talkie chirped suddenly for his attention. The voice on the other end was Fuller's.

"How're we doing, Rock?"

"About done."

"You're finished? You've chained every gate to the Village?"

"All except the Main. Nichols just left, but the girl's still inside."

"Watch her till she leaves, then lock the rest of 'em in. I've had all the Latin American surprises I care for on this trip, understand?"

"10-4."

4:20

Not far away, over near Jacob's Well, Sylvie was wheeling herself laboriously up the hill, struggling mightily with pain and nausea. Sweat was getting in her eyes, dropping from the end of her nose. Grunting with determination, she paused and clung to one of the lampposts for a moment in an effort to catch her breath. More and more, her thoughts were tormented with the idea of waking the next morning without having seen Jesus again. Of hearing these damned jackals, these cold calculating scholars and administrators, report calmly over breakfast that all had gone well, that the machine had performed flawlessly, that he was gone now and forever out of her reach. These thoughts stirred panic again and she released her hold on the cold iron pillar. Bucking up her small reserve of remaining strength, she pulled herself forward once more, weak and cramping. Could she live with that? Could she face her remaining days with the knowledge of having missed such an opportunity—an opportunity beyond all imagining? She didn't know. Likely she wouldn't *have* to live with it long; she knew that very well. She felt like dying this minute, in fact. But not without asking her questions! Please, God, not without confronting the man! Not without holding him in front of her again, making him stop and stand still, staring at him, looking and looking until it all made sense. Just as she reached the well, the left wheel of the chair stuck firmly between two of the cobbles in the street. She yanked at it, blasphemed violently, hammered at the top of the tire. Finally, she just broke down and cried again, sinking backward into a heap, wholly overcome with exhaustion and despair.

And then Jesus appeared, walking quietly up from behind and touching her shoulder softly. "Oh my God," she said quietly.

Jesus did not reply, but instead grasped the handles of the chair firmly and, with one short motion, pulled the recalcitrant wheel easily loose.

Sylvie stopped crying right away and rallied elaborately, concerned for her appearance. She wiped her nose with the corner of the Navajo blanket and, after a minute or two of silence, tried speaking again.

"What are you doing here? I mean—I'm surprised to see you."

Jesus answered calmly, with his soft and pleasing Hebrew accent. "I need your help, Sylvie."

"You need—you need *my* help?" Sylvie might actually have laughed if she hadn't felt so bad.

"My friends in the Village are about to begin a long journey. They've learned a great deal in a short time, but they need a more experienced disciple in their number. Someone who knew me before all of this. Someone like you."

This struck Sylvie as so absurd that it almost made her angry. And Jesus just stood there, his dark brown eyes reflecting the flames of the gas lights dotted all around. She snapped back at him, speaking more freely than she meant to.

"Someone like me? Hell, I'm not even sure I believe in any of this! I mean, if you were the real Jesus you'd know what a lousy disciple I'd make. A heroin addict? Come on!"

"That makes no difference."

"Maybe not to you, it doesn't. But it sure does to me!" Her thoughts were dragged back to her symptoms again, which were getting more and more strident. She was longing for some smack, plain and simple, and loathing herself for it. She spoke again, still in an accusatory tone.

"People always assume I'm asking 'Why me?' I don't ask that. I ask, why *anybody*? I mean, why do these things happen? If there's really a caring, Almighty God out there someplace why is there so much evil in the world?"

Jesus looked away briefly; for a moment it looked to Sylvie like he was deciding whether to offer any answer to this at all. But he did speak finally, in words that might have seemed flippant in the mouth of another speaker but were strangely compelling here.

"If there is no God," he said softly, "why is there so much good?"

"But why don't you do something to stop it?"

"Why don't you?"

Sylvie gaped for a moment, then just turned away frustrated, getting teary again. "You haven't seen the things I've seen," she said harshly. "Heard the things I've heard."

"Haven't I, little daughter?" said Jesus, smiling sadly. "Haven't I?"

Sylvie was still churned up, still kicking out, though she wasn't quite sure why. Finally, she just blurted out the two words that were closest to her heart—which were also the words most accusatory, most demanding.

"Heal me."

Jesus paused only briefly, then responded with similar brevity.

"No."

Sylvie was surprised at the level of shock and disappointment she felt at this answer—deep inside, underneath the skin-crawling and painful cramps.

"I thought you answered prayer!"

Jesus met her blistering gaze with one of relentless compassion. "I did answer. The answer is no."

The girl would not take this for an answer. She now dropped all pretence at dignity or grown-up-ness; like a three-year old, she simply threatened Jesus—though with what she had not yet decided.

"Heal me or…or…"

"Or what? You'll stop believing in me?" The Nazarene shook his head patiently. "That won't change anything, Sylvie. I'll still be here."

Sylvie relaxed at last, defeated. She resumed her crying again—and felt better for it. Jesus dropped to one knee next to her and took her hand.

"You must trust me, Sylvie. Believe that I can see even better, even farther than you can."

The words seemed to bubble up from someplace deep within, deeper than thought or consciousness itself, and she choked them out between sobs: "Lord, I do believe." And as she heard herself say them, they shot back down into that same place, like a sonar ping, and returned back to the surface of her soul carrying the second half of a Bible verse memorized years ago: "Help my unbelief."

Then Jesus smiled again, tears in his own eyes now.

4:21

In spite of his promise to Spaz, Caleb did not go directly back the Time Cave. He passed by the Main Gate of the Village first, where he ran into young Dominguez lugging two heavy suitcases.

"Where's Rabbi Silverberg?" he asked.

"No hablo Ingles, Señor."

"Silverberg, Silverberg," Caleb repeated irritably. "Have you seen him?"

"No lo se."

The scientist turned away in annoyance. At that moment however, two yellow headlights came rushing over the cobblestones and Fuller's car whished through the Gate, headed into the Village. Caleb caught a glimpse of Carter Nichols behind the wheel and determined to follow him on foot.

Sylvie, meanwhile, was still inside the Village at the Well. She saw the car approaching and watched Nichols park nearby and get out.

"That's Carter!" she said, in a much more hopeful voice. "Oh, I wish you could speak to him, too." Sylvie had directed this last phrase at Jesus, but when she turned, smiling, to face him again she found that he had disappeared.

"There you are!" Nichols called out. "Thank God."

"Hello, Carter!" said Sylvie brightly.

Nichols was pleased, but decidedly surprised. "Well, hello there. Gee, you seem better. What's happened?"

"I don't know where to begin. I only know…I'm not so afraid anymore."

"Well, before you get started let me give you the screaming headline. Things are finally starting to make sense around here."

"What headline?"

Carter drew in a breath, as if starting a prepared speech. "I've just come from Fuller's office. He came clean at last, just as I thought he would."

"Came clean about what?"

"Jesus is an actor! I would say a two-bit actor, but actually he seems to be rather a good one. He's got a shelf full of awards back in his apartment in Jerusalem."

"What are you saying?"

"I'm saying that this whole thing is nothing but a set-up. A hoax. Fuller admitted it to me a little while ago."

"A hoax? What kind of a hoax?"

"Our so-called 'Jesus' is actually Schlomo Davidtz, age 29, professional thespian. Fuller found him in the State Theatre Company of Israel about two years ago. Have a look at this."

Carter produced a fat manila folder and handed it to Sylvie. Even in the dim gaslight Sylvie could see that it was full of info about Schlomo Davidtz, including an 8X10 black and white headshot. He was, of course, a dead ringer for the man to whom Sylvie had just opened her heart. Yet in the photo he was completely out-of-costume, a modern, stylishly dressed Israeli citizen.

"I don't believe it," she said, voice wavering. "I—I can't believe it. He's lying. He's lying to you."

"Why would he lie about something like that? And anyway, which sounds more like a lie—what I'm telling you now, or some cock and bull science fiction yarn out of H.G. Wells?"

"But I *know* it's him!" said Sylvie vehemently. "I've felt it—I've seen him in my visions! What about the nail?"

"What about this 'Vitamin X' they're been feeding you? Do you know what it is? Did you even ask?"

"No, I…"

"Well, I can tell you. It's a powerful derivative of LSD, developed by Fuller himself. It produces *hallucinations*, Sylvie. Very vivid hallucinations. That's what it's for."

"But why?" asked Sylvie, her voice tremulous with confusion. "What would be the point? MacDonald has spent billions out here!"

"MacDonald is also a nut—or hadn't you noticed? Those cameras I helped put up everywhere? They're not just for security. They're *filming* everything. This is his idea of Reality TV or something. A sociology experiment—'The Psychology of Religion' or some shit."

"Even if that were true," Sylvie responded, "why would they admit it to you?"

"I figured it out on my own. He couldn't keep up the sham anymore. Anyway, it wasn't my reactions he was after."

"Whose then?"

"The Theos, of course," said Carter, with a look on his face like he was passing a paper mill on the highway. "The joke was on them right from the start. *They* were the ones under the microscope, not this phony Messiah." Sylvie was staring dully at the 8X10 glossy now, entirely at a loss for words. "No harm done there, I guess," Carter continued. "MacDonald will sit 'em all down tomorrow and admit there's no Santa Claus after all. Then they can all go home, write their best-sellers about the experience—probably go on the lecture circuit. Fuller made me promise not to spill the beans to them, had me sign a couple of papers, but other than that I'm free to go. He even gave me the keys to his car."

Abruptly, Donophan appeared on the square, still searching for Silverberg. He looked worried, disturbed, but he was glad to have caught up to Carter. Carter saw him and pointed him out to Sylvie.

"Here you go. You can get it straight from one of the plotters themselves."

"Plotters?" asked Caleb, stepping up to the Well.

"Yeah. We just found out about Schlomo Davidtz."

"Who the hell is Schlomo Davidtz?"

Carter reclaimed the folder from Sylvie and handed it to Donophan. "You tell me."

Caleb flipped briefly through the contents, then slapped the folder closed and handed it back to the security tech.

"Fuller gave you that."

"About an hour ago."

"I don't know what he's up to," Caleb said calmly, "but he's feeding you a line of bull for some reason. I can assure you, my machine is the real thing."

"And you always tell the truth, don't you?" Carter replied. "It's not like you're both on MacDonald's payroll or anything."

The chief technician's eyes flashed brightly as his Irish temper flared up. "I don't give a rat's ass whether you believe me or not, Carter. Think what you like."

"How about her?" asked Carter, indicating the girl. "Do you care what she believes?"

Sylvie's eyes met Caleb's. He saw right away that she was teetering visibly on the brink.

"That's the worst part of all this," Carter continued. "You've been toying around with people's hearts out here."

Sylvie spoke to Caleb, smiling weakly. "Mr. Nichols is worried about me, Caleb. His favorite cynic has gone all gullible on him."

"Look, Sylvie," interjected Carter. "I didn't say you were gullible. I'm just saying that you're...vulnerable. God knows, anyone could understand. History's most famous miracle worker here in person? If I were in your situation I'd try to believe in it myself."

Sylvie started to shiver again, her face already turning white. Caleb gave her the folder which Carter had refused. "Listen, guys," he said, "this stuff is all forged! It's some kind of cover story they've arranged in case things should go wrong."

"You're guessing?" Carter asked.

"I don't get involved in the security arrangements! I never have."

Carter shrugged. "Okay, maybe they've been playing you for a sucker, too. I don't know. I don't care. All I know is, I don't want any part of this anymore. I'm leaving. Right now."

Caleb watched helplessly as a single tear welled up in the corner of Sylvie's eye. "Sylvie, listen to me," he said, hoping to intervene. "The time machine is for real. They couldn't fool me on something like that. Given its design, the principles involved, it couldn't *not* work."

"Then can I come and watch tonight?" she asked hopefully. "Watch you send him home?"

Caleb looked very uncomfortable here. "I'm…afraid that's not possible. There's, um, been a delay."

Carter turned toward the car, disgusted. "Let's get out of here, Sylvie."

Sylvie was sweating again, and the look on her face was proof enough that the nausea had returned as well. Caleb was truly upset now. He spoke again, desperately in earnest.

"Jesus is for real, too, Sylvie. I swear to God. Who he is, what he is, what it all means—I don't know anymore. But the man we've got here is the man from the Bible stories. That much I can promise you."

Stepping between them, Carter returned and crouched in front of Sylvie's chair. "Come with me," he said tentatively. "I'll—I'll take care of you," he promised. "From now on, if you want."

Sylvie hardly noticed. She reopened the manila file and looked very deeply and very carefully into the smiling face of Schlomo Davidtz. Caleb could almost hear the gears grinding in her head. Furrowing her brow, she narrowed her eyes in a pained expression, scrutinizing the picture with all of her remaining energy. Then she closed the folder again and looked off into space, eyes darting unfocused across the Village facades. There was a final, incalculable moment of choice—like the last instant before a piece of iron springs to the magnet—and then suddenly, a moment of release. She relaxed her features and gave it up. It had happened again. Caught with her britches down one more time. She laughed at herself silently, bitterly, smiling another crooked smile. This one, however, was not at all endearing, but was instead, one of the most chilling things Caleb had ever looked at. He did not want to hear, he knew, what was coming next, but it came anyway.

"I need a hit."

The girl stuffed the folder into one of the pockets in the chair and, taking hold of the wheels, began to push herself slowly away.

"You're going to Fuller again?" Carter asked.

Sylvie did not respond. She turned her back on the two men, hell bent for the exit. Carter and Caleb were left standing side by side, the picture of futility, watching her inch painfully toward the gate.

"Let me help, then" continued Carter. "At least let me push."

"No thanks," Sylvie said, not looking back. And as she did, Caleb noticed that she tossed some small object onto the ground nearby. Carter caught up with the chair for a moment.

"Alright, look," he said. "I'll go back to the dorm and get our stuff. I'll load up the car and meet you at Fuller's office. Then, when you're ready—when you come out, that is—we'll go."

There was still no answer. Carter, choosing to take this as a "yes", got back into Fuller's car, not bothering to take leave of Donophan, and drove away.

Caleb followed Sylvie haltingly, a few sad steps. Then, bending over, he picked up her discarded article. It was, of course, the little silver cross. He stuck it into his pocket. A few moments later, while walking back through the Village, he ran into Dominguez again, still carrying suitcases. He approached him a second time.

"No se, Señor," he said, begging off again. "No se!"

"Forget about Silverberg," Caleb replied. "Where's Ramirez? I need to see Santiago Ramirez..."

4:22

The door to Fuller's darkened suite was ajar. Shivering violently, Sylvie rolled up to it and shoved; it swung easily open and she entered.

"Hello?"

Silence. Sylvie cried out in despair.

"Oh God, no! Where are you, you evil bastard?"

She noticed that the second, inner door was open as well. Hastily, she crossed the dimly-lit living space and passed into the private medical lab. Right in the center of the room sat Silverberg, tied to an office chair with electrical cords. His head was covered with a clear plastic bag; both of his wrists were slit and the blood—every last drop of it—had drained into porcelain medical basins sitting on the floor. Off in the gloom to one side, Sylvie saw Lance Fuller hunched over a countertop—shot glass in one trembling hand, bottle of Jack Daniels in the other. He noticed her presence after a moment and responded in a shaky voice.

"Sylvie. I wasn't expecting..."

Fuller screwed the lid back onto the bottle and stowed it under the counter.

"Oh, I know why you're here! You need your booster shot, don't you? Well, I think we can manage that."

The Administrator got up and stepped to the opposite side of the lab where he procured a medical bag with a hypo and several prepared doses of "X". Sylvie was not watching; she was staring instead at the pale, waxy corpse of the Rabbi, looking at it with a great deal more than mere physical horror. This whole chamber, this antiseptic hole, was crawling with sensible evil; it tingled across her clammy skin like static electricity. Fuller had done murder here—but it wasn't just Fuller! She felt another presence in the room, another mind behind the scenes; restless, powerful, malevolent, drifting through the air like a poisonous gas. Fuller had spoken of psychic experiments taking place here—but who, Sylvie now wondered, was experimenting upon whom?

Fuller, interpreting her reaction as simple shock at his crime, turned apologetic. "Oh. I'm sorry about that, but it couldn't be helped. He was trespassing! We caught him using my private telephone!"

There was a plaintive quality in this outburst, an appeal for sympathy that struck Sylvie as terrifyingly sincere. Fuller was somewhat affected by the booze, it seemed to her, but she also suspected—though she'd put nothing at all past him by this point—that he'd never killed anyone before. She thought of trying to escape—but it was nonsense, of course, for a 96 pound girl in a wheelchair. Even moreso than it would have been otherwise, given her weakened condition.

"It looks ugly, I know," continued Fuller, in a tremulous voice. "But it was the only way out, really—and the best way for the Rabbi himself. Exsanguination isn't a bad way to go. You just get listless and drowsy, finally you drop off to sleep. Death can be a lot worse, believe me—usually is, in fact."

He peered into Sylvie's face for some sign of understanding, and found, of course, only repulsion and dismay. A note of anger, then, had entered his speech when he spoke again. "You're not seeing me at my best. I never expected to—I mean, they've thrown me a major curve here tonight. I'm still trying to pick up the pieces!"

All at once, the Ghostly Voice crackled out of the speakers again; still female, still with the Russian accent, but not soft or dreamy now. The tones were forceful this time, imperious, full of icy authority.

"Lance! Who is that with you?"

"This...this is the girl I told you about. The seer. The medium."

Sylvie would never have used these terms herself; she always tried to distance herself from the attention-starved drama queens who usually wore these titles on TV. Yet she was certainly too stunned to quibble under the present circumstances.

"Is it really?" asked the Voice, with a deep, unfeigned curiosity. *"Bring her in here. Bring her to me."*

Sylvie turned to see the red light flashing above the dark inner door. The door itself was standing wide open now.

4:23

Caleb approached the guard at the tunnel checkpoint. The officer on duty was Burgess, the genial black man who had taken Sylvie's photo ID.

"Glad you're back, Doc," he offered with relief. "They've called three times from inside, asking about you."

Caleb smiled perfunctorily. "Um, look, Dave," he said. "Can you buzz me back through from your end? I left my badge at the office."

Burgess hesitated a moment, then pushed a hidden button releasing the gate arm. "Yeah, c'mon through," he said, grinning. "I guess we can cut the Time Lord a little slack on the last night."

"Owe ya one," said Caleb, passing inside.

4:24

Fuller piloted Sylvie under the flashing red light and into his final, secret inner chamber. It was a dark, ominous place, full of beeping medical equipment, like the ICU ward of some hopeless terminal hospital. One object, however, was brilliantly lighted: a large flat table in the center of the room, almost like an operating table, with the outline of a headless female form painted onto its surface. Had the situation been less horrific, it might have made Sylvie think of the old electric "Operation" game for kids, since the location where each organ should have been was clearly indicated and a complex network of wire leads sprang upward from the outline to a central harness above. A second look revealed another, more disquieting network; a spidery web of fleshy cords crawling across the surface horizontally, corresponding roughly to a central nervous system. At right angles to the table itself, standing upright where the head should have been, was a flat glass box about five inches thick, divided vertically into eight parallel compartments. To use, once again, the iconography of childhood, it looked to Sylvie like an overgrown ant farm—but there were certainly no ants inside. The box was stuffed instead with a spongy mass of pinkish-gray material that looked, upon close inspection, as if it had *grown in place*, grown into long rectangular blocks in order to fill every cubic centimeter of the space provided. Sylvie squinted to look even closer and saw, with a gag reflex of physical disgust, that the gray stuff was interlaced throughout with pulsating blood vessels, fed by a pump below the table.

"Holy God, what is that?" asked Sylvie, shrinking in her chair.

Fuller looked simultaneously proud and defensive. "Well, it's a breakthrough, is what it is. In about five fields at once." Still at the helm of Sylvie's chair, the Administrator began making a long, slow orbit around the display. "It's a very advanced piece of cloning, to begin with. Not my own work, for the most part, I must confess, but it *is* the fruit of ten years with the HGP and a lot of terrific connections in the large and very active human cloning underground. Three ounces of iffy bone marrow, Sylvie—three ounces produced a nearly complete human nervous system grown to a functioning state. Now, *that*...is pretty cool, don't you think?" Sylvie, of course, said nothing. "Secondly, it's the most powerful instrument of psychic mediation ever created. The donor of the

DNA—posthumously, of course—was the greatest medium of all time, Madame Blavatsky herself."

Sylvie's eyes flashed recognition at the name. "The voice we heard…"

"Oh, not the voice you heard just now. That silly, dithering woman you heard the other day—*that* was Madame Blavatsky. She only comes through when the apparatus is not in use. When it's *idling*, so to speak."

"Who then?"

"The Madame would have called it a 'Spirit Guide.' Earlier generations knew them as gods or angels. The reality is, this technique has opened a line of communication to someone older, wiser than we are; an ancient planetary intelligence that has always been here, sharing this world with us, but never reliably accessible until now. The Madame channels it for me."

"Take me out of here," begged Sylvie, terror-stricken.

"Not yet," crackled the Ghostly Voice, louder and clearer than before. *"Not yet. Let me look at her a bit more…"*

Fuller shoved the chair closer. When he did, Sylvie got another powerful flash of psychic insight, almost stunning in its intensity. She saw precisely what Silverberg had seen in the synagogue: the frozen, murdered body of Christ drifting through a void deeper than interstellar space. Sylvie could feel the cold of absolute zero, as if her space capsule had just depressurized halfway to the moon. The vision lasted only seconds, but when it passed her eyes had widened, her horror deepened.

"The time machine!" she gasped.

"Yes," said Fuller coolly. "This is how it all came together. Donophan's know-how, MacDonald's money—and his pathetic obsessions. My new Mentor showed me how to make the connections, not long after the Madame here introduced us."

"Then…it *is* the real Jesus."

Something uncanny happened in response to this phrase: Fuller and the Ghostly Voice responded *in unison.*

"Of course it is."

Perhaps it was a coincidence; Sylvie pressed on with her next question.

"So your 'Vitamin X'…?"

"Increases psychic sensitivity," said the Administrator, speaking once more alone. "I've been taking it myself—in low doses—since I developed it in the mid-Nineties. It's how I first conceived the cloning methodology."

Sylvie was still very frightened, still suffering physically—but the light seemed to come back into her eyes now and she sat a bit straighter in her chair.

"You know, it's funny," Fuller continued, "I suffered from migraines as a teenager. Invented the 'X' purely to get some relief. But it did much more than that—it opened up a whole new world. That's when I first began to detect the presence of the Ancients, and to cultivate a dialogue with them."

The girl spoke up at last, turning inside the chair as best she could in an effort to confront her captor face to face. "I don't know who this Mentor of yours is, Fuller, but it's driving you to assassinate God!"

Fuller seemed genuinely stung by this, genuinely shocked. "No, no! That was never the idea. We just wanted to discredit the Jesus superstition, bring in a new era of peace and enlightenment. That's been the driving ambition in all of my work—to contact the Ancients, to use their wisdom and advanced techniques to clear away some of the refuse of the ages, all the things that hold us back as a species. I mean, dammit, we could have put a bullet in his head the very first day, couldn't we?"

The voice of Fuller's Mentor interrupted very suddenly at this point, speaking on its own. *"Lance. I'm seeing something through the cameras. Yes, I'm seeing something."*

A bank of security monitors came to life in one corner, much like the station in Carter's office, though on a more limited scale.

"Multiplexer 115," said the Ghostly Voice. *"Camera 6."*

Fuller stepped away from Sylvie's chair and pulled up the camera in question. It was an image of Caleb Donophan in the Cave, monitoring his equipment.

"Your man Donophan bears watching tonight."

4:25

Caleb was, indeed, back at his station at stabilization control. The bright-eyed Spaz—freckled, enthusiastic, and surprisingly ambulatory for a man of his bulk—stepped up behind him.

"We're ready to bleed anytime you are, Boss."

When Caleb did not immediately respond, Spaz peeked over his shoulder at the charge meter, sitting on 99.99 percent.

"God, look at that," he said. "We been waitin' a long time for that kettle to boil, haven't we? Don't seem right to dump it all this close to the finish line. Kinda sad."

These words seemed to shake Caleb loose somehow. He blinked and turned to his young assistant with new orders. "Let's run that safety check one more time," he said.

Spaz raised an eyebrow. "The one we just finished?"

"Yeah. That one."

Spaz turned compliantly, with a distinct "O-kay" expression on his face, but said nothing. Just then, Ross Rocklynne entered the chamber and, without speaking to anyone, took up a post near the door. Caleb noticed but chose merely to continue the monitoring of his instruments.

4:26

Anson MacDonald's ears pricked up at a few soft footsteps. He turned away from his ragged old boyhood Bible (opened to the 24th chapter of Matthew's Gospel) and with a quiet thrill saw Jesus himself enter the room. And the room in question was not just any room—not MacDonald's office but the elaborate wax crucifixion scene in Bible Land where the billionaire was seated on a bench provided for weary tourists. He'd come here, indeed, to collect his thoughts—but for MacDonald it was something more. This was a sensual experience for him and intensely comforting: the moody lighting, the familiar smell wafted gently through the chilly air by an antique air conditioner, the immemorial feel of the varnished wood under his hand; all of these were tangible links to his vanished adolescent self and to the emotions which had once engulfed him in this place. Now, MacDonald watched in wordless wonder as the real-life Redeemer drifted slowly over to the rail and began to examine the inconceivable spectacle laid out before him.

The wax Savior from the lobby was crucified between two thieves, with a glowering red sky for a backdrop. A quaint hand-lettered sign, rendered long ago by some local Arkansas sign-painter, hung above the tableau: *"Father, forgive them for they know not what they do."* The live Jesus standing in front of the scene gave every indication of intense curiosity about what he was seeing: this was the climax, MacDonald realized, of the 1st century life he never finished leading. Crucifixion, to a man of his time and place, would not have been a religious symbol. It was simply a degrading and ignominious form of capital punishment. The familiar quotations on the signs—words upon which a whole civilization had been built—were not familiar to the visitor at all. He hadn't coined them yet and was, in fact, at this very moment encountering them for the first time. Even MacDonald's years of close association with the time travel concept did not prevent his brain from reeling at these thoughts.

Jesus stared at the scene a long time. What passed through his mind during these meditations MacDonald could scarcely imagine. Finally, the Nazarene noticed the red "Push Me" button off to the right. As he complied,

MacDonald observed the scene with silent awe as the customary (to him) music track and primitive 1960s special-effects came noisily to life.

"Hushed and humble with sorrow," the narrator began, to the accompaniment of a mournful wind and rumbling head of thunder, *"we stand before the soul-rending scene that depicts the agonizing and bitter termination of the Master's mission upon earth: death upon the Cross at the hands of enemies he forgave with his passing breath. This was the foreordained sacrifice, the ransom for sins that brought forgiveness to the world..."* What minimal lighting had decorated the room up to now faded almost to black. MacDonald's view of Jesus was completely obscured, the darkness punctuated only by the flashes of an off-stage strobe light, meant to simulate lightning and the wrath of God. The glimpses provided by this pulsating illumination, almost like the flicker of a silent movie, revealed that Jesus' gaze had turned to the foot of the cross, where wax figures representing his mother Mary and his friend John were bowed in sadness. And though the stiff costumed manikins bore little resemblance to their real-life counterparts back home, Jesus himself began to tear up at the sight. MacDonald, mistaking these emotions for fear, called out for the first time.

"Don't you worry about that, Lord," he said, rising to his feet. "That will never happen to you. I won't allow it. I'm going to protect you."

Jesus' smile cut though his tears with great warmth and sincerity. "Are you now, Andy?" he said. "Does this mean that you and I are friends again? We were once, you know. That's why I've come to see you tonight."

4:27

Fuller's car was parked in front of the dorms. Carter dropped the last of several suitcases into the trunk and slammed the lid. As he did, he heard the unmistakable sounds of approaching helicopters in the distance.

Santiago Ramirez heard them, too, as he and his friends rushed up *en masse* to the Main Gate of the Palestinian Village. They found it solidly chained, the fence very high and surmounted with razor wire. Many of the women, trained by long experience to a general fear of authority figures, whimpered as the sound of the choppers grew louder and more threatening. The young Dominguez ordered one of the maintenance men to go and get some bolt cutters to use on the fence. Ramirez, meanwhile, pulled out one of Caleb's walkie-talkies and awkwardly started pushing buttons, as if using it for the first time.

"Come in, Mr. Donophan! Come in, please."

4:28

Deep in the Time Cave, Caleb's own handset chirped; Rocklynne and several of the techies noticed right away. The scientist held the walkie close to his ear and answered as discreetly as possible.

"Go ahead."

"The gate is closed with a chain! We can cut it open but it will take time."

Glancing around, Caleb saw several of the techies murmuring amongst themselves.

"Fast as you can, amigo. For His sake. Fast as you can."

Just then, Caleb's closely-watched ammeter finally hit the top; a set of red letters appeared on the display:

CHARGE COMPLETE.

Caleb began flipping switches and turning dials immediately—and not, it would seem, exactly the same ones needed for the sell-off procedure. Spaz noticed this right away and stepped over to his boss' side.

"Um, what exactly are you up to?" he asked in a hushed voice. "Sir?"

Caleb continued his work, but responded in a low, conspiratorial tone of voice. "In about three minutes Señor Ramirez and company are going to come down here, get Jesus out of his cell with my security badge, and bring him to us."

"Is that a fact?" asked Spaz, with a carefully masked amazement. "I thought they wanted to bust him out of here altogether, take him on his triumphant world tour or something?"

"I haven't told them everything. Just that he's in danger and I want to help."

Spaz cast a nervous glance at Rocklynne, who had turned to tinker with the controls of the small bank of security cameras mounted here in the central chamber.

"In about 30 seconds," continued Caleb, "I'm going to walk over to the motherboard and start firing this thing up. You're going to stay here and run modulation."

"I take it Fuller and MacDonald would not approve..."

"Not at all. But what are they going to do? Fire us?"

Spaz grinned. "Count me in."

4:29

Although the monitor in Fuller's lab was zoomed in on Caleb and his assistant the voices were muffled and unintelligible. Nevertheless, the steely voice of Fuller's Spirit Guide seemed, when it spoke again, little deceived by their secrecy.

"He's turned on you, Lance," said the sharp, female instrument. *"He's going to start up the machine."*

"So what?" said Fuller brusquely. "What difference does it make? MacDonald was dumping the power anyway, and we've got the Man himself locked up tight."

"Stop him. Tell Rocklynne to stop him."

"Why?"

Sylvie, fists clenched against her withdrawals, suddenly knew the answer. "It needs the power! Your Master there. It needs the power to open the—what did you call it?—the Hellmouth! A door into limbo."

Fuller was incredulous. "For what reason?"

"To dispose of the body! To put it someplace safe this time, where even the angels can never find it!"

"You're crazy. I told you..."

"Yeah, you told me. Your 'Guide' could have killed him right away. But I don't think it works like that. It didn't in the old days, anyway. I don't think he's *allowed* to strike at him directly. He has to tempt some human being into doing it for him. Just like before. Just like Judas Iscar..."

Fuller reacted with visible horror at this name, actually putting his hand over Sylvie's mouth before she could finish.

"You can't say that!" he shouted. "She can't say that, can she? Can she?"

The voice from the loudspeaker did not respond.

"It's not like that!" Fuller cried. "Is it?"

"You need your medicine, Lance," said the Spirit Guide at last.

"What?"

"It's time for your shot."

4:30

One of Donophan's techies realized that though his boss was certainly doing *something* to the equipment, he wasn't following the sell-off protocols. Stepping up, he began to ask.

"Um, Caleb, I couldn't help noticing, but…"

Spaz took hold of the man's shirttails and put one finger to his own lips in the traditional shushing motion. Several of the other techies saw this, too. Unfortunately, Rocklynne saw it as well.

"What's going on over here?" he asked, moving towards Donophan.

Spaz stepped between the two men, allowing Caleb to continue working his instruments. Surprised, Rocklynne paused, then shoved the redheaded geek roughly aside. Caleb only glanced up.

"You better stand back there, Rock. I can't be interrupted now, this is delicate work."

"What do you think you're doing?"

The tense moment was broken by the chirp of another walkie, Rocklynne's this time.

"Go," he said, answering.

It was the voice of Farmer, his squad captain. *"You better get up here, Rock. We've got visitors."*

"What visitors?"

"Three helicopters. Black helicopters, right outta Art Bell's radio show."

"What do they want?"

"They want the containment field dropped. The pulse is interfering with their equipment and they can't get through. They insist on coming aboard."

4:31

Fuller extracted the needle from his own arm and revealed a set of tracks which put him in quite the same league with Sylvie herself. Sylvie, on the other hand, who had gone without her dose, was watching the procedure closely, with a look of suppressed animal hunger on her face. Fuller bit his lip and sighed a deep, involuntary sigh of pleasure—but when he spoke again it was in complete and uncanny unison with the female voice on the loudspeaker.

"Yes. That's much better."

Swinging aggressively back around to the camera console, he picked up the microphone and called out to his man in the cave.

"Rocklynne. Rocklynne, can you hear me? This is Fuller speaking."

His voice boomed out over the P.A. speakers in the time chamber. In response, Rocklynne looked up at one of them and answered.

"I'm here."

On his end, Fuller saw the Security Chief from above, as a small figure shot from one of the ceiling cameras.

"Arrest Caleb Donophan. Get him away from that machine. He's betrayed us. Stop him now."

Rocklynne moved in on Caleb immediately. Spaz stepped up again, pretty bravely for a fat guy with a Ph.D in tensor calculus. Rocklynne simply punched him in the stomach and dropped him to the floor. Several of the other techies had begun to gather, however, and seeing Spaz go down, leapt onto Rocklynne's back as a body—dogpile on the security goon. Caleb stayed at his work, only glancing from time to time at the nearby melee.

Fuller was watching via the security monitors. For several minutes Rocklynne struggled with, but finally shook off the last of Caleb's nerds, at which point he pulled out a big automatic, backing them all away at once. Fuller shouted through the mike.

"Shoot Donophan! Shoot him immediately!"

Still winded, Rocklynne looked up at the camera in disbelief.

"Shoot him? He's the only one who can operate the machine!"

"Do it now!" Fuller insisted. "Get him away from those controls!"

Seeing a chance, Sylvie grabbed at the cord and yanked the microphone out of Fuller's hand.

"Silverberg is dead, Caleb!" she said, shouting into the mike. "Fuller's killed him!"

Fuller tried to reclaim the mike; Sylvie wheeled around for an extra moment of communication.

"Jesus is next, Rocklynne! Jesus himself is next!"

In the cave, Rocklynne heard a scuffle over the speakers, then the P.A. went dead.

"It's a plot, Rock," said Caleb, not looking away from his equipment. "Has been, right from the start. It's a plot to erase our whole history—all the way back to Year One."

The gun in his hand was still threatening, but Rocklynne himself seemed torn and wavering.

"Go get him, Gunny," urged Caleb. "Get Jesus down here so I can send him back where he belongs."

Rocklynne lowered the gun and took a step or two back, as if moving toward the exit. The move was far from decisive, but the moment he made it a loud whooping fire alarm tore through the air and filled the huge echoing chamber with sound. A flashing strobe signal went off and then great clouds of gas rushed into the room as if fired from a multitude of extinguishers all at once.

"It's the halon system! Fuller's set off the halon fire extinguishers!"

Rocklynne, near the door, saw it begin to close automatically. He rushed boldly into the gap and tried valiantly to hold it open. Failing, he rolled out of the way…and into the tunnel outside. Out in the hall, he found the keypad and attempted to reopen the door from there. The only response was the flashing red phrase:

"ACCESS DENIED." Flipping open his walkie, Rocklynne called out to Caleb.

"Donophan, can you hear me?"

Inside the Cave, the machine chamber was filling quickly with the suffocating gas. Several of the geeks were crowded around the exit door, hammering at it, trying to escape.

"I hear you," said Caleb, responding to the walkie.

"It won't open from out here either!"

"Did you try the override code?"

"Yes. Fuller must have scrambled it. What about Nichols? He could open it, couldn't he?"

"Well, I hope you can see him from where you're standing because we've got about one minute to live in here. You can't breathe this stuff, you know!"

Frustrated, Rocklynne spied a regular fire extinguisher hanging in the tunnel; he grabbed it up and used it to bang (uselessly) on the back side of the door. Halon, meanwhile, was still pouring down into the Time Cave, and was already choking the panicked geeks. One of the monitors inside the Cave showed Rocklynne out in the tunnel, pounding and pounding. All at once, Caleb got a flash of inspiration. He dashed across to stabilization control and looked down at the panel solemnly.

"Rocklynne," he said, calling into the walkie. "Forget the door. Go get Jesus—you've got him in a cell now, is that right? Get him and bring him down here as quick as you can."

"What're you gonna do?"

"I'm gonna clear the air around here."

4:32

Sylvie was shaking with sickness and frustration as she watched the time chamber fill up with gas via the security monitor. "It's the power," she said between sobs. "You're willing to gas them all just to save the power!"

Suddenly, the monitor flared white as the Cave exploded with a searing brightness—Donophan had activated the time machine! After the iris in the camera had time to compensate, Sylvie saw the blackness at the center of the hub torn open, and a blinding eruption of sunlight shooting up into the Cave from below. The pressure in the chamber dropped suddenly as well, sucking the toxic gas instantly from the cavern along with much of the air. Wild-eyed, Lance Fuller hammered at the countertop with his fists.

In the Cave itself, it was as if the entire room had been constructed inside an airborne B-52 and somebody just opened the bomb bay doors. In spite of a painful popping-of-the-ears, the geeks rallied instantly; laughing, giddy.

"It's incredible," one of them shouted. "That's mountain air I'm smelling!"

"That's Jerusalem air," Caleb corrected, both hands still on the motherboard. "First century A.D. and 3000 feet above sea-level. The difference in altitude acts just like a vacuum!"

Looking down into the hub, the tiled surface of the Temple Plaza could be seen twenty feet below. Everyone in the chamber cheered lustily and even Caleb found time for a smile.

"No time for celebrations, though" he finally said. "We've got roughly six minutes to get our man down that hole before I'll have to shut this thing off for another three months!" Spaz staggered to his feet, still shaky and coughing. Caleb shot him an order. "Can you get on modulation, Spaz? And the rest of you guys—get that door open now! Try hot-wiring it from the side panel."

4:33

Still in his lab, Fuller pulled up a different feed, producing an image of Rocklynne running down one of the cave tunnels. Stopping at a formidable steel door, the Security Chief opened it with his swipe card and entered Jesus' cell—but only for an instant. He re-emerged into the hall immediately and barked into his walkie.

"He's not here! Donophan, he's not here. The cell's empty!"

"You're kidding, right?"

Fuller couldn't believe it either. "That's impossible. I've got a camera inside that cell!"

Punching another button or two, the Administrator pulled up video from said camera...and it showed Jesus seated placidly on the edge of his cot, hands on his knees. Sylvie managed a smile through her shivers.

"More camera loops, eh?"

"Damn it!" shouted Fuller.

"There never was any hacker, you clown. It's been Jesus himself all along. He knows more about time manipulation than any of you."

Fuller seemed almost to growl.

"You'll never stop him, Dr. Fuller," Sylvie continued. "Or whoever you are. You're out of your league."

Fuller's face grew steely. "You think so, eh?"

He tapped the keyboard again, producing a whole new set of video feeds. He selected one of them with a flourish.

"Aha! I thought as much."

The real Jesus was just where Fuller guessed he might be: still at the Wax Museum with MacDonald. Both of them were seated on the bench at the Crucifixion scene, talking quietly. The Administrator grabbed up the handles of Sylvie's chair and whisked her toward the exit. He spoke again and as he did Sylvie again heard the eerie echo from the speakers overhead—Fuller's "Spirit Guide" aping his every word. Or was it the other way around?

"We'll see who's outclassed. And you might as well come along for the show, young lady."

4:34

As soon as Rocklynne reached the top of the tunnel he saw that two of the black helicopters had chosen to set down right outside the north gate of the containment wall. Any attempt, however, to dismantle the door or take it off its hinges would take hours, he reflected, since a breach in the wall would negate its effectiveness as a fail-safe and the gates had been designed accordingly. Beyond the choppers, Rocklynne thought he detected more interlopers approaching: multiple sirens and dim flashing lights coming down the narrow black highway that led across the desert back to civilization. Just as he was preparing to dash away in a desperate search for the wayward Messiah, Rocklynne ran smack into Ramirez and his party, coming (as they thought) to the rescue. The Mexicans, surprised at the sudden appearance of the Security Chief, eyed him with trepidation. Ramirez flashed Caleb's missing security badge.

"We've come for the Master, Señor Rocklynne."

"He's not here. Isn't he with you?"

"No, Señor."

Rocklynne flipped open his walkie. "They don't have him, Donophan!"

"Then tell them to start looking! Spread out, search everywhere. Can you hear me, Ramirez? Spread out and find him! Find Jesus!"

Ramirez agreed instantly, turned and shouted instructions to his followers *en Español.*

"And Rocklynne," Caleb's voice continued. *"We're not getting anywhere with this door, so I need you to go after Nichols. If he's still onsite at all he oughta be headed for Fuller's office."*

Rocklynne acknowledged the new instructions and dashed away alone.

4:35

The hasty trip through Bible Land was a phantasmagorical blur for Sylvie, wracked as she was with sickening withdrawal symptoms. Through her tears she glimpsed fleeting visions of Noah and his ark, Jonah and his whale, David and Goliath, Elijah fed by the ravens. It was a waking dream, a strange kaleidoscopic recapitulation of the whole of sacred history, leading very obviously, as Sylvie now saw, up to some kind of painful and purgatorial climax. When Fuller finally pushed her through into the room where the Son of David himself, not wax at all, sat ministering to MacDonald, the line between fantasy and reality smudged away into nothingness. Christ and MacDonald rose to their feet in response to the sound of their arrival. Sylvie watched it all play out like a movie.

"Lance," said the serene MacDonald, a note of puzzlement in his voice. "What are you doing here?"

Fuller pushed the chair past them and stood with it, near the exit to the next room, as if barring the door to further progress. He then pulled a .38 caliber pistol out of his medical bag and pointed it at Jesus.

"You there," he said. "Step away from Mr. MacDonald."

MacDonald moved between the two men.

"Fuller, have you lost your mind?"

"Just you stand back there, Mr. Davidtz. The police are on their way."

"Police?" exclaimed MacDonald.

Fuller's voice grew pained, compassionate. "I don't know how to tell you this, sir. Dammit, I'd rather shoot myself than break your heart this way! But—this man here, this 'Christ'—is nothing but a plain fraud. He's an actor, hired by Donophan to deceive you."

Wide-eyed now, Sylvie interrupted loudly.

"Don't listen to him, Andy! That's a lie!"

"It's not a lie!" cried Fuller. "You shut up, young woman!" He directed his words to MacDonald again. "She's in on it, too, sir. Donophan paid her to help put all this over, to convince you with her phony psychic routine."

MacDonald turned to Jesus now, casting a questioning look.

"Donophan's machine was a boondoggle," continued the Administrator. "He got it built and it didn't work. He wasted every penny of your money. So he thought to cover it up with this cheap hoax."

"That can't be," said the billionaire, beginning to look shaky. "I saw the Extraction myself."

"You saw Donophan's people haul an actor up through a hole in the floor. That's all."

MacDonald questioned Jesus directly now. "What do you say to all this?"

Jesus spoke quietly, but with great firmness. "What do *you* say? You know me. You've known me all your life."

"More fog," said Fuller. "And more lies. Here. Here's some facts for a change."

He produced another stack of "Schlomo Davidtz" material and handed it to MacDonald. The magnate thumbed through it a moment, then sank back onto the bench, eyes glistening.

"Oh my God," he said. "What is this?" Looking up at Jesus again, he repeated the question. "What is this I'm looking at?"

Jesus said nothing now. He went totally silent.

"Why don't you answer?" asked MacDonald, in anguished tones.

"He can't answer," responded Fuller bitterly. "Because he's a fake, and he's ashamed! Just another religious fraud. Just another David Koresh."

MacDonald looked up sharply at this phrase; Sylvie recalled his words from earlier in the day…

A fire. In Texas.

She could almost hear something break inside him.

4:36

Winded, Rocklynne ran up to the front of the Administrator's office just as Carter Nichols arrived in Fuller's car. The younger man rolled down the electric window and draped his elbow over the door just as if he were out for an evening drive. "Where's Sylvie?" he asked. "Have you seen her?"

"I don't know, man, but we need you at the Time Cave. Right away."

"Look, I'm out," said Nichols, shaking his head. "I resigned this afternoon."

"This is life and death, Carter."

"For who? Schlomo Davidtz?"

"For all of us, maybe," said Rocklynne, exasperated. "You gotta trust me on this."

"I'm done trusting around here."

"Then do it for Sylvie. She'd want you to come."

Carter hesitated, but then unlocked the doors so that Rocklynne could get in. The car shot off toward the Cave, with the noises of police activity outside growing more and more pronounced.

4:37

Caleb truly had both hands full now at the mixer board, with Spaz actively engaged as well, standing at his own set of controls nearby. A low frequency hum had been building in the Cave for several moments and the edges of the hole seemed slightly less distinct than they had been earlier. Caleb called out to his first assistant.

"Wave-packets?"

"Getting a little loose," responded Spaz. "380 on the Bloch vectors. 220 on the downside. Whatya think—three more minutes?"

"Three *safe* minutes, maybe." Caleb glanced at the door. "Where is everybody?"

Several of the younger techs had drifted over to the rail by now, looking worried and helpless. Peering down through the time hole, they were surprised to look directly into the eyes of three curious 1st century Jews who had ventured bravely into the space beneath. The two sets of men blinked at each other dully. These must have seemed a curiously purposeless set of angels to the profoundly religious men below; the nerds in the sky simply gawked and wished their fire door open, relieving them of any further responsibilities as an ersatz heavenly host.

4:38

MacDonald was muttering to himself, shaking pills out of one of his bottles and fumbling them hurriedly into his mouth. Jesus spoke to him; firmly, with his manly Hebraic accent, but with profound gentleness as well.

"We can leave here, Andy. None of this is written in stone. If you will it we can take Sylvie out of here and go."

"Shut up! Shut up!" MacDonald cried. "I can't think anymore!"

Sylvie piped up in her own shaky voice. "He's telling you the truth, Andy! It's Fuller here who's the fraud!" She turned and glared at the Administrator, who wasn't even trying to seem innocent anymore, but simply glowering at her from beneath a lowered forehead with a look on his face to peel paint off the walls. "Tell him who you really work for, Lance," she shouted fearlessly. "Tell him who's pulling your strings!"

Fuller paused a moment, then opened his medical bag again and began rummaging around in it.

"Well," he said condescendingly. "You know, Sylvie's got her own alternate reading of what's going on here. She's perfectly entitled to her own opinion, of course."

Here, Fuller produced another of his pneumatic injection guns and carefully fitted a small bottle of clear fluid onto the top. As he did, he continued to speak. "She'd tell you, I think, that I had those documents printed up for your benefit. She'd say that in spite her hopeless *drug addiction*—"(He spat these words with great contempt, knowing full well he was every bit Sylvie's equal in that department)"—you ought to take her word on this." Fuller was getting worked up as he went, more and more angry and heedless of his appearance. "That this man really is God's own Son, but that you, Mr. MacDonald, ought to fling him back into the sea of time anyway so that he can stay safe from proof or disproof eternally! That way, the whole damn world can go on groveling at his feet forever, on the *off chance* that Hell is real after all and that by signing onto this fairy tale you might just keep yourself out of it!"

Sylvie wondered how MacDonald could possibly miss the wild, devilish glint that had come into Fuller's eyes now or the malevolent emotions that were turning his face into a mask of hate. MacDonald, however, was focused on the injection gun.

"What's that?" he asked hesitantly.

Fuller seemed to shake himself free of his rant and calmed down quickly. "It's the only way to find out for sure."

Awestricken at the implications of these words, MacDonald now looked at the device in terror. "That—that would be murder!" he exclaimed.

"If he's for real," consoled Fuller, "you can't harm him. He'll rise gloriously from the dead, just like in the movies. But if he's just another con man like I said—well, then he deserves worse than this. Just like your Pied Piper out in Waco."

Jesus took a step towards the wheelchair, clearly intent on taking Sylvie out of harm's way. Fuller backed him off by pointing the .38 at Sylvie's head.

"Not another step, my Lord, or I'll solve her drug problem once and for all."

Fuller handed the injection gun to MacDonald, who accepted it meekly.

4:39

Fuller's car roared to a stop at the entrance checkpoint. The guard Burgess was waiting as Carter and Rocklynne got out.

"Have they come through yet?" inquired Rocklynne of his subordinate. "Ramirez and his people?"

"No sir, only some of the Theos. They were looking for..."

"Theos? Did they have...Him with them?"

"Who?" asked Burgess dully.

"You know."

"No sir, they didn't."

"Dammit!" Rocklynne turned to Carter. "Okay, I've gotta go find him. Give me the keys."

"Listen, I..."

"Just give me the keys, Carter. I'll be back in a minute, God willing. Just you get down there and open that door! Quick as you can, man!"

The Security Chief jumped back into the car and peeled out. Burgess admitted Carter through the gate and he sauntered down into the tunnel as if nothing at all were at stake.

4:40

MacDonald moved slowly up to Jesus' side, holding the injection gun gingerly. "Do a miracle," he said. "Some kind of miracle so I can know the truth."

Jesus answered nothing.

"Actors don't do miracles, Mr. MacDonald," said Fuller. "Rock stars, maybe. Elvis Presley, perhaps."

MacDonald lit up for a moment at this. "Wait a second, Fuller! An actor wouldn't stand here and be killed, would he?"

Fuller merely grinned. "You make a good point, sir. But then, maybe I'm an actor, too. Maybe that's just a load of sugar water there in your gun and he knows it. How could you ever be sure? Unless there was a body to examine afterward…"

Still there was no response from Jesus. Sylvie, in the meantime, had slipped her hand stealthily down into the side pocket of her wheelchair; she fumbled sightlessly amongst the junk that had collected there, searching for something with which to defend herself…and (dare she imagine it?) to defend Him.

"Just one small miracle," begged MacDonald. When silence was still the only answer, he grit his teeth in tortured frustration. "You're bringing it on yourself!" he cried.

A hint of distress showed on Jesus' face now. He looked at the poisonous gun with a troubled, uneasy expression. MacDonald moved the device toward him and he instinctively took a half-step toward the door. Fuller shoved his .38 against Sylvie's temple.

"Stand still, my Prince. Stand patiently, or it will be the girl instead of you." MacDonald, half-crazy now with doubt, watched the confrontation miserably. "The math is simple," Fuller continued. "Your life for hers. Cooperate with me here and the girl goes free. Word of honor."

Jesus seemed to accept this somehow, as if Fuller's word of honor meant one blessed thing to anyone. But Sylvie emphatically did not accept it. Without warning, her hand shot out and she jabbed a long yellow Ticonderoga pencil about two inches into Lance Fuller's thigh. He cried out and faltered—but only for an instant. Recovering, he kept the gun pointed firmly at Sylvie.

"You see there," he said, grunting against the pain. "These Christians are all hypocrites. With the mouth it's all 'Love thy neighbor' and 'Turn the other cheek.' But when push comes to shove..."

4:41

Caleb and Spaz were elbow deep. The hefty redhead was sweating profusely, his eyes fixed on one of the iffier gauges.

"Getting some spontaneous emissions here, Boss. Yeah, this is definitely gettin' kinda active. Where are we on the time?"

"We're okay," said Caleb, without looking at any timepiece. "We're all right."

One of the other techs gave a much more precise answer. "Six minutes are up in—five, four, three, two, one."

"That's it, Boss," said Spaz. "That's the limit."

"That's the *book* limit," corrected Caleb. "We can stretch it. Quite a bit if we have to."

Just then, his walkie-talkie chirped again. His hands were not free to respond.

"Somebody answer this for me."

One of the techs stepped to his side and took the handset off his belt. "Go ahead," he said. It was Ramirez on the other end.

"Mr. Donophan, is that you?"

"He can hear you," said the technician. "Go ahead."

"We're not finding him, Señor."

Caleb did not speak; he just stared at the time hole and kept his hands moving.

"What about that last building?" asked the Mexican plumber. *"That big warehouse without any windows?"*

"The wax museum. That's it!" Caleb cried. "Tell him yes! Tell him to use my badge and go in there!"

"Dr. Donophan says go in there," relayed the geek. "Use the badge."

There was no further sound from the walkie. Caleb seemed encouraged and called to Spaz again.

"Conductor plates?"

"Hot," said his assistant. "Way too hot."

"It'll hold a while longer. Just stay cool and everybody do their job."

One of the younger technicians seemed close to panic. "But the exit doors," he said. "We can't get through if…"

Caleb stopped him in an irritated voice. "Just cool it, okay? Nichols is coming. Give him a minute."

4:42

Approaching the problematic door from the other side, Carter ran into Kent, Breen, Flammerion, and several of their assistants choking the narrow tunnel. Hearing him arrive, they turned and faced him confrontationally.

"Nichols," said Kent, with a tinge of disgust in his voice.

"Where've you been?" demanded a panicky Breen. "Where's everyone hiding? Fuller? MacDonald?"

Carter was laconic. "I dunno. Don't care. What's eating you?"

Breen pulled out a small pistol of his own and pointed it at the security tech. "Maybe you'll care about this!"

"Dr. Breen!" cried Flammerion, deeply shocked.

Kent put his hand on the gun, restraining his colleague. "Hold on, Joe," he said quietly. He turned to Carter and took charge of the questions. "Haven't you seen those helicopters at the wall? There's a raid on, young man, in case you hadn't noticed."

Carter was dismissive. "A raid?" he said. "Shoot, that could be anything. That's probably the INS looking for green cards!"

"It's the police," said Breen. "And they'll arrest us for all this. They'll tell the world what we've done!"

Flammerion broke in, trying to be the voice of reason. "We *ought* to tell the world! Joe, Kelvin, it's what I've been saying! Let's just turn ourselves in. We should have been open with this from the start—brought it all under UN supervision. A thing like this is too big for any one man to..."

"I don't know who it is," Kent interrupted. "It could be the police, could be some crazy fundamentalist militia out of Ruby Ridge. All I know is I'm not taking the fall for this and none of us scholars should." He took Carter by the shirtsleeve. "You're the closest thing to an administrator we can find in this ghost town right now. I'm marching you topside, through that outer gate, and then *you* can explain what's been happening in here."

Kent turned Carter around, Breen put the muzzle of the gun between his shoulder blades, and the group walked back up the tunnel, away from the all-important locked door.

4:43

MacDonald, still hovering near Jesus, had stopped listening to anything but his own inner demons. Mumbling to himself, cursing at the wax figure on the Cross, balling and unballing his fists, Sylvie wondered if a stroke might not overtake the struggling billionaire first and rescue Jesus after all. Fuller, in the meantime, opened his bag again, pulling out another hypo.

"I think it's finally time for me to keep my promise to you, Sylvie, and spare you any further emotional distress." He held the needle at eye level, carefully measuring the dosage. "It's Vitamin 'X', of course—the purest, most powerful batch ever concocted."

The Adminstrator began tying off Sylvie's arm; she struggled, of course, but feebly now—frantic with desire for the very thing she was resisting. Between hunger for the needle and horror at the scene playing out before her, Sylvie was half mad as her eyes darted to and fro and she scrunched backward in her seat as far as she could possibly go.

"Relax, Sylvie," said Fuller, just before the stick. "You don't need him. I've got your ticket to heaven right here."

The Harvard neurophysiologist jabbed once, then inserted his needle into the girl's arm all the way to the hilt. Sylvie gasped loudly and sat up stiffly in her chair, her big eyes rolling smoothly back into her head. Another deep sexual moan crawled out of her throat; wholly involuntary, contrary to every rational thought.

"There. That ought to keep her out of trouble a while."

Just then, MacDonald swung around again, completely oblivious to Sylvie's situation, and questioned Fuller directly once more.

"He's expecting it, isn't he? I think he's calling for it! It must be God's plan. How could I be punished for fulfilling God's plan?"

Amazingly, Sylvie forced her eyes open again and fixed them on Jesus, hard as she could, squinting as if trying to focus. Another second and she was biting her own wrist—very hard—in a furious attempt to regain something like sobriety. MacDonald, meanwhile, moved even closer with the injection gun. Jesus' eyes were closed. His lips were moving in something like prayer, though no one could hear the words.

"And we *can't* send him back, can we?" cried MacDonald. "I mean, that's clear now, isn't it? That really would change the past, with all that's happened here. I think I'm supposed to prevent that. It's destiny I believe!"

"Oh, just do it, you stupid old fool," said the exasperated Fuller. "Do it for Beth—and for the baby."

MacDonald went nearly blind with tears now. He grabbed Jesus roughly by the collar and shoved the muzzle of the injection gun against his bare neck.

Jesus opened his eyes. "I love you, Sylvie. Promise me you'll never forget it. I'll always love you, forever and ever."

Sylvie heard, grunted, grabbed the arm of her wheelchair savagely and actually *rose to her feet* in an effort to intervene. Fuller watched her incredulously, stock still with astonishment. The girl teetered a moment, attempted one single, pathetic step—and crashed to the polished floor with a smack. Jesus lifted his eyes to heaven.

"Father, into your hands I commit my spirit."

MacDonald pulled the trigger—and Jesus, too, crumpled heavily to the floor.

But something was dreadfully wrong.

MacDonald watched in revulsion as Jesus *did not* die, but began to writhe back and forth in terrific agony. His body was convulsed with spastic jerks, his head thrashing backwards and forwards, knocking heedlessly against the cold, bare floor.

"Fuller!" he cried out. "What's wrong? You promised me this would be painless!"

"Nothing's wrong," said the Administrator coldly. "You were right to begin with, MacDonald—it's all destiny. And the parallel is perfect now."

"What parallel?!"

"He had to die in torments, didn't he? Just like on the cross! You can't just put the Son of God to sleep—like a sick kitty or something."

"You don't mean you did this deliberately?"

"Of course I did. That injection was a torture chamber in a bottle. And he deserves it, too, for what he did to me and my kind!"

MacDonald was beyond shock, beyond terror now.

"Oh, don't fret," continued Fuller. "He'll die—eventually. And after that you, Lance Fuller, and Mr.

Wonderful there can all go down to the pit where you belong."

Fuller turned now and simply sat on the bench to watch, as Jesus struggled, gasping for breath. Yet MacDonald only waited a moment. He leapt onto his Administrator's back like an enraged animal and the two of them fell to the floor, locked in a violent struggle.

Sylvie, meanwhile, lying not far from Jesus, opened her eyelids heavily but could do nothing except reach out toward him, trying to touch him with her fingertips.

4:44

The spinning time hole shifted abruptly, like a 45 record shifting off center without its little plastic ring. As it did, it tore away a portion of the capacitor banks around the barrel, sending showers of sparks everywhere.

"We're losin' it, Caleb," advised Spaz. "We've got to pull the plug."

"Not yet," yelled Caleb. "Can you boost the Y axis?"

Spaz hesitated, scanning his own panel quickly. "I guess so, but you'll never use this thing again if I do. You'll burn out the whole discharge manifold."

Caleb cast another tense, hopeless look at the back of Carter's door…then said, "Boost it."

4:45

The wrestling match between Fuller and MacDonald came to a climax quickly. Though much older, MacDonald was heavier and still a powerful man. He wrested the handgun out of Fuller's grasp, forced the younger man's head against the floor, and put the muzzle to his temple. Just as he did, the ghostly voice from the lab called out again—not from Fuller's mouth this time, nor even from any loudspeaker, but simply from thin air.

"Go ahead. It makes no difference now."

Suddenly, Fuller's eyes seemed different; he became the disoriented scientist with the shot glass again. Peering up at MacDonald quizzically, it was as if he'd just beamed in from some other planet.

"Mr. MacDonald?"

MacDonald fired, creating a sunburst splash of blood and brains on the terrazzo behind. Rising to his feet, the billionaire turned his attention to Jesus—who was still moaning, hissing, and crying out piteously.

"The doctors have gone!" he said to Sylvie. "They left this morning!" His expression grew crazed, frantic. "This is my fault! This is all my fault!"

Jesus rose to his knees, his nose bleeding profusely from repeated collisions with the floor. As MacDonald watched, a sudden terrible shiver coursed through his body and his bladder evacuated involuntarily—a pitiful stream of urine piddling from the crotch of his jeans and pooling on the ground.

"Sylvie, forgive me!" MacDonald cried, brandishing the .38 again. "I've got to—to put him out of his misery now. It's my responsibility."

Weeping, he stepped over to Jesus and pointed the pistol at the back of his head. Closing his eyes tightly, MacDonald squeezed the trigger…and nothing happened. Appalled, he opened the chamber to find only the single empty cartridge he had expended on Fuller. He flung the gun away in terror.

"What do I do now?" he shrieked at the ceiling. "What am I supposed to do now?"

Looking around wildly, empty-handed, he seemed to get a flash of inspiration and then ran from the room, dashing back toward the museum entrance. Left by herself, Sylvie had been sobered enough by the sound of the gunshot to attempt another slurred phrase or two in response to the disembodied voice.

"You're beaten," she said, with an inappropriate tone of relaxation and ease. "With Fuller dead you'll never get Jesus to the time hole..."

Eerily, the voice responded, in a quiet conversational tone. *"Foolish child. There's no need to move the body at all. Thanks to your bumbling friend Donophan the hole will come to us."*

A few rooms back, MacDonald had arrived at Abraham and Isaac once again; the father sacrificing the son, the son who would become the father of Israel. The lethal-looking knife of brass glinted in the artificial lights, drawing the billionaire's gaze instantly. Climbing over the spilt-rail partition, MacDonald snatched the dagger crudely out of the patriarch's fingers, sending the wax digits crumbling in pieces to the floor. Then he scrambled back into the hallway and ran full tilt back toward the scene of the crucifixion. There must have been a storm gathering outside, for a peal of thunder rattled the museum heavily at just that moment.

4:46

The time hole widened somewhat and a sudden counter-clockwise twist from it yanked the metal of the surrounding spokes out of shape. Loud alarms were going off throughout the Cave; the halon, however, had already been discharged, leaving the several small fires in the wiring to burn unabated.

"This ain't happening, Boss!" yelled the hitherto steadfast Spaz. "Shut it down now—while you still *can* shut it down."

Caleb briefly scanned the faces of his men, all of them panicking and with no small justification. A look of resignation came into his features—resignation tinged with a deep, existential despair. Looking down at his instruments, he finally seemed ready to do as he was urged…when the locked door opened at last.

"Nichols," he cried. "Thank God!"

But it wasn't Nichols. Anson MacDonald entered the time chamber; dazed, shell-shocked, and covered in blood. His clothes were smeared with it and his hands were red up to the elbow.

"Where—where's Jesus?" Caleb gasped.

There was no answer.

Caleb shouted. *"Where is he?"*

"He's gone," MacDonald managed at last. "He's gone, Caleb. Gone from this timeline, anyway. But we'll fix it. We'll fix it, you and I!"

4:47

Rocklynne, Ramirez and company entered the Crucifixion room. They found Jesus dead on the floor, throat cut, at the center of an enormous pool of blood. Sylvie was lying head to head with him, lolling back and forth in the blood semi-consciously, holding one of his hands in hers. She was singing to herself softly.

"Jesus loves me, this I know, for the Bible tells me so..."

Rocklynne's own eyes filled with tears and from somewhere below his heart there issued a low, inchoate groan of desolation. The Mexicans cried out openly, fell into each others arms weeping. The teenager Dominguez collapsed onto his hands and knees but made no sound at all.

"Little ones to him belong, they are weak but he is strong."

The throat wound gaped open horrifically; a little white patch of larynx was even visible. So after a moment Rocklynne began looking for something with which to cover the body. Finally, he climbed over the partition and took the wax Christ's purple robe away from the soldiers who'd been gambling for it. He draped it gingerly over the dead Christ on the floor, leaving exposed only the canvas dock shoes on his feet and the blue jean pant legs below the knee.

4:48

The time hole looked like a *warped* record now, rocking and wavering drunkenly over the Temple Plaza below. And it was clear that Spaz, at least, had had enough.

"Caleb, for God's sake, close that hole before we're all..."

"No, don't close it," countered MacDonald. "Shift it backwards."

"Backwards?" Caleb spared a glance way from the motherboard.

"Move it back in time an hour or so."

"What good will that do?"

"I'll go back myself," said the wild-eyed Southerner. "I'll be there to meet Fuller as he comes through for the original extraction. Then I'll kill him again, leave Jesus where he was, and erase this whole godforsaken timeline!"

"You must be completely insane," was all Caleb could manage.

From across the room, still being held by the tech who'd answered before, Donophan's walkie-talkie signaled again. The young man answered with a shout.

"Go!"

"Donophan, it's Nichols," came the voice over the radio. *"Sorry I haven't got that door open yet…"*

Spaz worried that Caleb would explode with vexation. "Mother of—!" he yelled at the geek, "Hang up on him!"

"…but I just thought you oughta know, there's a whole gang of police or something outside and these Theos are about to open the outer doors."

"Police?" said MacDonald unhappily. He stepped over to the video station where he quickly confirmed the story: the remaining Theos had reached the North Gate, still escorting Carter at gunpoint, and were plainly preparing to admit the party-crashers.

"We can't allow that," said the billionaire, and he started pushing buttons on the security console.

"What are you doing?" demanded Caleb.

"I'm setting a new security code—for the whole complex. No interlopers right now. No interlopers."

The scientist cried out decisively. "That's it—I'm pulling the plug! You've just locked us all in here!"

"You're *not* pulling the plug," said MacDonald, with the tone of someone accustomed to being obeyed. "Look, Donophan, Lance Fuller just engineered the death of Jesus Christ! You wouldn't want to go out there anyway!"

Caleb looked like he'd been stunned with a blow to the head. "You said what?"

"I said Christ is dead! There's no one to put into your hole anymore *except* me!"

Was that even possible—scientifically speaking? Did the laws of physics allow it? Apparently they did, given MacDonald's current sanguinary appearance. Mentally, the floor fell from under Caleb's feet.

"Send me through, Caleb, and it won't matter what happens in here. I'll prevent any of this from ever taking place!"

A thirty-year's habit brought the answer quickly to his lips: the past can't be changed. Yet Fuller's whole plot had been based on the contrary affirmation—just as Silverberg had warned. To "wipe him from the pages of history" the Rabbi had said—"Get him back whatever it takes." But if Jesus was dead now there'd be no getting him back. Ever. Did that mean the pages had been wiped already?

Donophan began to stammer. "But I don't...I mean, no one's really sure if..."

"Have you got a better idea?" demanded MacDonald. And Caleb certainly had not. His eyes darted across the panel.

"I'm not even sure we *can* do it. This thing is right on the brink."

"We've got to try, Caleb! We've got to try, at least!"

Caleb blinked and turned his gaze inward, leaving his eyes blank and doll-like. For one brief, insane moment he toyed with another idea—that of moving the hole to a different now-changeable past, to one particularly painful evening in 1969. But would there even be a 1969 anymore?—nineteen hundred and sixty-nine years from a crucified Savior who wasn't going to *be* crucified any longer? Caleb shook off the lunatic thought—and then turned to his portly assistant.

"Okay, Spaz. Set your wave parameters at 478. Pull the modulator back and then *get out of here*—all of you!"

4:49

Kent was repeatedly pushing 911—to no avail whatever. He heard police band radios on the other side of the gate and the sounds of men tampering with the door.

"It's supposed to open! They swore to us that 911 would always work!"

Breen called out loudly. "Help!" he cried. "Can you open the gate? We're being held against our will!"

Carter looked back toward the center of the Compound where beams of sunlight were pouring up into the stormy sky from vents around the top of the Time Cave roof. Powerful gusts of wind were whipping down into the enclosure and periodic bursts of horizontal lightning shot from one side of the storm cell to the other, rocking the crucial containment wall with sonic booms of thunder. Soon, Carter realized that the Theos were ignoring him for the moment, so he took the opportunity to drift away, walking back toward the Cave entrance.

4:50

The geeks had gone now, including Spaz. Dust and debris were raining into the central chamber from the overhead, much of it dropping through about eighteen feet of 21st century air, and passing into the shuddering time hole, before coming to rest in 29 AD below. Caleb, meanwhile, was still manfully wrestling with the mixer panel, like a man heavily engaged in an intense foosball game.

MacDonald had shoved the winch mechanism into place over the hole, the one that had been used to lift Jesus into the present three months ago. It had a sort of catwalk on it and the billionaire had stepped out onto it. Lifting his voice to be heard, he called out to Caleb: "Let me know when you're ready." Strange waves were spilling out around the hole now, causing the structure to vibrate and thrum. Looking down, he noticed that the image of Herod's courtyard slipped momentarily out of focus from time to time.

"Get ready!" yelled Caleb.

Heaving thumping noises issued from the machinery, rattling the fluorescent lights overhead. The hole grew foggier, the city below indistinct. Suddenly, something on Caleb's panel shorted out with a snap. One of the capacitor banks caught fire and began emitting an acrid electrical smoke, choking to the nostrils. Worst of all, the sunlight in the hole went out. When it did, a waft of cold, dank air whooshed up, smelling like the grave. The pressure from it blasted MacDonald's hair, whipped at his clothes.

"No, wait," Caleb said. "Hold on..."

"What do you mean, wait?" yelled the agonized MacDonald. "We *can't* wait! I've got to go!"

With a flash, the sun returned; the plaza reappeared below—but only for an instant.

"Stop!" bellowed Caleb. "It's no good! It's getting away from us! It's too late."

MacDonald looked past his own blood-caked hands, saw the pit yawning below—looking not at all like a doorway to anyplace anymore. "No, that can't be possible," he shrieked. "What kind of an ending is that?" The hole *had* to work, had to offer an escape from this nightmare. Surely it *did* still work, since the alternative was unthinkable. "I'm going, Donophan! I'm going! Here I go!"

"Don't move!" Caleb implored. "You can't go down there now!"

MacDonald wasn't listening anymore. Shutting his eyes tightly, he opened them again after a second or two, stared off blankly into space, and then stepped out with one foot, dropping silently into the void. When he did, the time hole morphed instantly into an ugly, whirling Hellmouth—an indoor black hole, sucking the heat and air out of the chamber. Caleb was left alone with the thing...and its diameter began slowly but visibly to increase.

4:51

Rocklynne lifted Sylvie off the floor, intent on putting her back into her chair. She was still entirely out of her head, and, just like MacDonald, she had the blood of Christ all over her. Cradled like a child in his massive black arms, she gazed up into Rocklynne's face dreamily and spoke with a silly, girlish voice.

"Oh, hello. It's you."

Rocklynne was capable of no sound.

"You still love him, don't you?" asked the girl. "Your father, I mean." Here, she motioned to Jesus, still draped in purple on the floor. "He did, you know—still loved that old pervert. That's the hell of all this, ain't it? Love is the worst pain of all."

Now, the tears spilled freely out of the Security Chief's eyes, trailing down his cheeks. He carried Sylvie to the wheelchair and placed her gently in it. Elsewhere in the room, Ramirez had adopted a sitting position near Jesus' head, taking one of the Master's lifeless hands into his own and weeping like a little boy. Control, as always, had proved an illusion. And even with a time machine on the property, the final thoughts with which everyone was left to wrestle were the same as from time immemorial: too late, too little, if only.

And yet now...something incalculable began to happen.

The atmosphere in the wax museum had changed subtly. Rocklynne wasn't at all sure, but it almost seemed as if the artificial red sky behind the three crosses had begun to *brighten*. The air in the room had warmed as well and taken on, it seemed, a faint fragrance of roses. Noticing this, the gardener Reynoso, standing near the velvet rope, looked into the crucifixion scene and saw a fake rose bush (part of the scenery) beginning to blossom! It didn't take the other disciples long to begin watching this, too. More and more of the plastic fauna followed suit before their eyes—dead artificial vines, flowering branches, an eruption of rustling polyurethane ferns pushing up out of the trucked-in yellow sand. Every one of the Mexican workers crowded against the partition, agape with astonishment. Not only was the scenery springing to life, it was starting to spread, crawling everywhere, escaping from the wax tableau and pouring out onto the floor!

Hunched with sorrow until now, Ross Rocklynne rose to his full commanding height, new life rushing into his frame just as it had rushed into the lifeless simulacra. It was the energy of hope returning, lost since he left Mississippi. He saw tiny drifting lights appear in the air, weightless and carefree, almost like fireflies. They floated lazily among the disciples, glowing warmly, cheering and mysterious, until another heavier tide of warm wind rushed in, mussing hair and sweeping them away. The palpable change in the room finally got Sylvie's attention as well. She lifted her head, shook it, squinted, and looked around like a happy drunk.

"Is it just this shit," she inquired of no one in particular, "or am I really seeing what I'm seeing?"

Ramirez was the only one of the disciples who had not risen to watch the miracle, preferring instead to retain his hold on the Master's hand. But he dropped it now with a start—the hand had grown hot to the touch! Hesitantly, he took hold of the seamless robe and turned it back. He fell away in amazement when he saw that the whole body had begun to *glow from within.*

Something else was glowing, too. Even the security chief felt a wave of fear as he began to discern shadowy, half-visible figures standing in a circle all around, observing the scene from its darkened fringes, with large, unnatural eyes burning yellowish-white like the frightening globes in a glassblower's glory hole. Beyond that, Rocklynne could make out only their stature, which was that of 8-foot giants, and their basic form, which was not human but merely human-like. The big Marine had seen religious art all his life; greeting card angels and saints, muddy two-color printing in dusty old Bibles, naked infant cupids flitting around the head of the Virgin Mary. The figures he saw now, had they not been so alien, so somber and awful, would surely have made him laugh aloud by comparison.

The brightness around the body had increased, until it, too, looked like it was made of blown glass. Yet Ramirez extended his hand bravely…and found it cool to the touch. He looked around at the others with a smile of stupefaction. And the hideous wound around the neck was completely gone.

Something suddenly possessed Sylvie, still tripping gaily, to rally her wheelchair into motion. She scooted it backward a few feet into the doorway of the next room. There she found another "Push Me" button and, like Alice in Wonderland, did just as she was directed. The Bible Land choir launched immediately into Handel's famous

'Hallelujah Chorus' and the placid and earnest narrator began calling the play-by-play from across the sea of time:

"Here at the Resurrection, Christ won his victory over the powers of Hell and the grave. Delivered into the hands of sinful men, He humbled Himself and tasted death for our sakes, but God raised Him from the dead because it was impossible for death to keep its hold on Him…"

Stunned and speechless, Rocklynne looked up at the artificial Christ on the cross; the figure was no longer visible. It had been swallowed up entirely by fresh and flowering dogwood blossoms. The whole cross had become a living dogwood tree; no longer the symbol of death but a flowering staff of life springing out of the earth. MacDonald claimed the old tapes had been remastered, but the canned music sounded like the choirs of heaven now, accompanied by a massed philharmonic orchestra of saints with Handel himself waving the baton:

"For the Lord God omnipotent reigneth! Hallelujah! Hallelujah!"

Ramirez ventured to place his ear against Jesus' chest, listening for a heartbeat. His eyes widened and he backed away in fear, crossing himself devoutly.

"Dios mio!"

Jesus opened his eyes very suddenly; the golden aura faded away. Still in his blue jeans and sneakers, but clean now and unbloody, the Nazarene lifted himself onto one elbow, then extended his hand to Rocklynne for help in rising.

"…the kingdom of this world is become the Kingdom of our God and of his Christ, and of His Christ!"

Trembling, Rocklynne took the proffered hand and pulled Jesus to his feet. The two men stood face to face for a moment, barely a foot apart. Then the big Marine dropped to his knees, simply overwhelmed.

"My Lord and my God!" he cried.

"And he shall reign forever and ever, King of Kings and Lord of Lords!"

Jesus smiled. The others joined Rocklynne on their knees. In the back of the room Sylvie just allowed her head to fall back happily, singing along with the music (very badly):

"...King of Kings, Lord of Lords, forever and ever! Hallelujah, Amen!"

4:52

The ground above the Time Cave was rumbling heavily, shifting and emitting ominous crunching sounds from below the surface. Cracks began to form all along the base of the containment wall, an unsettling phenomenon which Kent and the other Theos devoutly hoped its designers and engineers had sufficiently anticipated. The powerful field above the wall was actually visible now, looking just like heat over a hot pavement. None of the Theos had noticed, even now, that Nichols, the company man upon whose neck they hoped to hang responsibility for the unfolding debacle, had long since vanished into the tunnel half a mile away.

Caleb down below opened a red and white striped emergency panel and threw the heavy switch inside; a curtain of steel plates descended in response from a ring-like slot in the ceiling, clamping down on the widening

Hellmouth like a giant tin can lowered from above. Carter Nichols wandered into the central chamber just as it slammed to the floor, having witnessed nothing more spectacular all day than a few circling choppers at the gates. Now, he saw the huge steel cylinder trembling and throbbing, sucking bits of paper and dust toward the cracks at its seams. Noticing his arrival, a shell-shocked Caleb merely shouted an update at the long delayed security tech.

"That won't hold the thing itself, but it'll keep it from sucking all the air out of the room right now!"

"That's wild, Caleb," said Carter, commenting on the shivering metal barrier. "How're you doing that?"

"With duct tape, jackass," said Caleb in disbelief. "And paper clips. How do you think?"

Carter looked around the chamber idly.

"I see the cameras are still running. What is this, the big season-ending cliffhanger?"

As if in response, the whole cave shifted suddenly, a twisting motion that wrenched the room itself out of shape. Carter grabbed a handrail to steady himself.

"Wow," he laughed, "that's better than the *Earthquake* ride at Universal!"

"You're not still clinging to your hoax theory?"

Carter stopped laughing, lashed out severely instead. "Look, Donophan, I'm just not buying this, okay? I'm sure the script has me get down on my knees at this point and ask Jesus into my heart, but I follow my own script, alright?"

The steel plates began to buckle around the base. They were growing hot from friction with the Hellmouth and Caleb saw clearly that they would soon soften and collapse.

"Get out of here, you fool."

"What about you?" asked Carter.

"I'm coming, believe me. But I think I can slow this down a little first—maybe buy you some time to open one of the outer gates."

Carter turned and approached the door through which he had entered—and it did not open. Closer inspection revealed that the twisting of the walls had crushed the frame out of shape.

"There's a topside hatch," Donophan said, quickly formulating a Plan B. "Right above." He indicated a small round opening in the ceiling, with a ladder and a dark shaft leading straight up. "There's a keypad at the top and the codes are all scrambled. So you'll still have to hack through that."

Carter appeared to hesitate, reluctant, it would seem, to get bent out of shape in front of the Chief Technician. He did, however, finally frown, scowl at Caleb, and hoist himself up into the escape tunnel with his one good arm.

The steel plates did sag, just as Caleb feared...and then failed completely, collapsing into a limp pile which was quickly vacuumed up by the resumed advance of the Hellmouth. The all-devouring anomaly now stood naked again, an empty, yawning maw, a bottomless pit sucking anything it could touch into infinity. Caleb gazed into it with morbid fascination, not unlike that of the proverbial moth for the flame. After all, with so many years of his life spent predicting it, calculating it, moving heaven and earth to guard against it, how could he do otherwise? It widened quickly and dramatically as he watched. It stirred up a swirling wind which tore at his clothes.

Caleb's walkie beeped one last time. He answered right away; it was Carter on the other end.

"I'm at the top," he said. *"Just a minute on the hatch."*

"Not sure if we've got one," said Caleb. "Call me if you get it."

Still turning his knobs, Caleb watched the Hellmouth swallow the winch device, the panels, remains of the capacitor spokes, Spaz's old control station.

"Call me if you get it," he repeated, quite unnecessarily.

The edge of the anomaly was only thirty feet away, now twenty-five—and just then the electrical power failed. This did not affect the Hellmouth, of course—it had already acquired a new and well-nigh eternal life of its own, and would roar on and on, out past Mars, Jupiter, and Neptune if the ringwall didn't hold—but the power failure did manage to plunge the time chamber into stygian darkness, punctuated only by the occasional shower of sparks as some piece of MacDonald's pricey equipment was consumed. At the moment the lights went out, Caleb surprised himself by laughing—just one damn thing after another, wasn't it? He laughed, too, to think that poor old Mintz had been right after all: the end *was* nigh, by God. But his laughter stopped when he thought of Sylvie. He'd long since quit expecting his own life to be fair and Sylvie herself, of course, felt the same way—or made out like she did anyway. And deep down inside, Caleb had always half-expected to wind up in the

Hellmouth one day anyhow, though he'd never have admitted that to anyone or even, consciously, to himself. But for *Sylvie* to end there, after the kind of hand she'd been dealt in life already—God, he couldn't bear the thought now. He felt the radio still in his hand; impulsively, he lifted it to his lips and called out for Rocklynne, hoping to hear, with everything in him, that the Marine had already taken the girl safely away.

"This...this is Rocklynne speaking," came the voice on the other end. Caleb groaned inwardly to hear it shaken, faltering.

"Tell me you're out, Rock. Tell me you've got Sylvie and you're both outside the ring."

"No, we aren't. We're still in the museum. With Jesus."

"What are you talking about?"

"He's here with us. And he's alive!"

"You mean he wasn't killed after all?"

"No. No, that's...not what I mean."

Those fantastic words had little time to sink in; just a few feet away Caleb heard the stabilization motherboard yanked loose by its cables and go clattering into the abyss—and that was the moment at which he knew for certain that he would not make it. "Oh, God," he said aloud, not really intending to be heard. "This is it, isn't it?" The mike on his walkie was still open. Rocklynne heard what was said, heard the howling vortex in the background, and quickly put two and two together.

"Donophan," the Security Chief shouted. *"Donophan, listen to me. He's alive – and he's stronger than death. Stronger than that thing in the Cave. You've got to believe that! He's proved it now and he's going to..."*

The signal died out, as if the radio waves themselves were being sucked into the unseen whirlpool of emptiness. Caleb steeled himself for the inevitable. But before it came, his eyes flew open again. He shoved his hand into his pocket and found Sylvie's little silver cross. He held it in front of his face and, standing with his back to the wall, began to repeat words he hadn't used since boyhood, the only such words he could remember:

"Our Father, who art in heaven, hallowed be thy name. Thy kingdom come, thy will be done on earth as it is in heaven..."

The Hellmouth was all around, a maelstrom, a whirlwind, a freezing breath of death.

"Give us this day our daily bread, and...um, forgive us our trespasses as we forgive those who trespass against us. And lead us not into temptation but deliver us from evil..."

Up at the top of the escape shaft, eerily lighted by red emergency lamps, Carter spoke into his own walkie.

"Donophan. Donophan, are you there?"

There was no reply.

Looking down, he saw nothing but blackness at the bottom of the tunnel. But the blackness was alive somehow—or was it a trick of the dim, colored light? No, this blackness was moving—creeping, crawling, rising up the shaft like a silo filling with frigid well water.

"God, that's creepy," said Carter to himself. "And realistic, too. I think I'd be getting concerned right now if I didn't...you know."

He continued punching at the keypad, trying to release the upper hatch. As he did, he couldn't help glancing from time to time at the security camera which was mounted, even here, at the top of the tunnel. It was pointed right at him as he worked.

"Davidtz," he said. "Schlomo Davidtz. I'll buy him a drink when this blows over. Coupla drinks."

The rising "water" was 20 feet below now, fifteen feet, ten. Finally, Carter gave up on the keypad. He turned directly to the camera, giving it an unobstructed fisheye-view of his face. Then he shot it a bird—the full, traditional-one fingered salute, right in the face. And he said, strongly and clearly, (his last words on earth, as it happens):

"Sorry to ruin the show. Sue me."

4:53

Rocklynne emerged from the wax museum just in time to see the Hellmouth erupt out of the ground in the distance, flinging great crashing breakers of earth seventy or eighty feet into the sky. This detritus then collapsed back upon the crater from which it came, falling not seventy or eighty feet but all the way into infinity. What had been the flat, sandy patch above the Time Cave was now a horrifying black void, a shaft leading, like Jules Verne's volcano, to the center of the earth—and beyond it *ad infinitum*. The hole, in fact, began immediately to act as a gravity well at the center of the Compound. The nearby Research Center was pulled in right away, rolling off into the abyss like an expensive California home falling victim to a mudslide. Other buildings rocked and reeled as well, having lost track, it seemed, of which way was properly down. Rocklynne stood transfixed at the spectacle; he turned away only when, over his shoulder and a few hundred yards away, the last airborne helicopter was pulled into the overtaxed dampening field and blew up, raining itself all over the western rim of the wall.

Santiago Ramirez exited the museum now, pushing Sylvie and followed by the remainder of the party, Jesus himself emerging last. That portion of the help staff which had remained outside (mostly women with small children) saw them as they came out and joined them on the wide exterior patio. Spaz and his techies saw them, too, and ran to join the band from a different direction. The exit area was situated on something of a rise, allowing a wide panoramic view of the entire site and a startling front row seat for the unfolding catastrophe below. Despite the glories of the last hour, much of the group gasped and almost panicked at the sight. Jesus, however, calmed them with a word. He surveyed the scene placidly, then turned and called for the big Marine.

"Your name is Rocklynne, is it not?"

"Yes, Lord."

Jesus smiled. "Very well, Ross Rocklynne, you *shall* be my rock. And on this rock I will build my Church. And the gates of Hell will never overcome it."

Rocklynne was wide-eyed, awestruck—but he did have questions. "But…what about your other life?" he asked. "Before you came to us?"

"Nothing has been destroyed, my friends. Nothing ever is. Something new has been created."

"But what about the ancient prophecies—of the Cross, the rich man's tomb?"

"There are prophecies for all possible worlds, including this one. And all of them come to pass somewhere in Creation."

"I don't understand."

"I know," said Jesus, smiling patiently.

Rocklynne dropped to his knees again, as did the others. In the distance, the Hellmouth could be seen generating actual tornadoes which spun away from the central crater and went careening through the Compound, destroying everything in sight. "A" Building crumpled like aluminum foil; "F" Building, the moment it was touched, exploded from its own interior air pressure. Fuller's car took a three-quarter turn in one of the twisters, then rolled along the desert floor on its wheels before crashing into the base of the very porch upon which the group was standing. Jesus took all of this in stride, inspiring his followers to attempt the same. He simply lifted his hands over the disciples in a gesture of blessing.

"Peace be with you. As the Father has sent me, I also send you."

He took Rocklynne by the shoulders and kissed both of his cheeks, reminding Ramirez of old movies about the Foreign Legion. Something seemed to happen to the Marine as Jesus did this; he looked up at the sky sharply, smiled, his eyes dazzled as if by a sudden infusion of insight. Jesus then turned to the others in a similar vein.

"Receive the Holy Spirit."

At these words, a new blast of wind whipped over the group—whether from spiritual causes or merely from the tornadoes no one was ever able after to say—but something supernatural certainly was involved in what happened next. A strange, delicate aura came to rest on every head, a weird, shimmering glow, and every face tingled with electricity. Their bodies felt suddenly weightless and a new health and energy filled every frame. There was, oddly, one exception: little Sylvia Fortune, shrouded in black and still crumpled heavily in her chair, was just conscious enough to realize she had been left out.

"Now," said Jesus brightly. "Take my people out of here, Mr. Rocklynne. Take them to a land I will show you. And be comforted. I will be with you always, even to the end of the world."

The moment Christ completed these words a hole opened in the cloud-cover above and a blazing shaft of light fell down upon him with a sound like the roaring of Niagara. He looked up into it, smiled, and lifted his hands in a gesture of welcome. Rocklynne looked up too, and he couldn't help but compare the strange manifestation to another hole in another sky, an event that now seemed to have been witnessed by a different man entirely, a lifetime ago. Weeping, the disciples fell back to a safe distance, Rocklynne falling back with them. The light showered onto the risen Christ like a cool spring rain. It seemed at first to bleach all the color from his garments, leaving him shining like silver and bright as an electric arc; then it swallowed him up so completely that he disappeared from their sight. There was a final flash of energy from the center of the column, then the hole closed with a clap of thunder, shutting off the light from above. Rocklynne and his people were left alone with the Hellmouth—and faced with a dash for the doors.

4:54

The entire Palestinian Village tumbled into the Hellmouth, digested without a trace. At the beach where Jesus taught, tornadoes were rushing out over the surface of the lake to become terrifying waterspouts. A discernable counter-clockwise rotatation could be detected within the chaos now, buildings and material swept up in an invisible whirlpool with the Hellmouth at its center. MacDonald's whole glittering Compound, with all its pomps and works, was literally going down the drain.

Rocklynne and his group came rushing toward the containment wall, a frightened exodus of thirty-five souls. South Street, leading to the largest of the several exit gates, was buckling and rolling, the ground under it liquefying as sometimes happens in a powerful earthquake. The pavement shattered—and Ramirez, pushing Sylvie's chair, could not keep up, falling swiftly behind the main group. He cast a spare glance over his left shoulder and wished he had not—the edge of the Hellmouth was approaching relentlessly, only a few dozen yards behind. It was Rocklynne who came to the rescue; seeing the crisis with the chair he turned, ran back, grabbed Sylvie out of it and threw her over his shoulder, leaving the chair behind.

It became a sprint at last—the last fifty yards or so to the gate at a dead run. Before they could get there, however, there was a final, deadly assault. A great churning tidal wave of destruction was rushing toward them from the east, like the second hand of a clock sweeping toward their "Noon" position. It was a rolling mountain of tarry surf embedded with brick, mortar, half-digested machinery, writhing waterspouts, and even the dead bodies of some of Rocklynne's security men. Piling ever higher, the terror of it could be seen on every face. The women and children cowered and screamed aloud, their sounds unheard in the general cacophony. Surely it would wipe them all away just about the time they could reach the gate.

They did reach it. The wave towered over their heads. Every face cringed until Rocklynne *shouted* and stretched out his hand, like a crossing guard stopping traffic.

"Stop!" he cried. *"Be still! In the mighty name of Jesus I rebuke you!"*

The roiling tower of death crashed into what could only be described as an invisible barrier, like that which Charlton Heston had invoked to hold back the sea in "The Ten Commandments." Rocklynne was in good voice again and his rhythm was perfect. The old skills, learned so long ago in the churches of Mississippi, came back as if no time had passed at all.

"I will say of the Lord, he is my refuge and my fortress: my God, in him I will trust!" The remnants of the shattered wave now sloshed heavily to either side, leaving the group standing in a V-shaped wedge of dry ground. *"Thou shalt not be afraid for the terror by night, nor for the arrow that flieth by day. There shall no evil befall thee, neither shall any plague come nigh thy dwelling!"*

Yet one of the waterspouts had broken loose from the main body and now threatened from behind. Ramirez turned to face this new threat and, emboldened by Rocklynne's example, shouted his own prayer of defiance—a memory from childhood, learned at his mother's knee.

"San Miguel Arcángel, defiéndenos en la batalla. Sé nuestro protección contra la maldad y los enganos del Diablo!"

The threatening spout slammed heavily into another invisible wall and instantly tore itself to shreds. Ramirez turned to Rocklynne, grinning like a small boy after his first home run.

They stood at the North Gate now. Rocklynne, still with Sylvie across one shoulder, stepped up next to Dominguez, who was repeatedly tapping 911 into the door pad—fruitlessly, of course. Though the threat from collateral damage had been weathered, the Hellmouth itself still crawled closer and closer from behind.

"Nada," announced the disgusted Dominguez.

Rocklynne put his hand on the pad and prayed. "In the name of Jesus of Nazareth, be thou loosed, and let these children pass."

No response. The door still would not open. Dominguez tried the code again.

Meanwhile, further along the wall, the Theos, still alive but backed up against their own stubborn gate, were hammering to be let out. If Rocklynne's gate were at straight-up "Noon" on the dial, these Theos were clawing away at the 11 o'clock position, about 100 yards to the west. Breen had been reduced to childhood, babbling and weeping without any restraint at all. Kent and his assistants were nearly as far gone. Dr. Flammerion, however, looked across at the other gate. She'd seen the approach of the giant wave, seen it rush unexpectedly past, though her angle had not allowed an unambiguous look at any invisible barriers. Now she saw Reynoso, the stout, earthy gardener, beckoning vigorously with his hands—an invitation to join the disciples. She hesitated, looked into the approaching Hellmouth for a moment, then decided to try and make it. She took off her shoes and ran, hard as she could.

Caleb had called it the "event horizon"—a term taken from astrophysics and his way of designating the outer edge of a runaway time anomaly. It was a mere 30 yards behind them now, quavering and rippling ever closer, turning Flammerion's path into a narrow curved chasm between the enclosing wall and infinity. It closed to twenty yards, to fifteen. At the North Gate, Dominguez was still pushing 911 and Rocklynne was out of ideas.

"It's no good," he shouted. "MacDonald reset the codes. He made up a new set of numbers and never told anybody what they were!"

Sylvie heard this and was just together enough to rally and generate a new thought.

"Rock," she cried. "Rock, sit me up!"

Rocklynne swung the girl down off of his shoulder and into a straight cradled position in his arms. Sylvie slipped her hand down into the pocket of her sweater; her fingers found MacDonald's snow globe. She squeezed it tightly in her hands, closing her eyes. An image rushed up right away: MacDonald's fingers typing in the new code.

"It's 4125! That was the street address for Bible Land—back in Hot Springs! 4125 Albert Pike."

The Hellmouth was nearly upon them. Ramirez called out the numbers in Spanish. Dominguez entered them as translated—4125. The Egress Door opened immediately.

The group rushed through one at a time, Ramirez standing back until the last of his people was through. Flammerion, however, still had not arrived. She was fifty feet away, forty, thirty…

A howling wind blasted out of the door. The vision of the Hellmouth filled the opening; impossibly black, mortally terrifying. Flammerion just slipped through—and then Ramirez slammed the door in the Hellmouth's face.

The wall dissolved in front of them. For a moment they feared that it would not contain the monster after all, that the devilish thing could not be stopped by anything and would proceed to devour the earth. But it didn't. The entire compound dissolved instead, leaving the group standing by themselves in an empty expanse of cool, moonlit desert. The sudden, nearly complete silence was eerie in the extreme.

No one spoke a word. It was as if the place had never been anything but desert to begin with. As their eyes adjusted to the new scene, however, the group saw that there was one thing left from the Compound—just one thing. It was Sylvie's wheelchair, standing by itself several hundred feet back, just where they had abandoned it moments before.

Still cradled in Rocklynne's arms, Sylvie saw the chair, too. He looked down into her face as if to search out her feelings. She met the searching gaze, her own eyes full of desperately conflicted emotions. She did, however, give her permission with a nod, before burying her face in the big man's shoulder.

Rocklynne carried her to the chair and placed her in it carefully. And when he did, Sylvie's features were transfigured immediately. She looked up at Rocklynne in wonder. She looked at the others, transfixed with amazement. Using her fingertips, she touched the armrests delicately, over and over. Tears were flowing freely now. Finally, she addressed Rocklynne directly with an expression of bittersweet delight.

"When—when I touch it," she said softly, "I can feel him in my arms again. He's right here with me."

She became aware of another feeling, too—with an almost comic double-take, she realized that she was straight and in her right mind again. She pushed up the sleeves of her blouse. Rocklynne used his keychain flashlight to illuminate her arms—and all signs of heroin addiction had disappeared. The big Marine took both of her hands, hugged her neck, and kissed the top of her head.

The manila folder was poking out of the side pocket; Sylvie took it out and opened it. Somehow, the Schlomo Davidtz material was gone. In its place were three big photos of Carter Nichols, Caleb Donophan, and Jakob Silverberg. Sylvie looked stung at the sight; she turned to Rocklynne with her questions.

"How did these get here?"

"He did it," Rocklynne decided. "Jesus put them there. For hope."

Sylvie looked back down at the pictures. Carter was still the bright, boyish geek. Caleb's was a faculty photo from MIT. Rabbi Silverberg was much younger, smiling warmly, wearing the uniform of an Army chaplain.

"We can pray for them, Sylvie. Like we never could before."

"Every day," said Sylvie, eyes glistening.

"Till we see them again."

R E V E L A T I O N

"These are the last words from the past. Let us go free...into the future."
Joanna and Timothy Leary, *Neurologic*, 1973

5:1

The thoughts of that long frosty night, in the hearts of the three dozen or so hushed souls now trudging across the vast emptied desert, were literally past telling. Once the jubilation of their escape died down, a profound stillness came over the group as each man and woman became lost in their own thoughts and mentally replayed every impossible moment of the previous twelve hours. No one spoke for a long time; they simply put their feet on autopilot and followed the big black Marine walking the point. Yet one by one the smiles came back and the mood of triumph returned. The ground under their feet, they noticed, felt solid—truly solid—for the first time anyone could remember. And any cares or uncertainties from their previous lives had apparently vanished down the Hellmouth along with everything else.

They'd been walking all night toward Reno, nearest human habitation to the south, and the temperatures had been quite cool. As the sky began to brighten faintly in the east, Ramirez could be seen pushing Sylvie's chair and

Reynoso, not knowing what else to do, had started trying to teach the Mexicans to sing "He's Got the Whole World in His Hands"—the only even vaguely spiritual song he knew in both English and Spanish. Rocklynne, who felt like singing too, scanned instead the slowly brightening landscape ahead with an increasingly puzzled look on his face.

"We ought to have seen the highway by now. We've been moving directly due south. I don't see how you could miss it."

In the dazed silence following the disappearance of the Compound, the group had walked for some time without thinking to look for the paved road. It had been proving elusive ever since and the mystery of its disappearance, for Rocklynne and a handful of the others, had gotten deeper and deeper the longer it stayed lost.

"How far to Reno?" asked Camille Flammerion, still barefoot and wincing at the occasional pebble.

"We should have seen the suburbs by now."

Shielding her eyes, the sole remaining Theo saw nothing but primeval desert on all sides, bare and forbidding.

"What about the radio?" asked Rocklynne, turning to a deeply fatigued Spaz, who was winded but keeping up heroically. "Still nothing on AM or FM?"

"Nothing," said Donophan's auburn-haired lieutenant, holding his expensive smartphone at eye level and fiddling with the touchscreen. "No GPS signal either."

Rocklynne frowned. "Could it have been EMP from the anomaly? Fried all the transistors, maybe?"

"Yeah, I thought of that, too. But this phone's not fried. It still works fine...runs all of my downloaded apps, no problem. It's just not picking up anything from the outside."

Rocklynne's gaze drifted toward the horizon again, his thoughts now turning to more exotic possibilities. "Okay then. Is it possible that *we* have travelled in time? Can that thing back there have carried all of us someplace—*somewhen,* I guess—where there's no satellite or radio yet?"

"I don't see how, Boss," said Spaz, unconsciously transferring Donophan's old honorific to his new chief. "That's not really what the Hellmouth does."

"Any way we can verify that?"

Spaz hesitated a moment and then took up the smartphone again. Tapping a few taps, he peered up at the sky intently and noted the positions of the remaining visible stars, before smiling, at last, the well-known smile of a geek proved right again.

"Looks like we're right where we should be, timewise. Same day we started, 6:32 AM." The Marine looked at him quizzically as Spaz, pointing screen in his direction, continued to explain. "It's an astronomy application. A sky map. Just give it your geographical position, the time and the date, and it shows you where the stars should be."

Rocklynne went silent again, as did Reynoso's singers who had paused in order to hear details of the conversation. But in the sudden quiet, a new sound could now be heard. Not over the radio, but in the distance, coming across the sands. A chugging and a puffing, almost like an old-time locomotive.

A vehicle was approaching from the west—but what a vehicle!

Only a dark silhouette at first, traced against an orange sky, it came at them from the opposite direction, a parallel course which would have missed them altogether had not the driver noticed. He did notice, however, and when it became clear that there would definitely be a meeting the MacDonald refugees closed ranks around Rocklynne. Wheezing and sneezing, belching smoke and cinders, the noisy conveyance looked stranger and stranger the closer it got. Long before it reached them, everyone in Rocklynne's party knew that it was quite unlike anything they'd ever seen before, on any world they'd ever known. More than anything else, it looked like a circus wagon. It was brightly painted, with weird, almost pre-Columbian designs; sunbursts, desert animals, warriors in battle, feathered serpents. It was steam-driven like a train, but there were no tracks. The numerous passengers were even more striking. There were four or five of them riding shotgun on top, with the facial features of Central American Indians, and each was armed with something like an old-time blunderbuss. Behind the wagon, struggling along in chains, were fifteen to twenty unmistakable prisoners; miserable-looking souls, men and women with faces Rocklynne thought looked more like native North Americans—Apache or perhaps Navajo. Two long pikes stuck out into the air at the front of the wagon. Sylvie blanched to see a human head displayed on each—also with the facial characteristics of a Southwestern Indian.

The driver stopped the wagon before Rocklynne. The man had a hard, savage face, elaborately tattooed in an evil-looking pattern, with teeth filed to a point. When he spoke, his language (highly reminiscent of ancient Aztec, as Flammerion thought) should have been wholly unintelligible...but it wasn't.

"Who are you? What are you doing in our country?"

Rocklynne turned to Sylvie with a smile of amazement.

"I don't know how, but I understood every word of that perfectly."

It was a tense moment. The Mexicans quite openly looked to Rocklynne for leadership. He paused, stood erect in a display of quiet dignity, and then extended his hand in an offer of friendship. And when he spoke, he spoke the stranger's exotic tongue easily, entirely without conscious effort.

"We are the ambassadors of a great king, Jesus Christ, Son of the Most High God. We come to you in peace."

The moment he said it, Sylvie knew, for the first time in at least eight years, who she was and what she would be doing for the rest of her life.

And she was happy.

"And I saw a new heaven and a new earth: for the first heaven and the first earth were passed away...And he that sat upon the throne said, Behold, I make all things new." – Rev 21:1, 5

THE CHRISTUS EXPERIMENT

If you enjoyed *The Christus Experiment* you may wish to read Rod Bennett's first book

FOUR WITNESSES; THE EARLY CHURCH IN HER OWN WORDS

From Ignatius Press, San Francisco, California
www.ignatius.com

Made in the USA
Lexington, KY
20 September 2019